Kane ... water ... decision ...

Struggling out of his coat, he snapped to Brigid and Grant, "Cover me!"

Grant echoed incredulously, "*Cover* you?"

Sucking in a lungful of air, Kane vaulted over the side, splashing feetfirst into the water. Helped by the weight of his Sin Eater, he sank quickly, his ears registering the muffled, multiple thumps of bullets striking the water around the boat. He swam beneath the sampan, back toward the dock. He came up under the pier and saw Erica's wet, dripping head break the surface.

Gasping, she clawed away the long black hair clinging to her face. She ignored a blood-oozing scratch on her right cheek. Her eyes were wide, but shining more with anger than fright or pain.

"Are you all right?" he whispered.

"I've been betrayed!" she rasped.

Other titles in this series:

James Axler
Outlanders®

HYDRA'S RING

A GOLD EAGLE BOOK FROM
WORLDWIDE®

TORONTO • NEW YORK • LONDON
AMSTERDAM • PARIS • SYDNEY • HAMBURG
STOCKHOLM • ATHENS • TOKYO • MILAN
MADRID • WARSAW • BUDAPEST • AUCKLAND

*For Will Eisner, Milton Caniff, Denny Colt and
Lai Choi San...Immortals without the benefit of rings.*

First edition November 2006

ISBN-13: 978-0-373-63852-9
ISBN-10:   0-373-63852-3

HYDRA'S RING

Special thanks to Mark Ellis for his contribution to
the Outlanders concept, developed for Gold Eagle.

I traveled over Qin Mountain one morning,
I met two fairies of brightness and beauty,
    riding on a white deer.
I realized they were immortals, and kneeled
    and begged for the Dao.
"Go west and climb and the Jade Terrace,
    there are gold pavilions and corridors."
They gave me an immortal elixir.
"Your longevity will match that of gold
    and jade and
You will never reach senility."
                    —Cao Zhi, 6th century AD

The Road to Outlands—
From Secret Government Files to the Future

Almost two hundred years after the global holocaust, Kane, a former Magistrate of Cobaltville, often thought the world had been lucky to survive at all after a nuclear device detonated in the Russian embassy in Washington, D.C. The aftermath—forever known as skydark—reshaped continents and turned civilization into ashes.

Nearly depopulated, America became the Deathlands—poisoned by radiation, home to chaos and mutated life forms. Feudal rule reappeared in the form of baronies, while remote outposts clung to a brutish existence.

What eventually helped shape this wasteland were the redoubts, the secret preholocaust military installations with stores of weapons, and the home of gateways, the locational matter-transfer facilities. Some of the redoubts hid clues that had once fed wild theories of government cover-ups and alien visitations.

Rearmed from redoubt stockpiles, the barons consolidated their power and reclaimed technology for the villes. Their power, supported by some invisible authority, extended beyond their fortified walls to what was now called the Outlands. It was here that the rootstock of humanity survived, living with hellzones and chemical storms, hounded by Magistrates.

In the villes, rigid laws were enforced—to atone for the sins of the past and prepare the way for a better future. That was the barons' public credo and their right-to-rule.

Kane, along with friend and fellow Magistrate Grant, had upheld that claim until a fateful Outlands expedition. A displaced piece of technology...a question to a keeper of the archives...a vague clue about alien masters—and their world shifted radically. Suddenly, Brigid Baptiste, the archivist, faced summary execution, and Grant a quick termination. For

Kane there was forgiveness if he pledged his unquestioning allegiance to Baron Cobalt and his unknown masters and abandoned his friends.

But that allegiance would make him support a mysterious and alien power and deny loyalty and friends. Then what else was there?

Kane had been brought up solely to serve the ville. Brigid's only link with her family was her mother's red-gold hair, green eyes and supple form. Grant's clues to his lineage were his ebony skin and powerful physique. But Domi, she of the white hair, was an Outlander pressed into sexual servitude in Cobaltville. She at least knew her roots and was a reminder to the exiles that the outcasts belonged in the human family.

Parents, friends, community—the very rootedness of humanity was denied. With no continuity, there was no forward momentum to the future. And that was the crux— when Kane began to wonder if there *was* a future.

For Kane, it wouldn't do. So the only way was out— way, way out.

After their escape, they found shelter at the forgotten Cerberus redoubt headed by Lakesh, a scientist, Cobaltville's head archivist, and secret opponent of the barons.

With their past turned into a lie, their future threatened, only one thing was left to give meaning to the outcasts. The hunger for freedom, the will to resist the hostile influences. And perhaps, by opposing, end them.

Chapter 1

The naked albino woman came from somewhere in the back of the Dai Jia Lou, sinuously weaving her way between the crowded tables.

Werner Musgrave squinted through the dark, round lenses of his spectacles, not sure if he could trust his vision, since his eyes stung and watered due to the haze of acrid smoke. Although he knew customs governing the exposure of the naked human body were only vague guidelines on Autarkic, he hadn't expected to see a nude female strolling through the most popular gathering place on the island, either.

The Dai Jia Lou was jammed and jumping even though it was only an hour past sunset. So many people stood elbow to belly that it was almost impossible to see the decor of the big tavern. A wooden bar spanned the far wall with nearly two dozen stools before it, not one of them exactly like any of the others. Musgrave figured they had been built, stolen or cobbled together over a period of many years. Behind the bar a cracked and fogged mirror within a gilt frame decorated with absurdly elaborate scrollwork only dimly reflected the overhead lights.

Small round tables filled the middle of the huge room, sprouting from the floor like a cluster of dark-capped mushrooms. The table section was lined on three sides by tall privacy booths. White curtains overhung by strings of bottle-green glass beads enclosed each booth. Four impassive Asians, tong security men, stood before the booths, their arms crossed over their chests. They wore identical black clothing with white detailing on the collars and cuffs. Their garb fit loosely, making it easy to conceal and to draw the weapons they carried. Strips of cloth bound their foreheads, all of them emblazoned with the red ideograph of Wei Qiang.

Musgrave knew Wei Qiang handpicked his men, selecting only hardened killers. The tong's preferred weapon for close-in fighting was a long-hafted, single-bladed hatchet. Each one of the men carried one, riding high in a red sash around his waist.

Musgrave idly wondered who might be within the privacy booths and whether they were important enough to warrant guards. One of the independent pirate commanders could be behind a curtain, dallying with a rented girl or boy, but he doubted it. Most of the pirate fleets had moved their bases of operations from the Cific to the Gulf of Mexico and they no longer paid Wei Qiang tribute.

The fourth wall of the Dai Jia Lou was occupied by a low stage holding a very old upright piano, a drum set and a brass-framed harp.

All the chairs and stools were filled with patrons. The red-jacketed wait staff could hardly move among the packed tables, but the naked albino woman didn't seem to have any problem making her way.

Upon a second glance, after fanning away the smoke produced by bronze incense burners, hookahs and long clay pipes, Musgrave realized the woman wasn't completely naked, but she had gone to some effort to make it seem as if she were.

She was perhaps five feet three with a mane of long white hair that fell down her back like a stream of snow. A strip of cloth of the same milky hue as her skin was pulled tight over her firm breasts, under her arms and knotted between her shoulder blades.

Aside from that, she wore only a G-string, or a greatly diminished version of one. From the rear of it arched a tail of brilliantly colored feathers that swayed with every suggestive move of her hips as she sauntered around the room.

Her skin, the color of polished bone, gleamed with satiny highlights as if it were oiled. Her eyes were enormous, the irises bright red, the lids painted a deep sea-green, a color repeated on lips that curved in either a seductive smile or a scornful grimace, depending on the man she looked at. She looked at many of them, first one, then another.

Her crimson gaze passed over Musgrave, paused for a fraction of a second as if waiting for a reaction from him, then moved on.

Musgrave wasn't surprised. He knew he was an unimposing presence in his drab, dun-colored coverall. He was under medium height and stocky of build with close-cropped iron-gray hair, and the expression on his coarse-complexioned face was studiedly neutral. He gave the impression that his expression would remain the same whether he watched a Cific sunset, a dying child or an almost nude woman. Behind the dark lenses of his glasses, his pewter-colored eyes were utterly cold and passionless.

Although the albino woman had done nothing but walk into the room, the customers broke into thunderous applause. Males and even females began chanting, "Misha! Misha! Misha!" and they hammered on the tabletops with their fists.

Misha lifted her arms over her head in acknowledgment of the calls and sauntered slowly around the perimeter of the floor, her hips snapping from side to side, the train of feathers swishing and rippling through the air. She arched her back and the points of her breasts strained against the thin cloth confining them. A steady, almost lethargic drumbeat sounded from the darkened stage.

Voicing a wild cry, a wiry little Hispanic man broke away from the bar and rushed toward her, grimy hands reaching lustfully for her hips, but the black-clad tong security staff intercepted him. Spiked knuckle-dusters flashed in the dim light. No one paid any attention as he went down under pummeling, metal-reinforced fists. Most of the customers probably figured the intoxicated man was fortunate, since the tong security men apparently didn't consider him hatchet worthy.

Without raising so much as an eyebrow, Musgrave

watched as the tong security men carried the maimed, moaning man to the door and heaved what was left of his body onto the rocky embankment upon which the Dai Jia Lou was built.

The sudden thunder of multiple drums filled the room, interwoven with the clang of a bell being struck repeatedly by a metal rod and the piping skirl of a Chinese woodwind, the *p'ai hsiao*. Glancing toward the stage, Musgrave saw that three musicians had mounted it while everyone's attention was focused on the albino woman.

The tempo of Misha's movements sped up, matching those of the drums and the bell. Her hips and arms and legs flashed in intricate movements in the hazy light. Her body curved, bending forward and backward as if her spine were made of rubber, her white hair touching the floor and the plumed tail quivering and arching.

In rhythm with the drumbeats and the clanging of the bell, Misha's lower body undulated, the muscles of her belly contracting and rippling. With a sharp cry of triumph, she ripped away the G-string and the breast binding in two savage motions, flinging both into the crowd.

Musgrave expected to see the bright plumage fall to the floor, but it didn't. To his unease, the feathers arched and shook as if they were part of the woman's body, attached to the base of her spine. The word *mutie* sprang to the forefront of his mind, and his stomach lurched in sudden revulsion.

As if aware of his reaction, Misha whirled on the balls of her bare feet and glared directly at him, her eyes blazing crimson with contempt. A challenge glinted there, as well, silently daring him to rise from his table and investigate his suspicion. She turned her back, defiantly frisking her bare buttocks and feathered tail at him.

A hard tap on his shoulder yanked Werner Musgrave's attention from Misha's gyrating pelvis and thrashing, colorful tail. He couldn't be sure if it was an artificial appendage or if the girl was indeed some kind of mutant, despite how biologically impossible he knew the concept to be. Bird and human DNA simply could not mix.

Cranio loomed over him, the same hatchet man who had met him at the docks and escorted him to the Dai Jia Lou. Although he was dressed like one of the tong, Cranio was not an Asian. Brown skinned, he was at least six feet three inches tall and over half of that wide.

His dark eyes burned with a kind of black fire under straight, equally black brows. His hair was tight against the scalp of his big head, like a coarse-curled black helmet. Musgrave guessed him to be of Polynesian extraction, probably a Maori, mainly because of the blue spiral designs tattooed on his cheeks.

Cranio said nothing, but his voice wouldn't have been audible over the racket anyway. He jerked a thumb meaningfully toward the door. Musgrave rose from the table, making certain the small briefcase was still securely chained to the metal bracelet around his right wrist. Although he didn't think it likely a thief would try to steal from a guest of Wei Qiang, the warlord's influence and reputation had waned over the past couple of years.

Musgrave followed Cranio through the crowd, the

people parting for the big man like waves before the prow of a ship. They stepped out into the cool night air and Musgrave inhaled it gratefully, despite the many strange scents it held. Over the horizon, black thunderheads massed and he glimpsed a flash of lightning within them.

The double doors were situated at a corner of the Dai Jia Lou, beneath a tall bamboo canopy that sported carved wooden ducks and egrets on the frontispiece. Scrollwork covered the window ledges and the shutters around them.

On the hills leading down to the waterfront, a variety of buildings stood against a backdrop of trees. Most of them were single-story structures, but the Dai Jia Lou rose four levels from the heart of the settlement, its size due to the fact it served as a combination of tavern, music hall, bordello, trading outpost and the only hotel within three thousand square miles.

The man beaten by the tong security men still lay on the embankment, his torn flesh spilling crimson across the dirty stones. Cranio ignored him, marching down the flight of wooden steps.

"Come," Cranio directed.

Musgrave fell into step behind the big man, following him along narrow, twisting lanes toward the wharves. The streets were narrow and deeply rutted. From booths and the mouths of alleys, raucous men and women of all ages and ethnic groups offered everything from goods to sexual services. When they spied Cranio, they fell silent or eased back into the shadows.

The anchorage was built around a long spit of land that stabbed out into the ocean over a shallow bay. None of the score of docks, like the furniture within the Dai Jia Lou, were of uniform size or shape. Torches thrust into brackets bolted to the pilings lit up the rippling waters with eerie, shifting highlights.

Looking out past the bay to the open water, Musgrave noticed the storm clouds had scudded closer. Lightning flared and he heard the distant boom of thunder.

Cranio's destination was a dock at the very tip of the land spit. Moored to the dock was a long wooden vessel riding high above the waterline, its profile all sharp angles, arches and buttresses. The planking and timbers had been heavily varnished and lacquered to the bright red color of freshly spilled blood.

Three masts held huge sheets of sailcloth that folded as neatly as a paper fan. They reminded Musgrave of gigantic window blinds. Chinese characters marked the junk's stern, but he couldn't read them. However, he knew that most of the junks and sampans tied up in port were part of Wei Qiang's fleet, his ships identified by bright scarlet chops painted on the hulls.

Not too long ago, even the most ambitious trader and vicious freebooter gave the Wei Qiang ships a wide berth due to a hard-earned fearsome reputation. Nearly sixty years before, Qiang and his tong had invaded the Western Islands and established a pirate and smuggling empire.

Werner Musgrave was aware that the term "Western Isles" was something of a misnomer. Back during the nuclear holocaust, bombs known as earth-shakers had been triggered, seeded months before by submarines along the fault and fracture lines of the Pacific Ocean. ICBM missiles had pounded the Cascades, from western Canada down to California. The concentrated destructive force had ripped that part of the earth to pieces.

Tidal waves swept inland and, pummeled by earthquakes and volcanic activity, much of California sank beneath the waves. When it was over, the Cific coast was barely twenty miles from the foothills of the Sierra Nevada range.

After a century, the sea had retreated somewhat, leaving islands in its wake where most of the landmass had once been. Many of the islands were the high points of old California, or regions that became more elevated with the shifting of the tectonic plates.

The two men crossed a gangplank spanning the black waters of the bay to the deck of the junk. Although Musgrave saw sailors lounging about among the rigging, he also saw several not quite hidden automatic gun emplacements, positioned to catch intruders in triangulated cross fires.

Cranio led to the way to the elevated superstructure of the foc'sle and gestured with one hand toward the open hatch. A pair of stone Fu guardian dogs snarled on either side of the hatch.

Without hesitation, Musgrave entered a dimly lit companionway, carefully climbing down the short ladder into a spacious cabin. From the wooden bulkheads hung brocades of the finest silk, and drifting wreaths of fragrant smoke covered the thick brine smell of low tide. The streamers curled from the mouthpiece of a gold-bowled water pipe atop a great teakwood desk.

The surface of the desk was intricately carved and inlaid with ivory and jade, depicting pagodas, tigers and elephants. A lean old man sat behind it in a high-backed chair of dark rootwood, puffing contemplatively on the pipe.

Werner Musgrave hadn't seen many truly old men. He had spent most of his life in Mandeville, as an assistant to the administrator of the Manufacturing Division. People in the villes or the Tartarus Pits did not as a general rule live much past fifty. Wei Qiang looked twice that age.

Illuminated by tea candles floating in large, water-filled glass bowls on either side of him, the old man's skin appeared somehow leathery and repellently moist at the same time. His complexion was like that of dark butter, and despite his rail-thin frame, his flesh seemed to hang off him as if it were several sizes too large. A thin white mustache trailed down on either side of the lipless slash of his mouth.

Wei Qiang's slitted eyes were old with an ancient wisdom, but they seemed oddly hooded, like those of a drowsing hunting bird.

Above a deeply furrowed but high brow, he wore a skullcap of black satin with a single coral pearl attached to the forepiece, which Musgrave knew indicated he held a rank of Chinese royalty, probably a Mandarin. He figured the ideographs embroidered in gold thread upon his high-necked blue jacket symbolized his high station.

A brown-furred marmoset perched on the old man's left shoulder, inspecting Musgrave with alert, bright eyes.

"I am he with whom you have sought an audience," the old man said softly. "I am Wei Qiang. I expect you to bow when you enter my presence."

Chapter 2

"I am Werner Musgrave," the dun-clad man said, inclining his head a fraction of an inch. He knew his short nod was more disrespectful than if he had made no acknowledgment of Wei Qiang's statement whatsoever.

The old Chinese didn't reply, but studied him closely, expectantly. With a slightly trembling left hand, he gestured toward a wicker chair. The flickering candlelight winked on the conical fingernail protector placed over the man's gnarl-knuckled thumb. It was made of interwoven strands of gold wire.

Musgrave sat down, placing the briefcase on his lap. He unzipped the collar of his coverall and turned the lapel inside out to reveal a small brass button pinned to it. The inscribed image was a stylized representation of a standing, featureless man holding a cornucopia, a horn of plenty, in his left hand and a sword in his right, both crossed over his chest. No words were imprinted on it, but none was necessary.

"I do not discuss business with a man whose eyes I cannot see," Wei Qiang said. "Please remove your spectacles."

Musgrave ignored the request. "Do you recognize this insignia?"

Wei Qiang nodded almost reluctantly. "It has been my misfortune to cross paths with representatives of the Millennial Consortium in the recent past."

The man's voice, although raspy and brittle, did not sound at all weak, nor was his English blurred by any kind of an accent.

Musgrave permitted himself a small, superior smile. "Yes, I read reports of the incidents. Last February, the crew of one of your privateer ships was seriously discommoded when it attempted to board a trading vessel under the protection of the consortium. And the following April—"

Wei Qiang interrupted, "Why are you here?"

"I will be blunt," Musgrave replied. "Your smuggling and piracy networks are in disarray. Since the fall of the baronies over a year ago, most of your contacts, conduits and client base have virtually disappeared, either dismantled or absorbed by local consortium branches. Your most powerful allies have deserted Autarkic. Many of your own people plot your demise, including your eldest son, whom you banished but who still has confederates within your organization…that is why you hide aboard this vessel."

For an instant, the membranous veils lifted from the old man's eyes, which flashed with surprising energy in the flickering candlelight. Their color was a true tiger green. "I do not hide. If assassins seek my life, they know where to find me."

Musgrave chuckled, a hint of condescension lurking

at the back of his throat. "If you say so. However, those who desire your death are not motivated by avarice or vengeance but only by business considerations."

"Business considerations," the old man echoed sardonically. "By that you mean chaos?"

"Anarchy does indeed run rampant around the baronies and through their former territories," Musgrave conceded. "But for those with the proper vision, there are opportunities for both power and profit in chaos."

Wei Qiang angled a ropy eyebrow. "Should I interpret your words to mean I lack that vision?"

Musgrave replied smoothly, "The unfortunate truth is that in today's realities, you are an anachronism, a curiosity. There is no place for you or your quaint criminal enterprise in the modern, postbaronial world. You must adapt to changing conditions or be overwhelmed by the growth of more up-to-date operations, like the one I represent."

"You threaten me, consortium man?" Wei Qiang's tone was silky soft.

Musgrave shook his head, lips curving in a cold smile. "By no means. I simply state circumstances as they are."

"You state circumstances only as you perceive them to be," Wei Qiang retorted contemptuously. "There is a vast divide between your perceptions and realities. You know nothing."

The smile that stretched Musgrave's lips became almost pitying. "I might surprise you."

Qiang arched a supercilious eyebrow. "Then do so, consortium man. Surprise and enlighten me with your knowledge."

Flatly, Werner Musgrave stated, "I know that Wei Qiang is only an alias, one of hundreds you have adopted in a life that began in China's Yellow River valley over five thousand years ago.

"Then you were known as Huang-ti and later as Xuanyuan Shi, the Yellow Emperor. You developed legendary skills in warcraft and allied yourself with the most powerful lords in Asia to create a vast empire. You also found a means that, for all intents and purposes, rendered you immortal."

Wei Qiang sucked on the mouthpiece of the waterpipe hose, his seamed face showing only mild interest. The marmoset nuzzled his ear. "Go on."

"Over the centuries you adopted many names, many guises," Musgrave continued, "and embarked on many life paths as Shiwan Khan, Wu Fang, Yen Sin, Lo Pan. According to my research, you were quite infamous in the early twentieth century when you were known by the melodramatic euphemism of the 'Devil Doctor.' During that period, you saw to the formation of the most pervasive Asian criminal organization in the world, the Si-Fan. The list of your alter egos is endless…as are the crimes you perpetrated under those names.

"History has hailed you as both a visionary and a criminal mastermind, a genocidal monster and a liberator. Now, as Wei Qiang, you are merely an enfeebled old patriarch who cannot die but can only be killed. Your position is truly untenable. You stand now, at long last, upon the brink of doom."

The old Chinese eyed him speculatively and exhaled twin streams of smoke through his nostrils. "I have heard similar sentiments pronounced over my humble person more often than you can possibly count, and yet I sit here talking to you."

"Talking, perhaps," Musgrave replied stiffly. "But not listening. Do you deny or confirm the extraordinary biography I just presented to you?"

Wei Qiang raised a thin left hand, the skin looking like damp parchment ready to fall off the bone. He scratched the marmoset under the chin with the tip of the fingernail protector. "Why should I do either, consortium man? Your fantasies bring a passing entertainment to, as you say, an enfeebled old patriarch."

Werner Musgrave placed his briefcase flat atop the desk. "If I speak only fantasies, then you should have no interest in my gift."

"First you spin a fable for my amusement, then you present me with a gift." Wei Qiang's tone was edged by icy sarcasm. "Why has the consortium so blessed me?"

Unlatching the locks, Musgrave said, "This blessing does not come from the Millennial Consortium. In this instance, we have agreed to act as intermediaries for another party."

"Oh? And who might that be?"

Musgrave didn't answer. He raised the lid of the case and Wei Qiang leaned forward slightly, then froze. The consortium representative pretended not to notice the expression of stunned incredulity that settled over the old man's face like a mask.

A heavy ring lay within a molded cushion of foam rubber. The metal was coppery in appearance, the strands shaped to form nine intertwined serpents, the horned heads holding the tails in their jaws. Delicate splinters and veins of jade traced along the twisting reptilian bodies, fused cunningly with the metal. The nine pairs of eyes were cabochon-cut rubies.

The ring was abnormally large, several sizes too broad to fit on even the thickest finger of a very large man.

Uttering a wild, gargling cry, Wei Qiang seized the ring with both hands. The marmoset recoiled at the sight of it, baring its tiny teeth and chittering in fear. Clutching the ring between his bony fingers, Qiang stared at it with a surprise so intense it was almost stupefaction. Holding it before his eyes, he studied it, turning it about in the candlelight, his respiration coming hard and fast. He lifted a questioning, imploring gaze.

"The Hydra's ring, yes," Musgrave said, unable to completely repress the gloating note in his voice. "One of nine. I believe you wore them first some four thousand years ago, when you donned the Kai Bu Xiu, the Armor of Immortality, and they were attached to the fingers of the gauntlets. Once every five hundred years thereafter you wore the rings and lay encased within the armor for a day and night—until the end of the fourth century A.D. Since then, the rings have been denied to you. Eventually, old age came upon you, but not death. That was the final gift of the rings and the armor…or their curse."

Wei Qiang's lips stirred as his fingertips continued to fondle the ring, as if trying to convince himself it was real and within his grasp. He tried to speak, but his vocal cords seemed paralyzed by shock. Musgrave realized what he was he was trying to ask.

"Yes, I know the location of the other eight rings, just as you know the location of the Kai Bu Xiu. So as I hope you understand, we have a mutually beneficial situation here."

In a faint, hoarse rasp, Wei Qiang asked, "Are you certain it is genuine?"

Musgrave nodded. "There is no doubt."

"How can *I* be sure?"

The dun-clad man lifted a shoulder in a casual shrug. "If you are indeed the man I claim you to be, then you know how to test its authenticity."

Wei Qiang fixed Musgrave with a brief, unblinking glare of pure malice and unspoken threat. Musgrave only smiled. Reaching into a drawer beneath the desk, the old man withdrew a thin-bladed knife, scarcely more than a thorn of steel. With its tapered tip, he pricked the ball of his left thumb.

A bead of dark red blood oozed from the puncture and he smeared it over the horned Hydra heads on the ring, masking the jeweled eyes. He slipped the band of metal onto the third finger of his right hand and waited, holding it up before his face. The ring hung loosely, askew in the web of flaccid flesh between his fingers. He stared challengingly at Musgrave. "I am waiting, consortium man."

Suddenly tiny lightnings played over the ring, blazing like a miniature aurora borealis. Nine pairs of eyes flashed with a bright yellow glow. As if the metal had come alive, the serpentine bodies coiled around his finger, altering in diameter, tightening and contracting. Laughter rose from Musgrave's throat, triumphant and not a little relieved.

Wei Qiang stared dispassionately across the table, meeting Musgrave's dark-lensed gaze. He breathed deeply, regularly, his chest rising and falling. His respiration became labored. Then Qiang's body went into a series of strange, almost mannered convulsions even though he remained sitting upright. The tangled rootwood of the chair squeaked and creaked.

His hands gripped the edges of the desk so tightly the knuckles stood out like small ivory knobs. The marmoset uttered a high-pitched screech and bounded from his shoulder in terror, taking refuge upon an overhead timber.

With each spasm of his body, Wei Qiang changed, the flesh of his face tightening, the breadth of his shoulders spreading beneath the jacket, his chest swelling. The man shuddered violently as the shriveled skin stretched taut over his cheekbones, the deep creases and wrinkles smoothing as if all the loose epidermal tissue on his face had been gathered in a knot at the back of his head. The prominent ropy veins on his hands sank into firm flesh. Liver and age spots faded. His mustache and eyebrows darkened to a charcoal-gray.

When the convulsions ceased, Wei Qiang panted deeply and harshly, breathing through his thin, high-bridged nose. His lips peeled back from his bared teeth, air hissing between them. Sweat glistened on his high, pale brow. He sat motionless, hands spread on the desktop, a dim yellowish-green flame flickering in his narrowed eyes.

"Are you convinced?" Werner Musgrave asked, sounding completely unperturbed by the transformation he had just witnessed.

Wei Qiang tentatively fingered his face, coughed and murmured hoarsely, "I am not young."

"No," Musgrave agreed. "Only the other rings working in tandem with the Armor of Immortality will restore your youth and vitality. The effect of one ring cannot reverse the deterioration of your body—it can only hold it at bay."

Eyeing him suspiciously, Wei Qiang rasped, "You say you know where the other eight rings can be found?"

Musgrave nodded. "Within Great Pyramid of China in Xian, in the vault that once served as the tomb of Shih Huang Ti…yet another one of your alter egos, or so I am told. Very clever, to masquerade as your own descendant."

"Who told you that?" Qiang snapped, his voice growing stronger and more vibrant with every word.

Waving away the question, Musgrave declared, "I have been instructed to inform you that if you agree to retrieve the eight rings from the pyramid in Xian, you must also agree to reclaim *only* the rings and leave whatever else you may find there untouched."

"Who has instructed you?" Wei Qiang's magnetic eyes fixed upon Musgrave's face.

"His identity is less important than the fact he will supply you with all of the means to succeed at this task.

Manpower, matériel, engines of war, all will be made available for your use."

"Engines of war?" Wei Qiang echoed doubtfully. "The pyramid has been abandoned for many centuries."

"No longer. Now it is occupied and heavily fortified."

Qiang's eyes widened as far as the epicanthic folds allowed. "By whom?"

Musgrave made a casual show of opening the bracelet of the handcuff around his wrist. "A woman who commands a well-armed contingent of troopers. She is called by them Tui Chui Jian."

Wei Qiang frowned. "The Dragon Mother. Rather a pretentious title for a woman to adopt."

"Perhaps," Musgrave replied. "But she is not Chinese. She is an American. Her true name is Erica van Sloan, and she will never willingly relinquish the means for you to regain your youth."

Wei Qiang nodded contemplatively, idly tapping the horned Hydra heads with the point of his thumbnail protector. "Then she must die."

Musgrave's lips quirked in a smirk. "Is killing and war an undertaking you are prepared to see through to the end, especially at your advanced age?"

Wei Qiang stared at him in silent surmise. In the sudden quiet, they heard only the lap of water against the hull of the junk and the faint creak of the rigging on the deck. Thunder boomed, sounding much closer.

With a sigh, the man pushed himself to his feet. He was far taller than Musgrave had expected, several inches over six feet. Qiang walked casually around the desk, tugging at the golden cone capping his thumb.

"I've seen more war and done more killing than ten thousand mortals you might meet," he said musingly. "And through it all I have learned two things—"

In one swift movement, he snapped away the protector, revealing a three-inch-long thumbnail, its edges beveled and curved like the blade of a scimitar. He slashed it twice across Musgrave's face, blood spraying from the deep lacerations that stretched from both corners of his mouth and curved up toward his earlobes. The man screamed as he clapped his hands to his face and fell to the deck, overwhelmed by pain and shock. His dark-lensed glasses fell from his face.

"No insult should go unavenged," Wei Qiang said in the same reflective tone, "and the punishment should always fit the crime, as Gilbert and Sullivan's quaint Mikado sang. If you enjoy smirking in the presence of your masters, then you should take solace in the fact that after tonight you will always do so."

Shaking his hand to rid the razor-keen thumbnail of blood droplets, Wei Qiang stepped on Musgrave's glasses. The lenses cracked and crunched beneath his foot. Coldly, he stated, "And the second thing I have learned is to always finish what you start."

Wei Qiang fondled the molded Hydra heads on the ring as a clap of thunder shook the timbers and planks of the junk. He couldn't help but smile at the melodramatic irony of the timing.

Chapter 3

Thunder boomed in the distance, a long, loud roll. A fireball bloomed amid an explosion of pulverized stone. Erica van Sloan flinched, shielding her eyes from the flurry of grit.

Seng Kao yanked her into the niche, away from the observation post, sheltering her body from the concussion of the high-explosive shell as it punched a huge smoking crater in the face of the pyramid. Through the tumble of falling masonry, Erica glimpsed the wheeled light-artillery piece down by the riverbank, flame and smoke belching from its bore.

"They are only finding the range," Seng Kao said softly but admonishingly, "but you must be more careful. Without you to inspire our troops, all is lost, Tui Chui Jian."

Erica brushed dust from her heavy, ankle-length cloak of dark green. "The troops who haven't deserted, you mean."

She didn't bother lowering her voice, despite the presence of three other imperial troopers within the

niche. Like Lieutenant Seng Kao, they wore black
boots, helmets and coveralls of midnight-blue with
facings of bright scarlet. They carried compact
SIG-AMT subguns slung over their shoulders. The faces
under the overhangs of the helmets were of an Asian
cast. They were all native Chinese, and Erica towered
nearly half a head above the tallest of them.

Her long, straight hair, confined by a high, sable-fur
tam set at a rakish angle on her head, spilled over her
shoulders. It was so black as to be blue when the light
caught it, much like the color of troopers' uniforms.
The mark of an aristocrat showed in her delicate, honey-
hued features, with the high arch of her brows and her
thin-bridged nose. Single-mindedness, intelligence and
the potential for cruelty glinted in her violet eyes.

She was tall, nearly six feet in her stilt-heeled boots,
and voluptuous in the tight-fitting uniform that clung to
her upper body. Ebony pants hugged her long, lithe
legs. Her waist was tightly cinctured by a red sash, and
the narrow shoulders of her indigo tunic were broadened
by tapered pads. The satiny fabric was tailored to
conform to the thrust of her full breasts, which were accentuated by crimson facings.

Carefully, she edged out of the niche and onto the observation platform again, lifting a compact set of binoculars to her eyes. She swept the ruby-coated lenses
over the thickly wooded valley roughly a mile across.
The Yarkand, a tributary of the Yangtze River, flowed
through it, the foaming waters cascading down a gentle
fall half a mile to the west.

The army of the invaders spread across the valley floor, sprawling nearly a quarter of a mile or more in all directions. A gray umbrella of smoke hung above the valley, the result of a hundred cook fires. The previous day the army had crossed the river, and all night the fires flared along the length of the valley. The wind brought the blare of horns and the sharp shouts of officers drilling the men.

Then, shortly after daybreak, the barrage began on the pyramid that had served as Erica van Sloan's home for the past two years. From her vantage point, on a small balcony halfway up its southern face, she could see only a small portion of the pyramid's staggering dimensions.

The immense structure was composed of countless blocks of seamlessly fitted stone, the top quarried perfectly flat. Early-morning sunlight played along its facade, lending an air of otherworldly majesty to the huge monolith. A broad expanse of trimmed gardens and lawns surrounded the base of the five-hundred-foot-high pyramid. Old pagodas and Buddhist shrines were hidden within the gardens. No walls or gates ringed the perimeter. They were not needed, since legends whispered in the dark of evening had taught all of the locals to keep away. Obviously the invading soldiers had not been pressed into service from any of the nearby provinces.

The pyramid was painted black on the north side, blue-gray on the east, red on the south and white on the west. The original colors had been restored shortly before Sam had undergone his transformation—or evolution—into Overlord Enlil.

In predark days, archaeologists had theorized the Great Pyramid of China was part of the tomb complex of Emperor Shih Huang. The purpose of the pyramid or tomb was never known, though Taoist tradition attributed its construction to a very powerful race called the Celestials, one of whom was reputed to be the first emperor of China, the legendary Huang-ti.

Whoever was responsible for its construction, one thing was certain—the great pyramid of Xian represented a cardinal point in the world grid harmonics, a network of pyramids built at key places around the globe to tap Earth's natural geomantic energies. That aspect of the structure's design was not conjecture. Erica knew it as a fact.

But one fact she still did not know was the true purpose of the army that had swarmed into her valley over the past two days.

The first reports of a very large and organized body of armed men marching from the port city of Kiangsu and across Honan had filtered into Xian sporadically over the period of a week. Verifiable intelligence from outlying provinces was not only difficult to come by, but the sources were also very hard to assess as to accuracy and simple veracity.

China was vast and without a centralized government, having reverted to a nation of divided fiefdoms and minikingdoms whose boundaries were determined by warlords. At first, Erica assumed the reports of Wei Qiang and his army were only distortions, fragmented exaggerations about one of the regional warlords seeking to expand his territories.

But the fragments, once assembled like a jigsaw puzzle, formed a coherent and terrifying image. Wei Qiang was whispered to be a direct descendant of Huang-ti, the Yellow Emperor, who millennia before had invented the four branches of military tactics concerned with mountains, rivers, marshes and plains.

To have reached the valley in Xian, Wei Qiang and his army would have had to contend with and cross all of those terrains, so she wondered if there wasn't some truth to the rumors about his lineage.

Erica van Sloan was not a historian, either by trade or inclination. More than two hundred years before, she had earned a Ph.D. in cybernetics and computer science. For years she worked as a models and systems analyst. During that time, she had learned through the process of punishment and reward to always take advantage of an opportunity when one presented itself.

She understood the motivation of the opportunist seeking profit and power far more than that of a military strategist. Wei Qiang's reasons for marching a quarter of the way across China specifically to lay siege to her small, isolated territory mystified her.

Although she more or less ruled Xian Province, Erica's position was not unique. She knew of at least two dozen families in neighboring Wuhan and Chengchow who, much like her, lived in sheltered, fortified estates protected by private armies. These families had prospered and grown powerful during the chaotic decades following the end of skydark, the generation-long nuclear winter.

Similar to the baronial system that took root in postnuke America, the families extended their estates by appropriating territory and absorbing into service the peasants who tilled and toiled in the fields. Almost all of central China was composed of a loose conglomeration of autonomous feudal estates, most of them far wealthier and expansive than her own.

But spies reported that Wei Qiang and his army bypassed the estates lying even along their invasion route, marching directly and single-mindedly to Xian, apparently not wishing to expend time and resources engaging the private security forces of the feudal lords. The army had no interest in liberating the peasants or even recruiting them into its ranks.

Since the arrival of the army, no attempt to communicate with Erica had been put forth. Couriers she dispatched never returned, and she assumed they joined the invaders. A number of her own troopers, at least a score, had vanished from their perimeter posts over the past two days, along with a substantial supply of ordnance from the armory. She suspected that, like the couriers, they had enlisted in Wei Qiang's forces, deserting while she slept.

Spying on the invaders from the pyramid's observation post, Erica was perplexed to see only Asian men among their numbers. She had expected a representative sampling of foreign mercenaries, like Russians and even Mongols, but apparently Wei Qiang was ethnically selective about his warriors.

The soldiers were exceptionally well armed and outfitted. Each man carried a handgun, a strangely shaped but deadly looking black autorifle, and wore a yellow uniform with three green pips on the high collar. The tunics bore the colors of blue and crimson in two very wide vertical bands that encircled their torsos. Erica guessed the colored bands were of Kevlar.

Their heads and eyes were protected by visored poly-carbonate helmets a deeper shade of yellow than the tunics, emblazoned on both sides by scarlet Chinese ideograms that, according to Seng Kao, represented the word *monarch*.

Erica could only roughly gauge the number of soldiers in the valley, but she estimated at least two hundred of them had crossed the river the evening before in flat, wide fan boats. Around a hundred men remained encamped on the opposite bank. The last roll call among her own forces indicated she could rely on a less than one hundred combat-ready troopers.

Until the shelling began shortly after daybreak, Wei Qiang's soldiers had undertaken no hostile action. Then, almost silently, they assembled in tight formation, facing the pyramid. They seemed to be waiting for a signal. Erica had no idea what the signal might be, but she could not help feeling impressed by their discipline. The invaders were not the usual ragtag rabble who swore al-legiance to a local warlord for as long as the loot held out.

A sudden metallic clatter and the rumble of engines reached Erica's eardrums, and she shifted her binocu-lars toward the sound. Like prehistoric creatures roused from aeon-long slumbers at the bottom of the sea, three dark shapes rose from the roiling surface of the river and came crashing through the undergrowth and reeds bordering the bank.

The low-slung, boxlike vehicles were propelled by eight massively treaded wheels, four to each side. The wet armor plate bristled with rocket pods and sealed weapons ports. At the end of jointed armatures sprouted two swivel-mounted .50-caliber machine guns like a pair of foreclaws.

Twenty feet long and nearly half that wide at their broadest points, Erica recognized them as Scorpinauts, omnipurpose Future Combat System vehicles that were designed to take the place of tanks in a variety of wartime situations. She had actually seen a few of them stored in the Anthill, shortly after the nukecaust. At the time she assumed they were nonfunctional prototypes.

From rectangular turrets protruded the tapered, ten-foot-long snouts of 40 mm cannons. The barrels were locked in a backward position, giving the FCS vehicles the aspects of mechanical scorpions, with the fore-mounted machine guns represented as claws and the cannon barrels the stinger-tipped tails.

The double thickness of their steel hulls showed no scoring of weapons fire. She received the distinct impression that the submersible FCS vehicles were experiencing their first combat trials. How such mil-spec ordnance had ended up in China was beyond her comprehension.

The formation of yellow-uniformed soldiers parted as the Scorpinauts chugged forward, leaving trails of water in their wake. The four vehicles braked to almost simultaneous halts.

A dorsal hatch on the turret of the center Scorpinaut rose, pushed open from within. As a figure emerged, an undulating wail burst from over five hundred tongues. The chant began slowly at first: *"Jun Zhu! Jun Zhu!"*

The words were shouted in an ever-increasing rhythm until they sounded like a voice tape sped up and on continuous loop: *"JunZhuJunZhuJunZhu—"*

Seng Kao sidled up behind her and said quietly, "They say, 'Sovereign monarch, sovereign monarch.'"

"I thought it was something like that," Erica said dryly, adjusting the focus on her binoculars. "So that's Wei Qiang himself."

She didn't ask a question, so Seng Kao didn't answer.

The surprisingly tall and lean figure of Wei Qiang was dressed colorfully in high boots of dyed yellow leather, blue leggings and a yellow silk tunic decorated with dragons worked in black thread. Fur-trimmed crimson gauntlets encased his hands and forearms. Light winked from the fingernail protector capping the thumb of the man's left glove and glinted dully from metal on his right hand. A long black cloak with a silk yellow lining fell from his shoulders, clasped at his throat with a chain of silver. He made an imposing, colorful figure, but there was something not quite right about him.

Taut, yellow-brown flesh covered his unlined angular face, stretched drum tight over the bones. The sharp nose was high-bridged, and the lipless mouth was a straight gash beneath a drooping mustache. His features reminded Erica of the results of a face-lift performed by a cut-rate cosmetic surgeon.

The tall man wore a black hat with a broad, upturned brim edged with pearls. She recognized it as the kind of headgear favored by Chinese royalty, dating back to the time of the Empress Dowager. The high crown glinted with same ideograph as that emblazoned on the helmets of his soldiers. He made a sharp gesture with his left hand, and the chanting throng almost instantly fell silent.

Wei Qiang struck a dramatic pose atop the turret of the Scorpinaut, fists on his hips as he surveyed the chanting men and the pyramid. His cold gaze traveled up across its smooth face, and Erica received the disquieting impression that the man was intimately familiar with the great monolithic structure.

He bent his head, his lips stirring as he spoke, and from the hatch another figure climbed up. Stocky of build and wearing a dun-colored coverall, he was the first Caucasian Erica had glimpsed among the invaders. He would have been completely nondescript except for two features—the round, dark-lensed glasses masking his eyes and the livid scars curving up from both sides of his mouth, as if his lips were perpetually lifted in a caricature of a smirk.

He handed Wei Qiang a monocular, and the tall man swept it up and over the facade of the pyramid. He fixed them on Erica's position, and his colorless lips twitched in a smile.

Tightening the focus of her own binoculars, Erica's attention was caught and held by sunlight gleaming briefly from a ring on Wei Qiang's gloved middle finger.

Recognition rushed through her like a flow of icy water. Made of thick, hammered copper, the ring was fashioned like nine serpents coiled in four loops, the dragon heads snarling balefully. Tiny, iridescent sparks danced within the eyes of gemstones.

As she stared, Wei Qiang lowered the monocular from his slitted eye and the thin, colorless lips parted in a taunting grin. He seemed to stare directly into Erica's soul, mocking what he saw there.

Then he turned his head to the right and shouted in a ringing, strident voice, *"Ben Teng! Jin Gong!"*

Even Erica with her limited understanding of Mandarin knew Wei Qiang had issued to the command to move forward and attack.

Chapter 4

The pyramid's defenders were stationed in camouflaged dugouts and trenches around the structure's perimeter, waiting for the order from their unit commanders before taking action. The commanders, in turn, were waiting for instruction from Tui Chui Jian, the Dragon Mother, before they opened fire.

Erica van Sloan stood and watched the movement of Wei Qiang's soldiers, weighing the proper time to activate the cybernetic implants in her brain, the superconducting quantum interface device, or SQUID.

As a predark cyberneticist, Erica had perfected the SQUID implants as interfaces between mechanical-electric and organic material. Over the past year or so, she had employed the SQUIDs to facilitate long-distance silent communication with her troopers as well as to exercise a degree of control over their thoughts.

She had implanted SQUIDs directly into the brains of her subjects herself. The devices measured only one-hundredth of a micron across and required very little in the way of invasive surgery. The nanomachines drew power from the electromagnetic field generated by the brain itself.

Uttering cries of *"Jun Zhu!"* the close-packed attackers poured up from the riverfront. Across the grassy field they swept, moving as though the pyramid exerted a magnetic attraction. Erica waited until the soldiers reached a certain point, then initiated the SQUID link with her ground commanders.

Almost at once, the black-clad troopers of Tui Chui Jian rose up from their trenches and fired a concerted fusillade with their SIG-AMT subguns, catching the first ranks in a triangulated cross fire. The soldiers reeled and staggered back in bloody confusion.

But the inexorable rush from the invaders in the rear vanguard pushed the second rank forward. The yellow-uniformed soldiers regrouped and split to either side, forming a wedge that curved around and flanked the trenches. Though a blizzard of high-velocity rounds struck them and knocked them down, more kept coming, trampling over their dead or dying comrades.

Against the swiftly moving targets, the defenders could only lay down their fire ahead of the onrushing lines, hoping that they judged close enough so the yellow-uniformed soldiers would run into the hailstorm of lead.

The range closed with alarming speed. The yellow-helmeted men leading the charge clutched at themselves and staggered, but the attackers behind them kept coming, pushing them headlong.

A series of eardrum-compressing detonations overwhelmed the cacophony of gunfire and screams. The cannon barrels of the Scorpinauts gouted smoke and flame, a sequenced volley that began with a vehicle on one end and pounded back toward the far end and then resumed with the first one again.

Two high-explosive rounds impacted within the trenches, flinging out dirt and men in billows of orange-red flame. The other two shells exploded against the base of the pyramid, the concussions causing dust and dirt to sift down from the ceiling of the niche that opened onto the observation rampart.

Closing her eyes momentarily, Erica transmitted another command through the SQUID interface. Within seconds, a group of black-uniformed imperial soldiers raced out of the pyramid, firing as they came. The blended autofire gave rise to a deafening, prolonged drumroll. Their fire was disorganized and too rapid, but it had some effect. A few of the invaders toppled and fell into the trenches, but the main body was not stopped.

The autorifles in the hands of Wei Qiang's soldiers roared in a stuttering rhythm of deadly syncopation. One of the Scorpinauts fired a shell that exploded in the center of the imperial troopers. Dark-uniformed bodies flew up amid a mushroom of fire.

Erica's throat constricted, and she felt her heart beat violently in her breast. Although intellectually she had accepted the fact her troopers were not as numerous or as well-armed as the invaders, she had refused to dwell on the possibility they would be so summarily slaughtered. They fought as courageously as their oaths of service demanded, but they could not overcome such superior firepower.

The FCS vehicles began rolling forward in unison,

the jointed armatures rising from the hulls and the swivel-mounted machine guns spitting tongues of flame. Erica caught only glimpses of her troopers spinning, clutching at themselves, falling as the high-velocity bullets clawed open their bodies, sending scraps of uniform, flesh and even bone flying in all directions, propelled by crimson sprays.

As the Scorpinauts rumbled forward, the cannons belched more rounds. Shell after shell detonated, until the smoke and dust boiled high and the explosions rolled together like many blended thunderstorms.

A tongue of flame licked from the hull of the vehicle that carried Wei Qiang. It gushed forth some fifty feet and engulfed a cluster of imperial troopers clambering out of a trench. Instantly they were transformed into screaming, careening scarecrows sheathed by flames.

Erica, all but blinded by the rising clouds of acrid smoke, remained at the observation post, knowing that if any of her troopers still lived down below, she would be invisible to them. Still, she was loath to withdraw, although she knew the invaders would breach the interior of the pyramid within minutes. Her stomach twisted in knots, a combination of frustrated fury and mounting terror.

"My lady! Please!" Seng Kao shouted desperately.

Reluctantly, Erica turned toward the niche just as she heard the slamming detonation of another cannon blast. The warhead impacted just below the observation platform, and the stone dissolved in a blinding flash, a clap of thunder and a blooming burst of hell-hued light.

Erica fell flat as ugly black fissures spread out in a spiderweb pattern around the mouth of the niche. Dust and gravel showered down from above. She looked back once to see the entire observation post falling away, breaking apart in hundreds of small pieces.

As she struggled to rise, the section of the floor beneath her collapsed with an earsplitting, crunching roar. A large portion of the pyramid face plunged downward and carried her with it. She clamped her jaws shut on the scream starting up her throat. Then a hand closed over her right wrist. Tilting her head back, Erica saw Seng Kao lying belly down with the edge of the floor digging into his armpits.

Erica seized his wrist, and Seng Kao snapped a sharp order over his shoulder. The other troopers held the man by the ankles, and they began to back away from the rim. When she was lifted to the point where she could rest her weight on the lip of the floor, more of the pyramid's facade had crumbled.

"Wei Qiang tried to kill you, blessed Dragon Mother," Seng Kao panted, his face expressing outrage at the very notion. "He does not seek terms—he seeks only your death."

Erica climbed to her feet, backing away from the edge, fanning dust away from her face. "If not for you, he would have found it. Thank you."

Seng Kao bowed. "I live only to serve my beloved Tui Chui Jian." He gestured behind him to the blank-faced troopers. "We all do."

Erica glanced at the three men. Their almond eyes

didn't even blink in the grit-laced air. They were little more than automatons, influenced by her thoughts only when she was awake. With a surge of despair, she realized the obedience instilled in them by the SQUID interface had definite limits, but she had never envisioned a scenario where they engaged in full-scale warfare with a superior enemy.

She didn't allow her emotions to register on her face or in her tone of voice when she declared, "They can best serve me by defending the entrance. Our enemies will not be stopped, but perhaps they can be delayed for enough time."

Seng Kao cocked his helmeted head quizzically. "Enough time for what, my lady?"

Erica brushed aside his query. "Send them down. You will come with me. Tell them not to surrender."

Nodding, Seng Kao snapped out orders in hard-edged Cantonese. Clutching at their weapons, the three troopers turned and jogged down one of the winding walkways that honeycombed the vast interior of the pyramid.

Wheeling, Erica ran in the opposite direction, her cloak belling out behind her. Seng Kao followed as closely as he could, having trouble keeping up with her longer stride.

They didn't run far. Rounding a corner, Erica paused before a wide shaft, like a smooth vertical groove cut into the stone wall. On the floor was a raised disk of a translucent, plasticlike substance about four feet in diameter. From beneath it emanated the faintest susurrus of electronic hums.

She stepped onto the disk and, when Seng Kao hesitated, she gestured impatiently for him to join her. He did so, moving with exaggerated caution. With the toe of her boot, she kicked a hidden trip switch on the upper rim of the disk and immediately it began sinking into darkness.

He didn't cry out in fear, but he uttered a brief murmur and then fell silent. The diameter of the disk was so small, he and Erica were jammed against each other, face-to-face. Although the man remained quiet, Erica could feel his heart pounding, either due to fear or the excitement of being pressed against the Dragon Mother's breasts. Perspiration pebbled his upper lip.

As the lift disk dropped swiftly down the shaft, Erica did not expend any thought about the breach of protocol. A riot of conflicting emotions warred within her. Fear, fury, humiliation and a rising sense of betrayal completely occupied her mind. Her stomach was twisted in adrenaline-fueled knots.

The disk eased to a hissing halt. As it did, she heard the heavy boom of artillery fire, interwoven with the staccato hammering of autofire. She stepped out into a dimly lit passageway, Seng Kao following an instant later. She looked around warily, drawing a 9 mm Makarov pistol from the red sash.

Although the emergency lift had deposited them on the ground level of the pyramid, they were in a section that only someone possessing an intimate knowledge of the layout could easily find. She suspected Wei Qiang of possessing that knowledge, but she hadn't devoted the time to formulate a theory on how he came by that

information. The most obvious answer was too mad—
and frightening—to entertain.

Thumping explosions compressed her ears, and the
corridor shuddered from the jolt of the shock waves. The
vibrations of the multiple detonations triggered a
shower of dirt and grit from above, sifting over her head
and shoulders.

"Our enemies have breached your fortress," Seng
Kao declared grimly.

Erica raced down the corridor, Seng Kao at her heels,
their feet clattering loudly on the flat stone tiles. The
passage was feebly lit by neon strips recessed into the
ceiling. She turned right down a narrow hall that dead-
ended against a tall set of double doors. They hung
open, and she rushed between them into a room of
black—the walls, floor and ceiling were the color of
ebony, like a view of deep space.

Erica sensed Seng Kao's hesitation and she spoke to
him in *pai-hu*, the simplest of the Chinese dialects
detached from Mandarin and the only one in which she
was fluent—cursing and insults. She hissed, "*Ben dan!*
Fool! *Nuo fu!* Coward! *Tong xing!* Faggot!"

At that, the man rushed forward to join her, apolo-
gizing breathlessly in the same dialect.

The room wasn't completely without light. A transparent sphere six feet in diameter occupied the center
of the room from floor to ceiling. The slowly revolving
globe glittered with thousands of pinpoints of light,
scattered seemingly at random, but all connected by
glowing lines. She knew the orb was actually a three-

dimensional representation of the electromagnetic power grid of the planet, as well as a targeting device.

Erica understood Seng Kao's reluctance to enter and cross the room, since it was a forbidden area of the Dragon Mother's fortress, a transgression punishable by death. Only one trooper had been executed over the past couple of years, and she had turned the manner of death over to Sam, who killed the man in a slow, painful way. He had kept the trooper fully conscious and alert to every sensation of his body. When he expired many hours later, eviscerated and mad from agony, the object lesson had been become an article of faith among the other soldiers.

Seng Kao followed her through a wide archway and came to a halt, blinking owlishly at the furnishings of the room. Under other circumstances, Erica might have been amused by the man's reaction.

Sam always referred to it as the Hall of Memory, and she never had reason to question that description. From the center of the floor rose a twelve-foot-tall, round sandstone pillar bearing ornate carvings of birds and animal heads. It was bracketed by two large sculptures, one a feathered jaguar and the other a serpent with wings. Silk tapestries depicting Asian ideographs hung from the walls. There were other tapestries, all bearing twisting geometric designs such as mandalas.

Ceramic effigy jars and elegantly crafted vessels depicting animal-headed gods and goddesses from the Egyptian pantheon were stacked in neat pyramids. Arrayed on a long shelf on the opposite wall were a dozen *ushabtis* figures, small statuettes representing laborers in the Land of the Dead.

Each and every item appeared to be in perfect condition and each and every item was beyond the ability of the mind to catalog. The huge room was an archaeologist's paradise, less a museum than a representative sampling from every human culture ever influenced by the Annunaki, the Tuatha de Danaan and the race known as the Archons.

"Guard the door," Erica commanded, handing him her pistol. "Let no one come near, not even our own men."

She rushed across the room to a far wall covered with shelves that held containers and boxes of wood, stone, gold, hammered silver and an abundance of jade. Some of the boxes were set with precious gems, others unadorned and all were stacked helter-skelter.

While Seng Kao stood by the entrance, Erica frantically lifted the lids of the containers and discarded them with no regard to their contents. Coins and jewels of all sizes and colors scattered and rolled across the floor.

The distant rattle of autofire ceased. Only a few cracking, single-shot reports floated down the corridor, followed by the faint tramp of marching feet.

Tensely, Seng Kao began, "My lady—"

Erica interrupted him by uttering a short, sharp cry of triumph. Turning toward her, Seng Kao saw Erica striding swiftly toward him with an ornately carved wooden box tucked under an arm. She swept past him out into the corridor, saying only, "Hurry!"

They raced down the passageway, their footsteps

echoing like the beat of faraway drums. The two people rounded a corner and reached the gateway unit, rising from an elevated platform. Six upright slabs of armaglass formed a translucent wall around it. The armaglass glistened as if ingots of gold had been melted down and applied to it like molten paint.

Erica pulled open the door on its counterbalanced hinges and pushed Seng Kao inside the chamber, his boots ringing hollowly on the metal hexagonal floor plates. The pattern was repeated on the ceiling.

She remained outside, quickly punching in a destination lock code on the keypad affixed to the door. Although Seng Kao had traveled via the mat-trans units before, he never grew accustomed to the concept, much less the practice. He said plaintively, "My lady—"

Erica opened the box under her arm and removed an object from within it, pressing it into his left hand while she took the pistol from his right. "You won't need that where you're going," she stated tersely. "It's best you arrive unarmed. And when you do, show them the ring and tell them I have the other seven. Say I ask their help."

Seng Kao gazed down with confused, disconcerted eyes at the ring of corroded copper in his hand. The band, resembling several intertwined serpents, was very wide. He noted absently that whoever had owned the ring in the past had to have been a giant, since its girth was several sizes too great for any normal human finger to hold.

"My lady," he said with a growing alarm. "Tell who about the other seven what?"

Erica stepped back and began swinging the door

shut. "You'll know who to tell when you get there. Tell them I have the other seven Hydra rings. You have one, and Wei Qiang wears the ninth. Explain what has happened and if they want to become involved, to seek me in Yichang."

Seng Kao opened his mouth to protest, but the door closed with a solid chock, the lock solenoids catching and triggering the automatic jump mechanism. He cried out, "But what of you, Tui Chui Jian? What of you?"

She didn't answer. Even through the armaglass Erica saw the disks in the floor and ceiling of the chamber beginning to shimmer. A vibrating hum arose from within the platform, climbing rapidly to a high-pitched whine.

Erica van Sloan didn't wait to see if the dematerialization cycle completed successfully. Pressing the wooden box between her left arm and ribs, the Makarov in her right fist, she dashed out of the room and down another corridor. She heard the distant thudding of grenades, the sharp crackle of machine guns and the heavier thud of rifle fire.

The floor became smoother and the square-cut blocks of stone on the walls gave to way a seamless expanse. The ceiling rounded overhead like an arch, winding gently to the left in an ever-widening curve. Behind her, she heard men shouting in Chinese, yelling something about finding the white whore. She didn't wonder whom they were talking about.

The passageway suddenly opened into a vast, domed space, a natural cavern beneath the pyramid itself. The unfinished stone of its ceiling gleamed here and there with clusters of crystals and geodes. The floor dipped down in a gradual incline and at the center, surrounded by a collar of interlocking silver slabs, lay a pool about fifty feet in circumference.

The inner rim was lined with an edging of crystal points that glowed with a dull iridescence. Sam had always called the pool the Heart of the Earth and in many ways it was, since it was a nexus point, a convergence of geomantic energy.

The pool served as a cardinal point in the world grid harmonics, a part of an ancient network of pyramids built at key places around the world to tap Earth's natural geomantic energies. She knew there were a number of hubs throughout Asia such as Angkor Wat in Cambodia and Chomolunga in Tibet, but none with the concentration of sheer power that lay beneath the Xian pyramid.

Only a few of the ceiling crystals sparkled with light. Some glowed steadily, others flickered feebly and still others were only multifaceted lumps of mineral. She knew that if all of them shone with the same light level, the interior of the cavern would have blazed as blindingly as a naked star.

Panting, Erica remained by the entrance, placing the box between her feet as she tried to catch her breath. She eyed the crystalline formations and the misty phosphorescence wafting within the pool with something akin to anger.

To her frustration and regret, she had never been able to manipulate the geomantic energies pent up within the

Heart of the World, or even figure out how they interacted with the targeting sphere.

Although she understood the principles, she lacked
Sam's psionic talents to engage the process. He had
promised to teach her the proper methodology, but like
so many of his other promises, it was only a lie to gain
her trust and cooperation for the furtherance of his monstrous plans.

In the year since Sam's true nature had asserted itself,
Erica made a promise of her own—that if she could not
learn how to harness the Heart of the World, then no one
else would have the opportunity, either.

Assuming a combat stance, holding the pistol in a
two-handed grip, she brought the block of C-4 into
target acquisition, aligning it with the front and rear
sights of her Makarov. The package of plastic explosive
was exactly where she had affixed it months ago,
jammed between a huge chunk of geode and a stalac-
tite a score of yards away. It had a percussion-charge
detonator, and a hard jolt was all that was required to
set it off.

Erica took a half breath, held it and squeezed the
trigger. The report of the pistol was a flat, lackluster
crack, as of the snapping of a wet twig in the distance.

There was nothing lackluster about the reaction when
the 9 mm round penetrated the percussion charge. The
ceiling of the cavern dissolved in a blinding flash, a clap
of eardrum-compressing thunder and a blooming burst
of hell-hued light.

A hurricane of hot air struck Erica in the face, driving

her breath painfully back into her nostrils. The wave of concussive force sent her staggering, her cloak billowing out behind her as if she faced a stiff wind.

A seething avalanche of rock slabs cascaded from the roof of the cavern. Great stalactites and crystal shards crashed onto the area around the pool, smashing and crushing the collar of interlocking silver slabs encircling it.

Inestimable tons of marbleized granite, mica and flint poured into the throat of the pool, filling it, clogging it, covering it. Small boulders rolled and bounced across the cavern. Squinting through the whirling clouds of dust and grit to make sure the Heart of the World was thoroughly buried, Erica picked up the wooden box and backed away from the entrance.

Dimly, above the grinding rumble of settling stone, Erica heard a series of pops. Bullets tore white gouges in the stonework above her head, sprinkling her hair with rock particles. She slid backward into the shadows, grimacing at the ricochets whining all around.

At the far end of the passageway dark shapes shifted through the planes of dust and smoke, little red flares twinkling in the gloom. Voices shouting in angry Chinese interwove around the autofire.

Taking a firm grip on the pistol, she stretched out her arm and fired in a steady roll at the indistinct figures milling in the corridor. She heard screams of pain and panic even over the gunshots. Then the slide of the Makarov snapped back into the locked and empty position. She flung herself behind the shield of a corner as the yellow-uniformed soldiers returned the fire. A sleet storm of bullets crashed into the stone, chipping out long, dust-spurting gouges.

More than one voice was raised in an infuriated scream about not allowing the dragon whore, Tui Chui Jian, to escape.

A cold smile creased Erica van Sloan's lips as she eased deeper into the shadows of the passageway, clutching at the wooden box. The rings rattled within it. "Too late, assholes," she whispered. *"Too late."*

Chapter 5

Mohandas Lakesh Singh was fuming. He was fuming and walking fast and talking all at the same time, which required a great deal of effort. Mainly he seemed to be cursing under his breath.

"That damned silly little twit," he muttered, the vanadium-sheathed walls of the corridor muting his voice. "She tricked me, sent me off on a fool's errand to the gymnasium. She tricked me!"

Brigid Baptiste, walking beside him, didn't even bother repressing a laugh. "Serves you right, Lakesh. You played tricks on a lot of people, me included, to get them here in the first place. Just because Domi turned the tables on you for once is no reason to throw a fit."

"I'm not throwing a fit," he snapped. "I'm expressing a victim's right to redress a grave grievance. The weekly security briefing was scheduled for today at noon, and Domi's nincompoopery has thrown my plans for the rest of the day seriously off model."

Brigid laughed again.

Lakesh scowled at her. He was a well-built man of medium height, with thick, glossy black hair, a dark olive complexion and a long, aquiline nose. He looked no older than fifty, despite strands of gray threading his temples. In reality, he was less than a year shy of celebrating his 250th birthday. He wore a one-piece white zippered bodysuit, the unisex duty uniform of the Cerberus redoubt.

"I'm pleased you take such pleasure in my discomfiture," he said sourly, his cultured voice underscored by a lilting East Indian accent.

"Like Kane keeps saying," Brigid replied, "you take yourself way too seriously way too often."

She was a tall woman less than half an inch shy of matching Lakesh's five feet ten inches. Her fair complexion was lightly dusted with freckles across her nose and cheeks, and her big feline-slanted eyes weren't just green, they were the color of brightly polished emeralds. Her high forehead gave the impression of a probing intellect whereas her full underlip hinted at an appreciation of the sensual.

A thick mane of red-gold hair fell in loose, lava-flow waves almost to her waist. She wore a military-gray T-shirt and jeans, which accentuated her full-breasted, willowy figure. Her bare arms rippled with hard, toned muscle.

They turned a corner and walked side by side down the twenty-foot-wide main corridor of the Cerberus redoubt, underneath great curving ribs of metal that supported the high rock roof.

Bright midsummer sunshine flooded through the square entrance, causing both of them to squint. The massive security door inset into the base of the mountain peak opened in accordion fashion and, because of the weight of the individual vanadium panels, the door was usually left partially ajar during daylight hours. Opening and shutting it completely required several minutes.

From the plateau outside the entrance wafted the murmur of several voices, Domi's among them. Lakesh heard her laugh, and by degrees his scowl turned into a rueful grin.

Turning toward Brigid, he inquired, "I suppose upon reflection my whole life has just been one big trick, hasn't it?"

Brigid nodded in smiling agreement. "So you'd better learn to relax and enjoy it while you can."

They continued walking toward the open door, passing the three heads of Cerberus. A large, luridly colored illustration of the triple-headed black hound of Greek myth was painted on the wall beneath the sec door controls. Fire and blood gushed out from between yellow fangs, the crimson eyes glaring bright and baleful. Underneath the image, in overly ornate Gothic script was written the single word *Cerberus*.

Brigid recalled when she asked about the artist shortly after her arrival at the redoubt some three years ago, Lakesh opined that one of the original military personnel assigned to the redoubt had rendered the painting. Although he couldn't be positive, Lakesh suspected a Corporal Mooney was the artist, since its exaggerated exuberance seemed right out of the comic books he was obsessed with collecting.

Lakesh had never considered having it removed. For one thing, the paints were indelible and for another, it was Corporal Mooney's form of immortality. Besides, the image of Cerberus, the guardian of the gates of Hell, represented a visual symbol of the work to which Lakesh had devoted his life. The three-headed hound was an appropriate totem for the installation that, for a handful of years, housed the primary subdivision of the Totality Concept's Overproject Whisper, Project Cerberus.

As a youthful genius, Lakesh had been drafted into the web of conspiracy spun by the overseers of the Totality Concept during the last couple of decades of the twentieth century. A multidegreed physicist and cyberneticist, he served as the administrator for Project Cerberus, a position that had earned him survival during the global megacull of January 2001. Like a number of other survivors, he spent most of the intervening two hundred years suspended in a form of cryostasis.

Brigid and Lakesh walked out onto the broad, tarmac-covered plateau. Behind and above them, the mountain peak raised gray stone crags and broken turrets to the blue noonday Montana sky.

On their left, the plateau debouched into grassy, wildflower-carpeted slopes, and the bright sun gleamed on the white headstones marking over a dozen grave sites. The fabricated markers bore only last names: Avery, Cotta, Dylan, Adrian and many more. Ten of them were barely a year old, inscribed with the names of the Moon base émigrés who had died defending Cerberus from the assault staged by Overlord Enlil. The surface of the plateau itself was still pockmarked by the craters inflicted by that attack.

On the far side of the plateau, the asphalt dropped away into an abyss nearly a thousand feet deep, plunging down to a riverbed. A two-lane blacktop road curled down to the flatlands, paralleling the forested slopes of the Bitterroot Range. The ragged remains of a chain-link fence rattled between rusted metal stanchions that bordered the lip overhanging the chasm.

Between two the stanchions a man-sized and -shaped target had been erected, a paper outline of a human being tacked to a flat piece of plywood.

A half dozen people faced the target, most of them wearing the white bodysuit of the Cerberus personnel. They were assembled behind Domi and Kane, who stood at the shooter's position—a two-by-four laid flat on the tarmac.

Tall and lean, long and rangy of limb, Kane resembled a wolf in the way he carried most of his muscle mass in his upper body. He wore a black T-shirt tucked into the waistband of drab olive-green camo pants.

His thick dark hair, showing just enough chestnut highlights to keep it from being a true black, stirred in the breeze. A faint hairline scar stretched like a piece of white thread against the sun-bronzed, clean-shaved skin of his left cheek.

Standing over six feet tall, Kane towered above the diminutive Domi. Her skin was as smoothly pale as fresh cream. An albino by birth, the girl's bone-white hair was cropped short and spiky, the eyes on either side of her high-bridged nose the bright color of polished rubies.

Every inch of five feet tall, Domi barely weighed one hundred pounds and at first glance, she gave the impression of being waiflike. But there was little of the waif about her compactly lithe body. High-cut khaki shorts hugged her flaring hips, and a red halter top concealed small pert breasts. Her bare waist was circled by a web belt from which hung a long sheathed knife and a canvas pouch. Domi's small hands held a pistol.

The pistol looked like an oversize toy made of aluminum. Responding to a softly spoken word from Kane, Domi leveled it at the man-shaped target ninety feet away. Although the weapon held the general configuration of a revolver, the exterior resembled dull, undetailed chrome and instead of a cylinder, a small round ammo drum fitted into the place where there was normally a trigger guard. The gun had no trigger, just a curving switch inset into the grip. The slender barrel stretched out to nearly ten inches in length.

"Fire," Kane said.

With a sound like a starched handkerchief tearing in two, a pellet no larger than a shirt's collar button zipped from the barrel. Very nearly simultaneous with the ripping noise, the outline of the target's head exploded in a flurry of splinters and paper.

All of the onlookers recoiled and Lakesh jerked in reaction, even though he knew what to expect. The rail pistol in Domi's hand utilized a complicated system of tiny electromagnets to launch an explosive projectile of tungsten-carbine at a fantastically high muzzle velocity.

A unit of energy inside the grip propelled the projectile out of the barrel at a speed of nearly fifteen miles per second. In a vacuum, the environment for which the pistol had originally been designed, the velocity would have been closer to thirty-five miles per second, with absolutely no recoil.

The amount of explosive material within the pellet was negligible, little more than that contained in a firecracker, but combined with the extreme speed of impact, the detonation was instantly lethal. Even a glancing wound to an extremity was fatal.

Kane glanced at the target and said wryly, "Not bad. Took off the whole head."

Domi frowned at the pistol. "Terrible shot for me. I was trying for between the eyes."

Kane took the weapon from her, hefting it in his right hand. Addressing Domi and the spectators, he said, "The trouble with firing the rail pistol is that you unconsciously tense up to reduce the recoil and since there isn't any to speak of, therefore you—"

"And therefore," Lakesh interrupted stridently, crossing the plateau, "you waste our rare and very limited supply of ammunition."

Kane and Domi turned toward him, both of them affecting expressions of wide-eyed innocence. The effect wasn't convincing, since Kane's blue-gray eyes held the color of cold dawn light on a sharp steel blade and Domi's resembled droplets of fresh-spilled blood. Born a feral child of the Outlands, there was a primeval vibrancy, an animal-like intensity about her.

"Something?" Kane inquired blandly, ignoring Brigid Baptiste's exasperated eye roll.

"You might say that," Lakesh stated in a flinty tone. "We were supposed to meet in the cafeteria for the weekly security briefing, remember?"

"We went there," Domi said earnestly, even though a smile tugged at the corners of her mouth. "But you never showed up."

"That's because you lured me down to the gymnasium on, in retrospect, a thoroughly ridiculous pretext and locked me in!"

Domi's porcelain features registered outrage. "I did not!"

"Which one didn't you do?" Lakesh shot back.

"Neither one. Either one. Did you *see* me ask you to meet me down there? Did you *hear* me ask you to meet me down there?"

"No, of course not." Lakesh's eyebrows knitted at the bridge of his nose. He refused to acknowledge the knowing smiles spreading across the faces of Kane and the other personnel out on the plateau. "Friend Brewster relayed the message that you requested my presence in—"

"Does he claim I *personally* gave him that message?" Domi broke in.

"You know he hasn't," Lakesh retorted angrily. "You were too clever for that. He wouldn't admit to being your pawn, not with the way you've got him intimidated."

"I've never intimidated him," Domi protested. "He might think he owes me some favors because of the way he tried to choke me to death when he was zombified a while back, but that's not the same as intimidation."

Lakesh didn't address the denial. Turning his glare toward Kane, he said accusingly, "You know I disapproved of practice with the rail guns and the quartz cremators. The ammunition for the pistols is in exceptionally limited supply, and it's far too time-consuming to manufacture more, not to mention we don't have the means or the materials accessible. So you willfully disobeyed me—"

As he spoke, the lazy smile playing over Kane's high-planed features vanished. Realizing he had chosen the wrong word with "disobeyed," Lakesh hastily amended his statement. "What I mean is you violated our agreement not to employ either weapon in practice sessions and reserve them for times of critical import."

The smile did not return to Kane's face. Coldly, he said, "That was only your assumption, Lakesh, not an agreement. I counted out the supply of rounds and figured we could afford to waste ten or so out of five hundred for the sake of a lesson."

Domi patted the canvas pouch on her belt, producing a faint clink of metal on metal. "We got plenty."

Kane indicated the other people with a jerk his head. "They need as much firearm instruction as possible in case we have another overlord incursion. This group was stationed at the Thunder Isle complex when Enlil came calling. They've never used any weapons, and they need firsthand experience with firearms. The rail pistols are a pretty safe introduction."

The personnel to whom he referred were expatriates from the Manitius Moon base who had chosen to forge new lives for themselves with the Cerberus exiles. Although many of the former lunar colonists had proved their inherent courage and resourcefulness, they wanted to get out into the world and make a difference in the struggle to reclaim the planet of their birth.

Nearly twenty of them were permanently stationed on Thunder Isle in the Cific, working to refurbish the sprawling complex that had housed Operation Chronos two centuries before and make it a viable alternative to the Cerberus redoubt.

Lakesh said darkly, "Still and all, you didn't need to trick me just so you could sneak out and pop away with the bloody thing, like disobedient children with a forbidden slingshot."

"There was no sneaking involved," Kane snapped. "We just wanted to circumvent the kind of pointless bitching that you're doing right now."

Lakesh glared at him and Kane glared back, fighting down his rising anger. At the moment, with the Manitius immigrants looking on in uncomfortable silence and Brigid regarding him with jade-hard eyes, Kane decided not to continue the feud that had begun on the day he and Lakesh had first exchanged words, some three years ago. Displacing the man from his position of total authority hadn't improved their relationship much.

Two years before, Kane, Brigid and Grant had staged a mini-coup d'état. Lakesh hadn't been completely unseated from his position of authority, but he was now answerable to a more democratic process. At first he bitterly resented what he construed as the usurping of his power by ingrates, but over a period of time he accepted sharing his command with the other Cerberus exiles. It was the only fair position to take, since the majority of them were exiles due to his covert actions.

Except for the former Moon colonists, almost every person in the redoubt had arrived as a convicted criminal—after Lakesh had set them up, framing them for crimes against their respective villes. He admitted it was a cruel, heartless plan, with a barely acceptable risk factor, but it was the only way to spirit them out of their villes, turn them against the barons and make them feel indebted to him.

This bit of explosive and potentially deadly knowledge had not been shared with the other exiles. Only Kane, Grant and Brigid were aware of it and they kept the information to themselves, not so much as a tool for blackmail but because they genuinely feared Lakesh might be lynched out on the very plateau upon which they stood.

Brigid stepped forward, breaking the eye-wrestling match. "Who tricked who about what is less important than the fact we have our security staff waiting for us in the cafeteria. And Grant said if nobody showed up in five minutes, he was gating back to Thunder Isle and then over to New Edo." She made an exaggerated show of consulting her wrist chron. "And that was seven minutes ago."

Kane gusted out a weary sigh. "All right, let's get it done."

Fixing a defiant gaze on Lakesh's face, he handed the rail pistol to Dana Troy, one of the émigrés. "Carry on. Just do what Domi tells you."

The statement was met with a chorus of "yes, sirs," which caused Lakesh's eyebrows to decline even further.

Domi grinned impishly, turning to face the people. "Got that, everybody?"

There were murmurs of agreement all around. Glancing over at Lakesh, still grinning, Domi asked, "How about you?"

With an angry, impatient snort, Lakesh heeled around and stomped back toward the redoubt's entrance.

Domi chirped cheerfully, "Yeah, he got it."

Chapter 6

Brigid hung back so she could walk beside Kane into the installation. She opened her mouth and Kane said peremptorily, "Don't start up with me, Baptiste."

She arched a challenging eyebrow. "I don't want to start up anything. I want it finished."

"If it makes any difference," Kane replied, "I didn't know anything about Lakesh being locked in the weight room until he mentioned it." He did a poor job of repressing a smile. "That was Domi's deal."

"If you'd known about it, would you have objected?" Brigid asked.

Kane shrugged. "Probably not, mainly because I'm getting tired of having to argue with Lakesh over every little point and detail before anything can be done here. You have to debate with him for twenty minutes about something that would take thirty seconds to accomplish."

They stepped over the threshold into the redoubt. "He's worried about our security," she said defensively. "He thinks the overlords are spying on us, learning about our ordnance and defenses. It wasn't that long ago since Utu tested our perimeter alarms."

Kane shook his head impatiently. "Whether the overlords know we have four rail pistols or four hundred won't make a damned bit of difference if they decide to come back against us in full force. You know that."

Brigid nodded reflectively. "I can't deny Lakesh been awfully A.R. lately."

Kane shot her a quizzical glance. "A.R.?"

"Anal retentive."

He nodded, smiling wryly. "Ah. I thought so."

As they strode down the corridor, they noticed heads of men and women turning toward them, the glances respectful and even embarrassingly admiring. Kane, Brigid, Grant and even Domi were considered something special among the personnel. The actions performed by the four of them had quite literally saved the world, more than once.

"Glamour," Kane muttered sourly. "That's what we've got. No wonder I like to spend as little time as possible here anymore."

Brigid nodded in understanding although she didn't speak. Although Cerberus had been constructed to provide a comfortable home for well over a hundred people, it had pretty much been deserted for nearly two centuries. When she, Kane, Grant and Domi arrived at the installation over three years before, there had been only a dozen permanent residents. Like them, all of the personnel were exiles from the villes brought there by Lakesh because of their training and abilities. For a long time, shadowed corridors, empty rooms and sepulchral silences outnumbered the Cerberus personnel.

Over the past year and a half, the corridors had

bustled with life, the empty rooms filled and the silences replaced by conversation and laughter. The immigrants from the Manitius Moon base had arrived on a fairly regular basis ever since the destination-lock code to the Luna gateway unit had been discovered. Whether the émigrés intended to remain in the installation or try to make separate lives for themselves in the Outlands was still an open question.

However, with the fall of the baronies and the rising threat of the overlords, most of the émigrés had shown a disinclination to wander too far from the Cerberus redoubt. As the installation became more crowded, Kane felt less content to stay there for any length of time. The pull of adventure, of exploring the remote places, grew stronger with every passing day. Despite the sense of danger, he also experienced a profound sense of peace while in the wild regions. Regardless of his growing sense of claustrophobia, he still considered the Cerberus facility his home.

Constructed in the mid-1990s, no expense had been spared to make the redoubt, the seat of Project Cerberus, a masterpiece of concealment and impenetrability. The Cerberus process, a subdivision of Overproject Whisper, had been a primary component of the Totality Concept. The researches to which Project Cerberus and its personnel had been devoted were locating and traveling hyperdimensional pathways through the quantum stream.

Once that had been accomplished, the redoubt became, from the end of one millennium to the beginning of another, a manufacturing facility. The quantum interphase mat-trans inducers, known colloquially as "gateways," were built in modular form and shipped to other redoubts.

Most of the related overprojects had their own hidden bases. The official designations of the redoubts had been based on the old phonetic-alphabet code used in military radio communications. On the few existing records, the Cerberus installation was listed as Redoubt Bravo, but the handful of people who had made the facility their home for the past few years never referred to it as such.

The thirty-acre, three-level installation had come through the nukecaust with its operating systems and radiation shielding in good condition. The redoubt contained two dozen self-contained apartments, a cafeteria, a frightfully well-equipped armory, a medical infirmary, a gymnasium complete with a swimming pool and even holding cells on the bottom level.

When Lakesh had secretly reactivated the installation some thirty years before, the repairs he made had been minor, primarily cosmetic in nature. Over a period of time, he had added an elaborate system of heat-sensing warning devices, night-vision vid cameras and motion-trigger alarms to the plateau surrounding it.

He had been forced to work completely alone, so the upgrades had taken several years to complete. However, the location of the redoubt in Montana's Bitterroot Range had kept his work from being discovered by the baronial authorities.

In the generations since the nukecaust, a sinister mythology had been ascribed to the mountains, with their mysteriously shadowed forests and deep, dangerous ravines. The wilderness area was virtually unpopulated. The nearest settlement was located in the flatlands, and it consisted of a small band of Indians, Sioux and Cheyenne, led by a shaman named Sky Dog.

Concealed within rocky clefts of the mountain peak beneath camouflage netting were the uplinks from an orbiting Vela-class reconnaissance satellite and a Comsat.

The road leading down from Cerberus to the foothills was little more than a cracked and twisted asphalt ribbon, skirting yawning chasms and cliffs. Acres of the mountainsides had collapsed during the nuke-triggered earthquakes nearly two centuries ago.

A network of motion and thermal sensors surrounded the Cerberus installation, expanding in a six-mile radius from the plateau, following an attack on the redoubt staged by Overlord Enlil.

Although a truce had been struck, a pact of noninterference agreed upon by Cerberus and the nine overlords, no one—least of all Lakesh—trusted Enlil's word, and so the security network had been upgraded over the past few months.

Brigid and Kane turned down a side passageway and entered the cafeteria.

They saw Lakesh, Bry and Philboyd seated at a table near the serving station. Grant stood before it, examining the food in the trays with a critical eye.

Donald Bry, who acted as Lakesh's lieutenant and apprentice in matters technological, had curly copper-colored hair and was a round-shouldered man of small stature. His expression was always one of consternation, no matter his true mood.

Brewster Philboyd, one of the refugees from the Moon colony, sat beside him. An astrophysicist in his midforties, he was slightly taller than Kane but very thin and lanky. Pale blond hair was swept back from a receding hairline, which made his high forehead seem very high indeed. He wore black-rimmed eyeglasses, and his cheeks appeared to be pitted with the sort of scars associated with chronic teenage acne.

File jackets lay scattered across the tabletop. Lakesh leafed through the contents of one, pretending to be so engrossed in the pages of text and satellite imagery that he didn't notice Kane and Brigid's arrival. Grant, however, glowered in their direction.

"Nice of you to rearrange your target practice schedule with the Luna-techs to join us," he said in a rumbling voice reminiscent of granite boulders settling.

Grant employed his pet term for the Manitius personnel, and Philboyd cast him a sour glance. "Very witty—or it was the first time I heard it, a year ago."

Grant grunted and poured himself a cup of coffee. "When you've got a good line, why mess with it?"

Grant loomed six feet four inches tall in his stocking feet, and like Kane, he wore a black T-shirt, tricolor camo pants and thick-soled jump boots that added almost an inch to his impressive height. The spread of his shoulders on either side of his thickly corded neck was very broad. Because his body was all knotted sinew and muscle covered by deep brown flesh, he did not look his weight of 250 pounds.

His short-cropped hair was touched with gray at the temples, but it did not show in the gunfighter's mustache that swept out fiercely around both sides of his tight-lipped mouth. Behind his lantern jaw and broken nose lay a mind of keen intelligence possessing a number of technical skills, from fieldstripping and reassembling an SA-80 blindfolded to expertly piloting everything from helicopters to the Annunaki-built transatmospheric vehicles known as Mantas.

As Grant sat down, Kane poured cups of coffee for himself and Brigid.

One of the few advantages of being an exile in Cerberus was unrestricted access to genuine coffee, not the bitter synthetic gruel that had become the common, subpar substitute since skydark, the generation-long nuclear winter. Literally tons of freeze-dried packets of the real article were cached in the redoubt's storage areas. There was enough coffee to last the exiles several lifetimes.

Pulling up a chair, Kane seated himself across from Brigid and handed her the cup, intentionally splashing a few drops on the printout Lakesh was pretending to study.

Raising his head, Lakesh glared at him and declared, without preamble, "Since this is a security briefing, there is no better time to express my dismay at the lack of forethought you showed by allowing our secret ordnance to be carried outside. You could seriously impair any element of surprise we might be able to bring to bear—"

"Give it a rest, old man," Kane snapped. "You know we found less than a dozen of the rail guns on the Moon base, only five quartz cremators and four Gyrojet rocket pistols. Even if the Supreme Council knows we have them, it wouldn't make them call off a full-scale assault if they have one planned."

"That's not the point, Kane," Lakesh argued. "It's your flaunting of the security protocols we all agreed to abide by after the last assault."

Kane stared angrily into Lakesh's bright blue gaze, but the man never flinched. He had only recently grown accustomed to dealing with a robust—relatively speaking—Lakesh, whose eyes weren't covered by thick lenses and whose voice no longer rose to a reedy rasp. He also had to consciously catch himself from address- ing Lakesh as "old man." It had become a habit over the past few years, and he found it was a hard one to break.

"You could look at it this way," Grant put in. "If the overlords know we have these kind of weapons, but not how many, they might think twice about mounting another attack."

Brigid nodded. "Grant has a point. But I'm afraid we might be leaning too far in the direction of paranoia here, overstating the intelligence-gathering capabilities of the Supreme Council. They've got more things on their plate than keeping us under surveillance."

Lakesh eyed her challengingly. "Utu dispatched a remote drone that very successfully penetrated our sensor net."

"And Domi very successfully shot the shit out of it,"

Philboyd interposed. "Whatever Utu was hoping to accomplish, either for himself or on the part of the council, he failed."

Lakesh fixed his bright blue gaze on the astrophysicist. "Supposition. Have you forgotten Tiamat?"

"How the hell could we?" Grant demanded gruffly. He tapped his chest and gestured to Brigid and Kane. "We're the only people at the table who actually saw the ship with our own eyes and went aboard her."

Tiamat was the inestimably ancient but sentient Annunaki starship in permanent Earth orbit, considered more of a goddess than a vessel by the overlords.

"Which makes your recalcitrance to accept a heightened awareness of security even more puzzling," Lakesh countered.

"Not really." Bry spoke for the first time, with an uncharacteristic degree of firm conviction in his tone. "We can't live every second of our lives expecting another attack. That's not preparedness, Lakesh—it's an obsession, dangerously close to mental illness."

Lakesh didn't respond, but only gaped in silent surprise as Bry picked up a file jacket. "If you're so worried, let's get on with the briefing and maybe your mind can be put at rest."

Kane didn't think it was only Lakesh's mind that needed placating, but he kept his opinion to himself, although he did exchange a brief, questioning glance with Grant.

Brigid leaned forward, propping her elbows on the table. "What have you got for us today, Donald?"

Opening the jacket, Bry said, "About what I've had for the past couple of months, ever since you got back from Africa. Locally, everything is in order. Nothing unusual has been reported by Sky Dog's scouts. There's little that indicates major movement on the part of any of the overlords. Nothing on the voyeur channel, either."

Bry employed his personal vernacular for the eavesdropping system he had developed through the communications linkup with the Keyhole comsat. It was the same system and same satellite they used to track the telemetry from the subcutaneous transponders implanted within the Cerberus personnel.

Bry had worked on the system for a long time and finally established an undetectable method of patching into the wireless communications channels all of the baronies used. The success rate wasn't one hundred percent, but he had been able to listen in on a number of baron-sanctioned operations in the Outlands. He monitored different frequencies on a daily basis, but ever since the fall of the baronies, all of the villes had been in a state of anarchy, with various factions seizing power, then being dispossessed by others. The radio transmissions were equally chaotic.

"What about activity from the Millennial Consortium?" Kane asked.

Bry shook his head. "I haven't heard anything about them on the ville comm channels. They've been keeping a pretty low profile since your run-in with them in Wyoming."

"Good," Grant stated with grim satisfaction. "I hate those guys."

The Millennial Consortium was, on the surface, a group of organized traders who plied their trade selling predark relics to the various villes. In the Outlands, it was actually the oldest profession.

Looting the abandoned ruins of predark cities was less a vocation that it was an Outland tradition. Entire generations of families had made careers of ferreting out and plundering the secret stockpiles the predark government had hidden in anticipation of a nation-wide catastrophe.

Most of the redoubts had been found and raided decades ago, but occasionally one hitherto untouched would be located. As the stockpiles became fewer, so did the independent salvaging and trading organizations. Various trader groups had been combining resources for the past couple of years, forming consortiums and absorbing the independent operators.

The consortiums employed and fed people in the Outlands, giving them a sense of security that had once been the sole province of the barons. There were some critics who compared the trader consortiums to the barons and talked of them with just as much ill favor.

Since first hearing of the Millennial Consortium a year before, the Cerberus warriors had learned firsthand that the organization was deeply involved in activities other than seeking out stockpiles, salvaging and trading. The group's ultimate goal was to rebuild America along the tenets of a technocracy, with a board of scientists and scholars governing the country.

Although the consortium's goals seemed utopian, the organization's method of operations was very pragmatic and cold-blooded. Their influence was widespread, very well managed and they were completely ruthless when it came to the furtherance of their agendas.

"What about Vela imagery?" Lakesh asked, sounding a little less impatient than he had a minute before. "Anything unusual transmitted from the Mideast or Africa?"

From a folder, Bry fanned out several photographs. "A couple of interesting things have turned up, but not from there."

"From where?" Philboyd asked.

"China."

That caught Kane's attention and he put down his cup, leaning forward to peer at one of the satellite photos. Although most satellites had been little more than free-floating scrap metal for well over a century, Cerberus had always possessed the proper electronic ears and eyes to receive the transmissions from at least two them.

One was of the Vela reconnaissance class, which carried narrow-band multispectral scanners. It could detect the electromagnetic radiation reflected by every object on Earth, including subsurface geomagnetic waves. The scanner was tied into an extremely high resolution photographic relay system.

A year's worth of hard work on the part of Bry had at long last allowed Cerberus to gain control of the Vela and the Keyhole. Knowing that the Annunaki empire had been originally established on the African subcontinent, Bry had programmed the Vela to transmit any imagery from there that fit a preselected activity parameter.

Kane couldn't really identify much in the grid-covered photograph, except a square, light-colored object centered in one quadrant. "The Xian pyramid," he stated, tapping it with a thumb.

Bry nodded, using a fingernail to trace a wavering pattern of light and dark. "It appears there is considerable movement here, a massing of people in the valley. This was just transmitted over the uplink this morning. I should have tighter views later in the day."

Grant frowned, eyeing the image. "Is Erica forming an army or what?"

Pushing his glasses up on his forehead, Philboyd squinted intently at a photograph and said, "Quite the opposite. I'd say her valley is being invaded by one."

Brigid picked up one the photos and turned it upside down, scrutinizing it keenly. "If it's an invasion force, it looks to be of considerable size." She lifted her emerald gaze to Lakesh's face. "We don't have much intel about China since skydark, do we? There isn't a centralized government, is there?"

Before Lakesh could answer, the trans-comm on the wall emitted a buzz, and from the op center Farrell's voice shouted in alarm, "We've got unscheduled gateway activity and an unidentified jumper!"

Hitching around in his chair, Lakesh faced the unit and demanded loudly, "Jumping in from where?"

"Gee, let me guess—" Kane murmured.

"Apparently from China!" Farrell exclaimed.

Kane pushed his chair back from the table. "That's just what *I* was going to say."

Appendix? ....

Kane and Grant sent back into the past. Think
forward when you can.

Chapter 7

Alarm Klaxons blared discordantly, echoing all over
the redoubt. People ran through the corridors in apparent
panic, but in actuality they were racing to preappointed
emergency stations as per the red-alert drills. Still,
Brigid, Kane and Grant had to dodge and sidestep to
keep from being bowled over as they rushed to the operations center. Lakesh, Bry and Philboyd followed as
swiftly as they could.

The central command complex served as the brains,
the nerve center of the redoubt. The long, high-ceilinged room was divided by two aisles of computer
stations. Half a dozen people sat before the terminals.
Monitor screens flashed incomprehensible images and
streams of data in machine talk.

The operations center had five dedicated and eight
shared subprocessors, all linked to the mainframe
computer behind the far wall. Two centuries before, it
had been one of the most advanced models ever built,
carrying experimental, error-correcting microchips of
such a tiny size that they even reacted to quantum fluc-
tuations. Biochip technology had been employed when

it was built, protein molecules sandwiched between microscopic glass and metal circuits.

The information contained in the main database may not have been the sum total of all humankind's knowledge, but not for lack of trying. Any bit, byte or shred of intelligence that had ever been digitized was only a few keystrokes and mouse clicks away.

A huge Mercator relief map of the world spanned the entire wall above the door. Pinpoints of light shone steadily in almost every country, connected by a thin glowing pattern of lines. They represented the Cerberus network, the locations of all functioning gateway units across the planet. As they entered, Lakesh and Bry cast quick, over-the-shoulder glances at the map. Both men discerned a tiny light blinking on the Asian continent.

On the opposite side of the operations center, an anteroom held the eight-foot-tall mat-trans chamber, rising from an elevated platform. Six upright slabs of brown-hued armaglass formed a translucent wall around it. From the emitter array emanated a sound much like the distant howling of a gale-force wind, rising in pitch. Bright flares showed like bursts of heat lightning on the other side of the walls, but they were safely contained.

Armaglass was manufactured in the last decades of the twentieth century from a special compound that plasticized and combined the properties of steel and glass. It was used as walls in the jump chambers to confine quantum-energy overspills.

Farrell, a shaved-headed man who affected a goatee and a gold hoop earring, rolled his chair back from the mat-trans control console on squeaking casters. The brown eyes he turned toward Lakesh and Bry were anxious.

"It's a standard gateway carrier wave," he said. "A unit to unit transmission, from China to here. The jump point of origin is the indexed unit in the Xian pyramid. Only one biosign, though."

Farrell stood up, allowing Bry to take his place at the console. Lakesh leaned forward, scrutinizing the monitor screen, which displayed a drop-down window. A jagged wave slid back and forth across a CGI scale. "You're right, friend Farrell. It's not the electromagnetic signature from the Heart of the World, acting as a tap conduit into the matter stream."

Eyeing the jump chamber speculatively, Kane said, "At least we know it's not Enlil."

"So who the hell is it?" Grant demanded.

Gazing at the image on the monitor, Bry stated, "Every piece of matter, whether organic or inorganic, that has been ever been transported to or from our gateway here has a computer record in the database. The image processor scans for patterns corresponding with those in the record and allows for materialization unless we physically locked out that pattern, redirecting it to a holding buffer."

Brigid smiled wryly. "In other words, whoever is coming into phase has been here before."

Bry nodded. "That's what I just said, isn't it? More than likely it's Erica van Sloan."

Philboyd speared Lakesh with a penetrating stare. "She has the destination code for this unit?"

Lakesh lifted a shoulder in a shrug. "Erica has had it for quite some time. After Sam—Enlil—deserted her, I saw no reason to go through the laborious process of changing the code once again."

Bry snorted disdainfully. "And you're the one complaining about our poor attention to security."

"She presents no threat to us," Lakesh shot back defensively. "On the contrary, she understands that Cerberus is her only potential ally against an overlord incursion. I've had diplomatic feelers out to her for months."

Crossing his arms over his chest, Kane commented dourly, "Not to mention you still want a piece of the Heart of the World Enlil left behind."

Lakesh cast him a challenging glance. "Is that so unusual? It's a vast source of untapped energy that needs to be studied."

"And manipulated," Grant rumbled. "But even if it is Erica who's coming to call, I don't think we should put out the welcome mat for her."

"We will still observe all due diligence," Lakesh agreed. Turning to Banks, who manned the main ops console, he ordered, "Turn off the alarms, but lower the security shields. Lock us down."

The young man's hands flew over a series of buttons on the keyboard. The alarm fell silent but the warbling was replaced by the pneumatic hissing of compressed air, the squeak of gears and a sequence of heavy, booming thuds resounding from the corridor. Four-inch-thick vanadium alloy bulkheads dropped from the ceiling and sealed off the living quarters, engineering level and main sec door from the operations center, completely isolating it from the rest of the redoubt.

Kane, Grant and Brigid moved quickly into the anteroom. After the mad Maccan's murderous incursion into the installation, it had become standard protocol to have at least one armed guard standing by during a gateway materialization.

To simplify matters, a weapons locker had been moved into the ready room. Opening the locker door, Kane removed a lightweight SA-80 subgun and tossed it to Grant. He threw another one to Brigid, who snatched it out of the air as she hurried through the door.

All of the Cerberus personnel were required to become reasonably proficient with firearms, and the lightweight "point and shoot" subguns were the easiest for the firearm challenged to handle.

The three people took up positions all around the room, shouldering the subguns, barrels trained on the door of the jump chamber, making it the apex of a tri-angulated cross fire if one was necessary. They waited tensely as the unit droned through the materialization cycle. Because of the translucent quality of the brown-tinted armaglass shielding, they could see nothing within it except vague, shifting shapes without form or apparent solidity.

The chamber was full of the plasma bleed-off, a by-product of the ionized wave-forms that resembled mist. Within seconds, the stuttering electronic whine melded into a smooth hum. They heard the clicking of solenoids, and the heavy armaglass door swung open on its counterbalanced hinges. Mist swirled and thread-thin static electricity discharges arced within the billowing mass.

The laser autotargeters mounted atop the subguns pierced the thinning planes of vapor with bright red threads and cast killdots on a dark shape at the rear of the chamber.

"Come on out, Erica," Kane called. "Very slowly and very carefully."

Nothing happened for a long tick of time. No one stirred or spoke from within the unit.

Standing at the ready room's doorway, Lakesh said loudly, "*Chu lai!* Come out!"

Looking like a backlit shadow emerging from a fog bank, a slightly built figure appeared in the doorway and unsteadily stepped off the platform and into the ready room, holding up his hands to prove he was unarmed. His right hand was clenched in a fist.

The three Cerberus warriors instantly recognized his midnight-blue-and-scarlet coverall as the uniform of Erica van Sloan's so-called imperial troopers. The Asian face beneath the helmet was also familiar, but only Brigid remembered his name. As the possessor of an eidetic memory, it wasn't difficult for her to draw the man's name from her prodigious mental index file.

"Seng Kao," she announced, not lowering her weapon. "Where is your mistress, the Dragon Mama?"

Seng Kao's eyes darted back and forth, like those of a wild animal. Although his expression was impassive, he exuded an aura of near panic. He had visited Cerberus nearly a year before and guns had been aimed at him then, too. But in that instance he was in the company of Erica van Sloan.

Lakesh spoke again, his tone impatient. *"Na baio Tui Chui Jian er?"*

Still keeping his subgun trained on Seng Kao, Grant turned his head slightly toward Lakesh. "What'd you ask him?"

Lakesh stepped into the ready room. "I asked him where Erica—the Dragon Mother—was."

Seng Kao stared, not responding to the question or reacting to the three bloodred dots shining on the chest of his uniform.

"The last time he was here," Kane remarked, "he spoke English. Now he doesn't even seem like he understands his own language."

Brigid studied him over the autotargeter and said, "I think he's in shock."

"What's that in his hand?" Grant asked.

Lakesh called to him in Chinese, but again Seng Kao did not reply.

Grant took an ominous, threatening step forward. "Maybe one of my boots on his scrawny ass will make him more inclined to talk."

Seng Kao's head swiveled toward him sharply and he inhaled deeply. Desperately, he blurted, "I will talk!"

He thrust out his clenched right hand and Kane said warningly, "Talk but don't move."

Eyes glinting with confusion, Seng Kao stammered, "My lady bade me show you this. If I do not, my talk will make no sense."

"Like that would be a change," Grant observed sarcastically. "All right, show us what you have. If we don't like the looks of it, you're a dead man."

Seng Kao swallowed hard, then slowly opened his hand. The overhead lights glinted on the round metal object nestled in the man's palm. Kane eyed it suspiciously and demanded, "What the hell is it? A baby's bracelet?"

Seng Kao shook his head. "A ring. Tui Chui Jian bade me to tell you she has the other seven and that Wei Qiang wears the ninth."

Kane felt a surge of surprise mixed with disbelief and glimpsed the same reaction on the faces of Brigid and Grant. "Wei Qiang?" he echoed incredulously. "What the hell does that old bastard have to do with—?"

Lakesh strode forward swiftly, marching up to Seng Kao, foolishly inserting himself between the Asian and three gun barrels. He peered at the ring in the man's hand as if transfixed.

"Get out of our way, Lakesh," Grant growled impatiently. "What are you, an idiot?"

Lakesh ignored him. Carefully, he plucked the ring from Seng Kao's palm, holding it between thumb and forefinger, studying it with wide, entranced eyes. Neither Kane, Brigid nor Grant saw anything particularly unique about the band of corroded metal except that it was ugly.

In a tight, breathless voice barely above a whisper, Seng Kao said, "My lady's fortress was overrun by the forces of Wei Qiang. She has fled Xian and seeks your help."

"Since when does Wei Qiang have any forces but his raggedy-ass tong soldiers on Autarkic?" Kane asked, casting a questioning glance over at Brigid.

She shook her head. "That's the last intel we have, and it's old."

Addressing Seng Kao, she demanded curtly, "Are you sure of the name? Wei Qiang?"

Seng Kao stammered, "There is no mistake. But it is believed that Wei Qiang is an incarnation of Huang-ti, the Yellow Emperor."

"Interesting," Lakesh said absently, turning the ring this way and that so the rubies would catch the light. "Lower your weapons. This man means us no harm."

"How do you know that?" Grant growled.

Smiling slyly, Lakesh turned toward him, holding the ring up to his right eye and peering through it. "Erica would have never sent him to us with one of the Hydra's rings, friend Grant."

"Looks like junk to me," Kane snapped. "Is it valuable or what?"

Lakesh's smile widened. "Only if you consider the Cauldron of Dagda, the Golden Fleece and the Apples of Indunn valuable."

Without waiting for a response, Lakesh turned toward Seng Kao, saying sympathetically, "Come along. We'll get you something to eat and you can tell us your story."

Seng Kao nodded gratefully. "Thank you. I am very hungry and have endured many hardships."

Grant, Brigid and Kane stood aside, mystified as

Lakesh led Seng Kao, flanked by Farrell and Banks, out of the ready room into the op center. Brigid looked after them, pensively nibbling her lower lip.

Kane asked, "Did any of that gibberish make sense to you, Baptiste?"

She smiled wanly, flicking on the safety switch of her subgun. "He mixed and matched references to immortality in various myths—the apples of Indunn from Scandinavian mythology, the golden fleece from the Greek and the magic cauldron or grailstone of Celtic tradition."

Grant frowned. "What do they have to do with each other?"

Brigid inhaled a deep breath before replying: "All of those magical items insured immortality in one fashion or another…and each one was guarded by a multiheaded dragon—a Hydra."

Chapter 8

The alert level was downgraded to yellow and the security shields raised. Lakesh, Farrell and Banks escorted Seng Kao to the infirmary, where he underwent a strip search cloaked as a medical examination performed by the redoubt's de facto physician, Reba DeFore. She pronounced the man both healthy and unarmed, and Lakesh took him to the galley so he could assuage his hunger.

Brigid, Grant and Kane remained in the op center with Philboyd and Bry. The two technical experts focused on downloading and interpolating the latest transmissions from the Vela while Brigid took a seat at a computer station networked to the main database.

Domi returned from the plateau, aware of the red alert and expecting an explanation. She joined Kane, Brigid and Grant at the computer terminal. The pair of men stood on either side of the sunset-haired former archivist as text and pictures flashed across the screen.

"Somebody want to tell me what's happening?" the girl demanded impatiently.

"An incursion," Grant replied casually.

"From where?"

"From China," Kane said.

Domi's crimson eyes widened and then narrowed to angry slits. Her hand made a reflexive grab for the Combat Master holstered at her hip. "Erica van Slut is here?"

Brigid chuckled appreciatively. "No, she sent an emissary—a man named Seng Kao. He accompanied her when she came to warn us about the overlords, remember?"

Domi nodded. "Did Enlil move back into her pyramid or what?"

"No," Grant answered. "According to her lapdog, Wei Qiang showed up at her doorstep at the head of an army."

Domi's porcelain features registered bewilderment, then disbelief. "That old pirate Chinaman from Autarkic?"

"Apparently he's not so old," Brigid said quietly, distractedly, her attention fixed on the screen. Words and images scrolled across it with a dizzying rapidity.

"I thought he was in his eighties," Domi continued.

"So did everybody else," Grant said. "He sure looked that old—older—when me and Kane faced him down in Autarkic a couple of years ago."

Domi ran her fingers through her bone-white hair in a frustrated scrubbing motion. "Don't get it."

"Neither do we," Brigid stated. "That's why we're…"

The computer beeped, signaling it had completed the search through the files in the database. On the screen flashed a dense block of copy and a very formal watercolor portrait of a mustached, aristocratic Asian man. He wore an elaborate robe and pearl-studded skull cap. The color yellow dominated his garb. His long, beringed fingers were steepled contemplatively beneath his chin.

Grant leaned closer. "Huang-ti," he intoned, stumbling a bit over the pronunciation. "The Yellow Emperor."

"That's the guy Seng Kao claimed Wei Qiang was the incarnation of?" Kane inquired.

"Yes," Brigid said dryly. "A very interesting person to reincarnate within the body of a tong crime lord…if that's what is really going on."

"Don't understand this," Domi complained. "Who cares if Wei Qiang attacks Erica?"

"We don't care particularly," Brigid said. "If it really *is* Wei Qiang who is doing the attacking."

Grant, Kane and Domi all eyed Brigid in confusion. "What do you mean by that?" Grant wanted to know.

Brigid manipulated the mouse, enlarging the image on the screen. "Look at his hands."

Although the artist's rendering was highly stylized, the nine rings encircling the fingers of Huang-ti all resembled coiled, multiheaded serpents.

"Hydra's rings," Brigid said unnecessarily.

"That's very interesting," Kane commented inanely.

"What is?" Domi asked.

"Coincidence," Grant grunted.

Brigid shook her head. "You know better than that."

"Better than what?" Domi demanded petulantly. "What are Hydra's rings? Who is Huang-ti?"

"He is," Brigid said, tapping the screen. "Huang-ti is the first emperor of China, one of the three Sons of Heaven mentioned in ancient Chinese records that arrived on Earth nearly five thousand years ago in a metal egg."

Domi scowled. "An egg?"

Brigid read aloud from the text on the screen: " 'An egg, created by magical forces of gods San and Bel, exited under the action of its own weight from the divine bosom of empty sky. The shell became a defensive armor. The casing defended like armor, and that became a source of strength for heroes. The inner casing became a stronghold for those who had dwelt in it…from the very center of the egg sprang a dragon's body, and from that came a human being, a possessor of magic force.' "

Casting a glance over her shoulder at Kane, she asked, "Should I assume that has a familiar ring to it?"

"A ship," he answered curtly. "An Annunaki scout ship made of smart metal…maybe even the body armor the overlords and the Nephilim wear."

Kane referred to the foot soldiers of the overlords. When the barons reached their final stage of evolution as the overlords, so too had the rank-and-file servant class of hybrids been transformed. According to ancient legend, the hybrid offspring of the cursed fornications between fallen angels and human women were called the Nephilim. They were believed to be soldiers in the armies of darkness.

Like soldiers, they wore armor but it was composed of smart metal, a liquid alloy that responded to a sequence of commands programmed into an extruder. A miniature cohesive binding field metallicized it from liquid to solid. Over the past year, the Cerberus warriors had learned that smart metal was a fundamental building block of Annunaki technology.

"And of course the reference to a dragon is another tip-off," Grant said thoughtfully.

"Not to mention," Brigid said, "that the Chinese gods San and Bel are probably derivations of the Sumerian Sin and Baal, two minor members of the Annunaki pantheon."

"Figures," Domi said tartly. "Goddamned snake faces are everywhere."

Hundreds of years ago, when humanity dreamed of roaming the stars, speculation about the extraterrestrial life-forms they might encounter inevitably followed. The issue of interaction, of communication with aliens, had consumed a number of government think tanks for many decades.

As Lakesh and his colleagues discovered in the waning years of the twentieth century, all of the hypothesizing was nothing but a diversion, a smoke screen to hide the truth. Humankind's interaction with a nonhuman species had begun at the dawn of Earth's history. That relationship and communication had continued unbroken for thousands of years, cloaked by ritual, religion and mystical traditions.

According to information gathered by the Cerberus personnel over the past few years, most myths regarding gods and aliens derived from a race known in ancient Sumerian texts as the Annunaki but also known in legend as the Dragon Kings and the Serpent Lords.

A species of bipedal reptile that appeared on Earth at the dawn of humanity's development, the Annunaki arrived from the extrasolar planet of Nibiru. With their advanced technology and great organizational skills, they conquered most of Europe and the African continent. They reared great cities, built cities and spaceports and influenced the evolution of Homo sapiens. They were also consumed by abounding pride, arrogance, and more than a few maintained an insatiable appetite for conquest and control. The Annunaki faction led by Enlil had developed and imposed complex, oppressive caste and gender systems on early human cultures to impose that control.

Philboyd sauntered over from the satellite-imaging station. "You're making a pretty big jump in logic, Brigid—from old Wei Qiang on Autarkic to the Annunaki overlords slithering around in China."

"I haven't reached a conclusion yet, Brewster," Brigid replied icily. "But we already know the Annunaki were involved in Asia. Ancient Chinese mythology gives us the tale of the dragon husband, where the dragon took the youngest daughter from a farmer. Here the girl witnessed the dragon-king dancing with delight, curling like a ribbon or a DNA helix and transforming into a human being. The Annunaki, particularly Enlil, enjoyed sexual dalliances with human females."

Snidely, Philboyd said, "I love that story. Too bad it's not pertinent to the point I'm making."

"Which is what again?" Kane asked.

Patronizingly, Philboyd stated, "It's part of scientific training to recognize that information obtained from only one source is never completely accurate. Even if we concede all the facts, we're still getting only one interpretation of them."

"We really appreciate the exercise in pedantry," Bry said with cold sarcasm, rising from the console. "You ought to know by now that we do a lot more here than sit on our laurels—and asses—and evaluate data from a safe remove."

Philboyd eyed Bry superciliously. "Some of us do, anyway. When was the last time you went out in the field—oh, wait…I know the answer to that. Never."

"I don't go out into the field because I know my limitations," Bry snapped waspishly. "Besides, I have an aversion to being cold-cocked, captured and then waiting around like a little girl to be rescued…unlike a myopic but arrogant astrophysicist I could name."

The back of Philboyd's neck flushed red at the reference to past incidents where he had suffered misfortunes when he accompanied Brigid, Kane and Grant on away missions.

Although Domi grinned at the exchange, Brigid interposed impatiently, "We don't have the time for this. Donald, what's up with the satellite imagery from China?"

Bry jerked a thumb over a shoulder toward the main ops console and the VGA monitor which dominated it, a flat LCD screen nearly four feet square. "Downloaded and printing out. I'll have hard copy in a few minutes."

Kane glanced at the screen. Across the right side scrolled a constant stream of figures, symbols and numbers. The screen was dark, yet it swarmed with little points of brightness, like flickering dust motes. Near the bottom left corner was a curving sweep of blue-green, mottled with wisps of white. Beneath the swirling clouds he saw Earth, her continents a hazy outline.

A few years before he had been given his first satellite view of Earth. Now as then, he was filled with awe and a sense of despair. The world still seemed shadowy, dim, with a lost look to it as though the universe had forgotten about it long ago. He saw large areas of the planet lying under an impenetrable belt of dust and debris. In some places, the belt looked like a dense blanket of boiling, red-tinged fog. The clouds were the last vestige of skydark, the generation-long nuclear winter.

"What do you expect sat pix to show?" Grant asked.

"An army leaves tracks," Brigid replied matter-of-factly. "If nothing else, we can find out where they came from and the kind of ordnance they're using. If it's recognizable, then we can formulate a theory, even if it's only provisional."

No one questioned her statement. A trained historian, Brigid had spent more than half of her thirty years as an archivist in the Cobaltville's Historical Division, but there was more to her storehouse of knowledge than simple training.

Almost everyone who worked in the ville divisions kept secrets, whether they were infractions of the law, unrealized ambitions or deviant sexual predilections. Brigid Baptiste's secret was more arcane than the commission of petty crimes or manipulating the baronial system of government for personal aggrandizement.

Her secret was the ability to produce eidetic images.

Centuries ago, it had been called a photographic memory. She could, after viewing an object or scanning a document, retain exceptionally vivid and detailed visual memories. When she was growing up, she feared she was a mutant, but she later learned that the ability was relatively common among children, and usually disappeared by adolescence. It was supposedly very rare among adults, but Brigid was one of the exceptions.

Since her forced exile, she had taken full advantage of the Cerberus redoubt's vast database, and as an intellectual omnivore she grazed in all fields. Coupled with her eidetic memory, her profound knowledge of an extensive and eclectic number of topics made her something of an ambulatory encyclopedia. This trait often irritated Kane, but just as often it had tipped the scales between life and death, so he couldn't in good conscience become too annoyed with her.

"Where are you going with your theory?" Grant demanded. "Are you saying there's a connection between Wei Qiang and Huang-ti?"

Brigid shrugged. "I'm putting the possibility out there. As it is, out of all the sons of heaven in Asian legend, it was Huang-ti who left the deepest footprint in Chinese mythology. The Xian pyramid was built as a tomb for one of Huang-ti's descendants, so a definite connection is there. Huang-ti himself was reputed to have a guardian dragon by the name of Changhuan."

"That's nothing special. All of the old Chinese royalty claimed to have dragons as guardian spirits," Philboyd said diffidently.

Brigid nodded. "Huang-ti's dragon was significant because, according to legend, it gave him armor that staved off the aging process of the human organism and granted Huang-ti an exceptionally long life."

Kane and Grant studied the image of the Yellow Emperor, trying to reconcile it with the memories of the ancient tong crime lord they had faced in his lair of Dai Jia Lou. Kane saw no resemblance, but that didn't necessarily mean anything.

"I suppose it's possible that there's a link to the Annunaki," he remarked musingly.

"Possible?" Brigid echoed with a hint of mockery in her voice.

"Probable?" Grant suggested.

Brigid pushed her chair away from the station. "Why don't we all go find out if it's possible or probable?"

Domi's scowl deepened. "'Bout time somebody said something like that."

Chapter 9

They found Seng Kao in the commissary, being treated like a traumatized, wayward child who had accidentally stumbled into the Cerberus redoubt after being separated from his Scout troop. Lakesh spoke to him softly and solicitously, plying him with cups of the green Bengali tea he favored.

Farrell had been drafted into service as a waiter, fetching bowls of boiled vegetables and a fried-rice concoction scooped out of an MRE package. He didn't look happy about his new role, but he did seem relieved when Domi, Grant, Brigid and Kane entered. He very quickly left the commissary.

Lakesh held the Hydra's ring possessively, clutching it tightly as the four people approached as if he suddenly feared they would snatch it from him. When they pulled up chairs and sat down at the table, Brigid declared, "We're waiting for more sat pix from China, but until we get them I figured Seng Kao could fill us in on the invaders. What have you learned so far, Lakesh?"

The scientist shrugged. "Nothing. I wanted to make our guest comfortable before we began interrogating him."

Flatly, Kane said, "If he's a guest, he's an uninvited one. I don't think the rules of hospitality really apply."

Seng Kao lifted his gaze from the bowl of rice. He looked much younger without his helmet and uniform. With a touch of defiant disdain, he said, "I do not seek hospitality. I have been sent on a mission by Tui Chui Jian."

"Which means exactly shit to us," Grant retorted in a low, grim tone, almost unconsciously slipping into his Mag mode—intimidating and menacing. He rarely had relapses, and when he did it was deliberate, or it seemed so.

For most of his adult life, Grant had been the penultimate Magistrate, in attitude, behavior and thought processes. Over the past ninety-odd years, both the oligarchy of barons and the Mags who served them had taken on a fearful, almost legendary aspect. Both Grant and Kane had been part of that legend, cogs in a merciless machine. Although they had been through the dehumanizing cruelty of Magistrate training, they had somehow, almost miraculously, managed to retain their humanity.

However, when it served their purposes, the two men could revert to the cold and cruel persona of the baronial enforcer.

Lakesh said hastily, "I'm sure our guest means to tell us everything he knows. That is, after all, the nature of his mission."

He patted Seng Kao on the shoulder. "Isn't it?"

The man nodded. "Of course. It was the wish of the my mistress the Dragon Mother that I come here, and I live only to fulfill her wishes."

Domi uttered a gagging sound and mimed being sick to her stomach by bending double, but she subsided when Lakesh shot her a warning glance, shaking his head. Brigid repressed a smile and said, "Let's hear your story."

As it turned out, Seng Kao's tale was maddeningly simple and short on details—the army of Wei Qiang appeared near the port city of Kiangsu and then began a single-minded march across Honan. They were well-equipped, well-fed and apparently well-trained. Up until that very morning, Seng Kao assumed that the Dragon Mother had no more of an idea why the army laid siege to the Xian pyramid than he did.

"She led me to the Hall of Memory," the man stated. "She took a box of rings and gave me one—" he nodded toward Lakesh's closed fist "—and took the others. She sent me here through the chamber of long crossings. Why she did not accompany me, I do not know."

Seng Kao sighed unhappily. "She bade me tell you to seek her in Yichang."

"Where's that?" Kane asked.

"It is a fishing village near the mouth of the Yangtze," Seng Kao answered. "Small and isolated."

"Why would she go there?" Lakesh inquired.

Seng Kao shook his head. "I have no idea." A beseeching, pleading note entered his voice. "Will you help my mistress against the evil forces of Wei Qiang?"

Grant grunted contemptuously. "If it's the same Wei Qiang we've met, he's no more evil than the so-called Dragon Mother herself. Whoever he is, if he's smoked Erica out of her rathole, he's got my thanks."

"Mine, too," Domi chimed in fervently.

Seng Kao's eyes glittered with sudden anger and he made a move to rise, but Lakesh laid a firm hand on his shoulder, holding him in place. "Let's not allow past hostilities to color our views of the future," he declared.

Grant snorted out a derisive laugh. "Past hostilities, my ass. Erica's pet bitch of a baroness, Beausoleil, tortured and damned near crippled me with an infrasound wand only a little over a year ago. That's not something I'm likely to forget."

"Nor should you," Lakesh replied smoothly. "But in order to move forward, it is an incident you should put behind you. After all, Erica was not the perpetrator of the torture, and the baroness no longer exists as such. Forgiveness is good for the soul."

"Be damned to that," Grant rasped bitterly, dark eyes glinting. "She can take her rings and see if they fit up her—"

"What's so important about those rings?" Brigid interrupted.

Seng Kao's lips pursed in a moue of confusion. "I do not know. It was sufficient that my mistress considered them of importance."

Kane cast a slit-eyed stare in Lakesh's direction. "I'll bet you know."

Lakesh bristled slightly at the hint of accusation underscoring Kane's tone. "I do have an idea," he admitted.

Brigid extended a hand. "May I see it?"

Lakesh hesitated, then reluctantly passed the ring to her. From the breast pocket of her shirt she withdrew the symbol of her former office as a Cobalt-ville archivist. She slipped on the pair of rectangular-lensed, wire-framed spectacles and eyed the ring critically. Although the eyeglasses were something of a reminder of her past life, they also served to correct an astigmatism. "This thing is too big for a normal human finger. And it appears to be very old," she commented.

"If it's what I think it is," Lakesh said quietly, "then it most certainly is…very, *very* old."

Leaning forward to peer at the ring, Domi wrinkled her nose. "It looks old to me, too…old junk jewelry. Lemme—"

She reached out and plucked it from Brigid's grasp, slipping it onto the third finger of her right hand. The hoop of corroded copper fit like a wheel on a twig. "It's heavy on top of being old and butt ugly."

Playfully, Domi spun the ring on her finger.

"Careful, darlingest one," Lakesh said in alarm, stretching his arm out toward the girl. "It's not a toy. Please give it back before—"

Domi evaded his hand and in doing so, the ring flew from her finger and clattered loudly across the floor tiles. It went rolling toward the open door, wobbling awkwardly.

"Damn you!" Lakesh exploded, rising swiftly from his chair.

As Grant, Brigid, Domi and Kane stared at Lakesh in sudden, silent surprise, Bry strolled in, a file jacket tucked under one arm. He glimpsed the ring rolling in his direction and very casually set his foot upon it.

Voicing a wordless cry of outrage, Lakesh rushed around the table and shoved Bry aside. The smaller man staggered, dropping a thin stack of glossy color photographs held together by a metal clasp. He barely avoided colliding with the coffeemaker and shouted angrily, "What the hell's wrong with you?"

Lakesh scooped up the ring and closed his hand around it. Sweeping everyone in the commissary with challenging eyes, he snapped, "This ring is an ancient artifact, not a cheap bauble dug out from the ruins of a department store's jewelry counter. I insist it be treated with care and respect!"

Bry picked up the photographs, saying stiffly, "I thought I was helping. Sorry I was so dense."

Lakesh blinked and a shamed smile slowly stretched his lips. "My apologies, Mr. Bry. I fear I allowed my concern for the ring's rather fragile condition to get the better of my restraint. However—" he cut his eyes over to Domi "—you playing with it in such a childish manner was inexcusable."

Domi stared at him in disbelief for a long tick of time, then ruby-red rage flared in her eyes. Springing up from her chair, she stamped toward the door.

Lakesh reached out for her. "Darlingest one, I was only—"

The little albino slapped his hand away and stalked from the cafeteria. Lakesh gazed after her, an expression of baffled embarrassment on his face. Clearing his throat self-consciously, he murmured, "Well, that was unpleasant. I'll make it up to her later."

As he sat back down, Kane said tauntingly, "If she'll let you without exacting some flesh and blood first."

Lakesh glowered at him. "You're in no position to offer editorial commentary on relationships, friend Kane."

Brigid said tersely, "Maybe none of us are. But you might want to explain why you went all Gollum on us."

Lakesh stared at her blankly, uncomprehendingly for a moment. Then he chuckled appreciatively at her reference to the ring-obsessed madman from *The Lord of the Rings*. If Kane and Grant needed an explanation, they didn't request one.

Instead, Grant demanded in a dark tone, "You have more than 'an idea' about why Erica thinks that ring is important, don't you?"

Lakesh nodded, gesturing for Bry to sit down in Domi's recently vacated chair. "Let's deal with one idea at a time, shall we? What have you to show us, Mr. Bry?"

Still glowering, Bry sat down and spread out six satellite photographs on the tabletop. From the pocket pouch on the leg of his bodysuit he withdrew a large magnifying glass. "I didn't have time for photo rectification and enlargement work, but I do have some multispectral imagery here. You'll just have to take my word for the rest."

"Word for what?" Kane asked uneasily, eyeing the bewildering pattern of contrasting textures and colors on the photographs.

With the point of a pen, Bry indicated a wavering, narrow line of a paler hue than the surrounding area. "This represents the army our visitor here has mentioned. Although most of the soldiers are on foot, they have some rolling stock. They moved into Xian very quickly, apparently with a minimum of interaction with settlements along the way."

Kane resisted the urge to ask why the tech could speak so positively. After working with Bry for years, he abided by the man's request and took him at his word. But he did inquire, "Along the way from where?"

"I backtrailed them," Bry replied. "And like Brigid said, an army leaves tracks. But I still don't know exactly where they came from originally...or rather from where they were recruited."

Lakesh arched quizzical eyebrows. "No?"

"No." Bry took three of the prints and held the magnifying lens over a certain section of each one. "These shots were taken about a hundred klicks from Xian Province over a period of a couple of days. I ran them through the thermal line scan and spectroscopic filter."

Everyone, including Seng Kao, leaned forward to peer at the small white smears, the edges of which were blurred and indistinct. Other images showed hues of red, white, yellow, blue and even violet. "What does this suggest to you?" Bry asked.

"Energy-output signatures," Brigid said. "Very intense but precise bursts."

"And coincidentally," Bry stated, "after each burst, the army of Wei Qiang grew."

Kane followed Bry's pen-point, noting how the dark mass swelled in size after the flares of light. Lakesh studied the photographs with narrowed eyes and intoned, "Now it's really getting good, isn't it?"

Grant frowned at him. "What do you mean?"

Brigid picked up a print and held it up before the big man's face. "Think about it, Grant. The army of Wei Qiang didn't march all the way across China. They didn't have to...not when they had access to an Annunaki threshold."

Chapter 10

Lakesh tugged absently at his long nose and said with slow reluctance, "I rather resist that quick identification, although I can't offer a reasonable alternative."

"Especially," Kane stated grimly, "since all of us know that Sam made the Xian pyramid his headquarters and that Sam was only a husk for Enlil."

Even a year after learning this information, the Cerberus exiles were still trying to come to terms with the full implications of the maneuvers and countermaneuvers undertaken by Enlil. In his various guises, the overlord had moved his chess pieces over a vast board of power plays that stretched across the world and through millennia. Through the centuries Enlil assumed many names and adopted many physical vessels in order to manipulate events and human belief systems to best fit the Annunaki agenda. He had been known in various religions and mythologies as Asmodeus, Set, Apep and Samyaza.

According to the Book of Enoch, Samyaza was the name of the leader of the rebellious angels who fell to Earth to corrupt humanity—by teaching the forbidden arts of sorcery and forcibly mating with the females.

Many thousands of years later, in the guise of

Colonel C. W. Thrush, a synthetic blending of machine, human and Annunaki, he moved easily through the oppressive times of human warfare and political chaos. He felt completely justified in setting into motion the atomic megacull because the Annunaki lived on Earth long before modern man. The world that emerged from the nukecaust fit the Nibiruan model.

As far as Enlil was concerned, the nukecaust was a radical form of remodeling and fumigation. The extreme depopulation, as well as the subsequent atmospheric and geological changes, approximated Nibiruan conditions. In the guise of Sam the imperator, Enlil set the stage for the reborn Annunaki to reclaim the nations and regions of Earth they had ruled three hundred thousand years ago.

"Not to mention," Grant supplied, "that we have reason to suspect the Annunaki planted thresholds all over the world."

Thresholds had been used by the Annunaki during their first occupation of Earth as a means of instantaneous transportation from point to point and to the orbiting Tiamat. Lakesh had opined the devices served as the templates for the mat-trans units of Project Cerberus.

"We always figured there was a connection between the snake faces and Asian dragon legends," Grant continued, "and if Wei Qiang is using Annunaki technology to besiege Huang-ti's pyramid, it looks like a stronger connection than we thought."

Seng Kao spoke softly, almost timidly. "In the lore of my land, Huang-ti was known as a dragon prince."

"And I've a notion that Wei Qiang may very well be Huang-ti," Lakesh said dolefully. "In some manifestation or another, perhaps in a way similar to how Sam was really Enlil."

Grant, Brigid and Kane stared at him expectantly. "Well?" Kane challenged. "Are you going to elaborate on what's led you to the conclusion that an old pirate is actually a four-thousand-year-old Chinese emperor?"

"It's not a conclusion yet, only a theory." Lakesh's eyes shifted to Brigid. "What do you know of Huang-ti?"

The sunset-haired scholar shrugged. "Only what I read in the database a few minutes ago."

Lakesh nodded to her. "Elucidate, kindly. I confess my memory on the topic is very spotty."

Brigid took a deep breath and said, "Archaeological evidence suggests that China is one of the cradles of the human race. According to tradition, Chinese civilization owes much to the legendary Huang-ti. Agriculture and animal husbandry simultaneously developed around 5000 B.C. when Huang-ti ruled. And it was in his age that the most ancient form of Chinese writing was invented."

"How is that significant?" Bry asked, frowning.

"Most ancient cultures claimed the art of writing was brought to humanity by divine entities," Brigid answered. "In Egypt, it was a gift of Thoth and Isis, while the ancient Greeks thanked Hermes for the written word. Huang-ti apparently was similarly driven to give the gift of literacy to the common folk."

Grant grunted thoughtfully. "He doesn't sound much

like an Annunaki or even a pawn. They wanted to keep humanity as ignorant as possible."

"Even so, Huang-ti was anything but a saint," Brigid retorted. "Ancient Chinese writings confirm that the Yellow Emperor was responsible for the invention of organized warfare. He supposedly fought seventy wars and pacified the entire nation, mainly by killing anyone he thought might cause him trouble, either in the present or the future. He was also the first to institute the feudal system of vassals and princes, each of whom originally bore the title of emperor...bringing the god-king system from Sumeria to China. He put four princes into power, granting them complete control over the four main provinces of China. Huang-ti was known to be strict and impartial—when one of the four princes murdered another, the Yellow Emperor was so indignant at the atrocity he ordered the entire family of the prince tortured and executed."

"Yeah, that's pretty strict, all right," Kane remarked inanely. "I don't know about the impartial part, though."

"From what I remember," Lakesh ventured, "the philosopher Lao Tzu attributed the creation of Taoism to Huang-ti, at least in an inspirational way."

"There was definitely a close association between Taoism and the Yellow Emperor," Brigid agreed. "That much is a historically confirmed fact."

"This is starting to sound more like the Annunaki MO," Grant observed sourly. "Creating a religion as a control mechanism for humanity."

"Not in this instance," Lakesh said. "Taoism is a way

of life rather than a religion. Its essence is strongly based on Lao Tzu's writings called the Tao Te Ching, the 'book of the way' and the 'book of virtue.' But over a period of years, a more religious interpretation of Taoism evolved, drawing strongly upon the ideas of yin and yang and experiments in alchemy, astrology and divination. It veered away from philosophy into occultism, fixated on jade as a curative and restorative…even as a method of immortality."

Brigid nodded. "The more magical version of the Taoist movement was sometimes known as Huang-Lao, named in honor of the Yellow Emperor and Lao Tzu. Mystics tried to cultivate powers that would transform stone to jade, and transform human qualities to the transcendent."

Bry, who had never made a secret of his impatience with matters esoteric, demanded, "Was this kind of knowledge given to Lao Tzu by Huang-ti? Maybe it was Annunaki technology."

Lakesh chuckled. "Who can say? Hard information about the Yellow Emperor is scarce. There are no first-person, contemporary accounts of the man, if he was indeed a man. Most Chinese considered him a mythological entity, not a real person. However, he was very different from other ancient heroes in Asian lore. He was an enlightener, teaching the natives all kinds of useful sciences, including acupuncture."

"True," Brigid said. "Huang-ti and his court were apparently dominated by the use of complex mechanical apparatuses. According to legend, the Yellow Emperor manufactured twelve gigantic jade mirrors of unknown nature and used them to 'follow the Moon,' whatever that means."

"Mirrors?" Kane echoed, alarmed.

Brigid smiled wryly. "I thought that would get your attention, after what we went through in Africa."

Her oblique reference to the ancient Annunaki artifact known in medieval legend as the Mirror of Prester John provoked weary groans from both Kane and Grant.

"Numerous other sources related that Huang-ti manufactured and used devices called 'miraculous tripods,'" Brigid went on. "The legends weren't clear on what they were used for or what was so miraculous about them."

"I have heard of the Yellow Emperor's tripods," Seng Kao put in. "The purpose of Huang-ti's tripods was to create a likeness of the Great Infinite, the Tao, the concealed engine of the universe. Hundreds of spirits filled their insides and they spoke with the voices of dragons."

Bry smiled slightly. "Maybe they were communication devices."

"Or computers," Lakesh said. "Perhaps the Annunaki version of laptops."

"And then there are the tales of Huang-ti's servants, known as Chi Yu and his brothers," Brigid stated. "Chi Yu had four jade eyes—at least, it was believed he did—six arms, or manipulators. The strangest of all was his head—it was made from copper and had tridents in place of ears. Chi Yu and his brothers were able to move in the rugged areas, and even fly for short distances.

"According to the local legends, Chi Yu went renegade and began killing villagers indiscriminately.

Huang-ti cut off his head and buried it separately. Years later this head continued to emit heat. On occasion a yellow steamlike cloud would come from the burial site, and the locals worshiped it as the essence of Huang-ti."

Lakesh tugged his nose again. "It sounds like Chi Yu and his brothers were autonomous mechanisms, akin to robots…very similar to the drone that probed our security network a couple of months ago. That's another indication of Annunaki involvement in ancient China."

Grant shifted his feet impatiently. "What happened to Huang-ti?"

"He allegedly ruled China for three hundred years," Brigid answered, "but some sources suggest that he lived for five hundred years. Where he spent the rest of his days, and what activities he was engaged in after he forfeited the throne, is open to speculation. There are Tao sources stating unambiguously that after three hundred years of rule, Huang-ti ascended to the heavens and became the lord of the Great Infinite, where his dragon guardian, Changhuan, rewarded his accomplishments by turning him immortal with a device that 'originates in the land where jade serpents are born.'"

She paused, and added almost apologetically, "Most scholars believe that land refers to the constellation Hydra."

Kane nodded in triumph, crossing his arms over his chest. "And now, finally, we get to the heart of this whole deal. The Hydra's rings."

"What is a Hydra supposed to be anyhow?" Bry asked.

"In Greek mythology," Lakesh answered, "the Hydra

was a nine-headed dragon with venomous breath. The destruction of the beast was one of the twelve labors of Hercules. Every time Hercules cut off one head of the Hydra, a new one would grow. Working with his nephew Iolaus, every time Hercules cut off one head, Iolaus would cauterize the stump of its neck, preventing new heads from growing back."

"Clever," Kane muttered sardonically.

"What about the immortal head?" Grant asked.

"Hercules buried it under a heavy boulder," Lakesh replied. "Certain esoteric traditions assert that the head was recovered and nine rings were made from the creature's skull. The rings were handed down among various cults of sorcerers."

Grant snorted. "We're jumping from ancient China to ancient Greece and I don't see the line of connection."

"It's subtle, but the why is indeed there," Lakesh argued. "Huang-ti was associated with the constellation of Hydra, so it's possible the myths of ancient Greece originated in China, and their dragon became a Hydra."

"Or vice versa," Bry said testily. "Hercules, the Yellow Emperor and jewelry made out of monster bone all seem pretty specious to me."

"Where have you been for the past few years?" Brigid asked with a dour smile. "All we've done is play connect-the-dots with various ancient cultures and Annunaki influence."

"Maybe so," the tech shot back irritably. "But this time the dots are damned hard for me to see. Maybe I need my eyes examined."

"Maybe you do," Brigid said dismissively. "The connection between the nine-headed Hydra and Chinese dragon myth is pretty obvious, particularly when you consider that there were nine specific kinds of dragons, the last of which was the jade dragon king. Nine dragons, nine barons, nine overlords...with Enlil as the Dragon King. Do you get it now?"

Bry's eyes widened in sudden comprehension. "To some extent. But what's with the fixation on jade?"

Lakesh took it upon himself to answer. "The mystique of jade has been paramount in the lives of the Chinese people for many thousands of years. The gem is an integral part of the country's history and society, especially in the royal courts. For millennia, the Chinese so venerated jade, they called it the Stone of Heaven, crediting it with spiritual powers, believing that it possessed the virtues of holiness and purity.

"Many Chinese mystics regarded the gem as a potent medicine and attributed to it incorruptibility, invincibility and even immortality. Emperors used to drink a mixture of pounded jade and herbs in an attempt to become immortal."

"It is said that both the Yellow Emperor and Queen Hsi Wang Mu partook of a jade elixir of life, and lived to be several thousand years old," Seng Kao put in.

Bry uttered a scoffing laugh. "More than likely drinking crushed jade gave them a serious intestinal blockage. If they lived to be thousands of years old, they probably didn't enjoy themselves."

Not responding to Bry's medical opinion, Brigid

said, "A number of rulers were so obsessed with the notion of jade being conducive to longevity that they arranged to be buried in suits of armor formed by thousands of pieces of jade held together with gold wire. In the old legends, the suits were known as Kai Bu Xiu, the Armor of Immortality. When nine dragon rings were placed upon the fingers..."

Her words trailed off and her eyes narrowed as her gaze focused on Lakesh's clenched fist. Slowly, he relaxed his fingers, displaying the ring in the palm of his hand. In a flat but quiet tone, he said, "When nine Hydra rings were placed upon the fingers, then immortality was bestowed upon the person within the armor."

After a long moment of silence, Kane stated, "And now we know what Wei Qiang wants...even if he's not Huang-ti."

Lakesh nodded, holding the ring between thumb and forefinger. The overhead lights struck glittering reflections in the jeweled eyes. "Wei Qiang has one ring, we have one ring and Erica has seven and, according to Seng Kao, she has fled to Yichang. So we know where he's going to lead his army next."

Grant eyed Lakesh and the ring dubiously. "I want to know why we should care one way or the other."

Lakesh stared at him in surprise. "Don't you care about immortality, friend Grant?"

"Mine," the big man countered blandly, "or anybody's in particular?"

Chapter 11

Mariah Falk straightened from the eyepieces of the spectroscope and said, "I don't know what the hell it is, Dr. Singh. It *looks* like a ring, but the BEC—background equivalent concentration—is only registering dirt. I'm not getting a background density mass per unit volume on the thing at all."

She turned on her stool to favor Lakesh, Kane, Grant and Brigid with a wry grin. "I'm no expert on costume jewelry, but my opinion is that your ugly ring here is high up on the unique scale."

A former geologist from the Moon base, Dr. Mariah Falk wasn't particularly beautiful or especially young, but she had an infectious smile and a relaxed, easy manner. Her short chestnut-brown hair was threaded with gray at the temples. Deep creases curved out from either side of her nose to the corners of her mouth. Dark-ringed brown eyes gazed up at him from beneath long brows that hadn't been plucked in years, if ever. Like the other lunar colonists, Mariah had been born in the twentieth century but spent almost all of the twenty-first and twenty-second centuries in a form of cryogenic stasis.

The woman sat a low trestle table in the workroom adjacent to the armory. Rows of drafting tables with T-squares hanging from them lined one wall, and various chassis of electronic equipment and tools lined the other.

"What are you saying, Mariah?" Kane asked, gazing at the color bands shifting across the screen of the spectrometer linked to the scope.

Mariah shrugged, gesturing to the machine. "In layman's terms, the quantitative-depth-profile function isn't able to make a determination between mass concentration and the BEC."

Grant's brows knitted together at the bridge of his nose. "*That's* in layman's terms?"

The woman laughed. "In scientific layman's terms. In layman's *layman* terms, it means that as far as the spectroscope is concerned, the ring doesn't exist. All it reads is dirt and rust particles, not the metal the ring is made of, or the minerals, like the gems and the jade inlays. It definitely is *not* what it seems."

"Big surprise there," Brigid murmured. "Then the question begs to be asked and answered—what is it?"

"I wish I could tell you," Mariah answered with a resigned head shake. "The material the ring is composed of is from a different atomic table than what the spectrometer can recognize."

She glanced over at Lakesh, her untrimmed eyebrows lifting meaningfully. "You don't seem surprised."

"In truth, I'm not." Lakesh shifted from one foot to the other uncomfortably. He leaned an elbow against a pedestal next to him. Atop it, enclosed within a locked transparent Lucite box, was an object resembling a very squat, broad-based pyramid made of smooth, dully gleaming metal. Barely one foot in width, the height of the interphaser did not exceed twelve inches.

"In my opinion," he stated, "the ring is of Annunaki manufacture, using alloys and substances that are not terrestrial in origin."

"Which means," Kane said dryly, "it's not made out of the skull of a Hydra."

Mariah squinted. "Made out of the skull of a what?"

Rather than answer the question, Grant stated, "Even if it's not made out of mythical monster bone, it still doesn't track that the ring can make humans immortal."

Mariah's brown eyes darted from Grant to Lakesh to Kane, then back to Lakesh. "I wish somebody would explain what you're talking about."

Brigid smiled wanly. "I'll do my best."

Quickly, but not leaving out any details, she told Mariah of Huang-ti, Wei Qiang and the legend of the Hydra's rings. By the time she was done, the woman's grin had faltered and become an incredulous frown. "How much of this nonsense do you believe?" Mariah demanded.

Kane managed to keep the surge of annoyance he experienced from being too evident in his tone when he said, "We've followed up on crazier-sounding nonsense than this before. If we hadn't, you and the rest of the Manitius moonies wouldn't even be here, would you?"

Kane's question was a rhetorical one. Investigating a scrap of information he and his friends found in the ruins of Chicago had led to their discovery of the lunar colony in the first place. The Cerberus exiles knew the stories about predark space settlements, even of secret bases on the Moon. One of the largest had been built in the Manitius Crater region. That particular site was chosen because of its proximity to artifacts that some scientists speculated were the shattered remains of an incredibly ancient city, once protected by massive geodesic domes.

A remote probe was dispatched first from Cerberus and it returned not only with evidence the Manitius base was still inhabited, but also was populated by a disaffected group of scientists, marauding packs of carnobots and both a flesh-and-blood devil and a machine known by the acronym of DEVIL.

The corner of Mariah's mouth quirked in an abashed smile. "Point taken. But why are you so sure the ring is of Annunaki make?"

"Mainly," Lakesh answered, "because of from where Seng Kao claims it was taken…the vault in the Xian pyramid. I was there before and what I was allowed to see of the artifacts in storage was only the merest sampling."

Mariah pursed her lips contemplatively and peered again through the scope's eyepieces. "We could try to chip a piece from it, penetrate the outer shell. That might tell us if the exterior is some kind of shielding formed around a technology."

"That's not an option," Lakesh replied sternly.

Mariah leaned back from the spectroscope and blinked at him in puzzlement. "Why?"

"I have my reasons." Reaching around to the side of

the spectrometer, Lakesh pulled open the examination tray and plucked the ring from it.

"If the ring is technological in nature," Brigid objected, "we should try to learn its operating principles."

"We don't have the time for that," Lakesh countered, slipping the ring into the pocket pouch on his bodysuit. "If the other artifacts in the Xian vault are technological in nature and Wei Qiang lays claim to them, he could stand upon the brink of power beyond limit."

Grant gusted out a sigh at Lakesh's melodrama. His massive chest rose and fell like a furnace bellows. "You say that about every fused-out slagger we go up against."

Lakesh regarded him gravely. "And aren't I usually correct?"

"Why are you so sure this time?" Brigid inquired. "The connection between Huang-ti and Wei Qiang, as compelling as I find the possibility to be, is sheer speculation."

"And even if it's not," Kane put in, "why are you so sure Qiang cares about anything in the pyramid other than kicking Erica out of it?"

Lakesh's lips compressed. "Are you forgetting the Heart of the World? If Wei Qiang is indeed Huang-ti, then he almost certainly conquered China with its power. Why do you think he wouldn't try again, particularly if he has access to Annunaki technology and weapons?"

"Question," Mariah said. "Did you actually *see* any weapons in that vault?"

Lakesh shook his head. "No, but I didn't see Hydra rings, either."

Kane rolled his eyes ceilingward in exasperation.

"Are you proposing that the three of us gate into the Xian pyramid and take an inventory?"

"Not gate and not the three of us." Lakesh tapped the transparent case enclosing the interphaser and gestured first to himself then to Grant, Brigid and Kane. "The *four* of us will make a phase transit to one of the parallax points in the vicinity. The entire region is a powerful vortex zone, with several overlapping vortices, as I'm sure you remember from your first and only visit there."

Grant, Kane and Brigid stared at him in mild surprise, their thoughts flying back to the incident he referred to, nearly two years in the past. According to Lakesh, Enlil in his guise as Sam had manipulated the energies of the Heart of the World, an encapsulated packet of the quantum field. He transported the three of them from Thunder Isle to Xian by opening a localized wormhole in the planet's electromagnetic grid at the instant they activated the mat-trans gateway unit in the Operation Chronos installation.

"Do we have a set of coordinates for that area?" Brigid asked.

Lakesh permitted himself a small, prideful smile. "They were some of the first that were indexed and downloaded into the interphaser's targeting computer."

The interphaser had evolved from the Totality Concept's Project Cerberus. Three years before, Lakesh had constructed a small device on the same scientific principle as the mat-trans gateways, designed to interact with naturally occurring hyperdimensional vortices.

The interphaser opened dimensional rifts much like

the gateways, but instead of the rifts being pathways through linear space, Lakesh had envisioned them as a method to travel through the gaps in normal space-time.

The first version of the interphaser had not functioned according to its design, and was lost on its first mission. Much later, a situation arose that necessitated the construction of a second, improved model.

During the investigation of the Operation Chronos installation on Thunder Isle, a special encoded program named Parallax Points was discovered. Lakesh learned that the Parallax Points program was actually a map, a geodetic index, of all the vortex points on the planet. This discovery inspired him to rebuild the interphaser, even though decrypting the vortice index program was laborious and time-consuming. Each newly discovered set of coordinates was fed into the interphaser's targeting computer.

With the new data, the interphaser became more than a miniaturized version of a gateway unit, even though it employed much of the same hardware and operating principles. The mat-trans gateways functioned by tapping into the quantum stream, the invisible pathways that crisscrossed outside of perceived physical space and terminated in wormholes.

The interphaser interacted with the energy within a naturally occurring vortex and caused a temporary overlapping of two dimensions. The vortex then became an intersection point, a discontinuous quantum jump, beyond relativistic space-time.

Evidence indicated there were many vortex nodes,

centers of intense energy, located in the same proximity on each of the planets of the solar system, and those points correlated to vortex centers on Earth. The power points of the planet, places that naturally generated specific types of energy, possessed both positive and projective frequencies, and others that were negative and receptive.

Lakesh knew some ancient civilizations were aware of these symmetrical geoenergies and constructed monuments over the vortex points in order to manipulate them. Once the interphaser was put into use, the Cerberus redoubt reverted to its original purpose—not a sanctuary for exiles, or the headquarters of a resistance against the tyranny of the barons, but a facility dedicated to fathoming the eternal mysteries of space and time. Unfortunately, Interphaser Version 2.0 had been lost during a mission to Mars to unlock a few of those eternal mysteries.

Brigid Baptiste and Brewster Philboyd had worked feverishly over a period of a month to construct a third one, but with expanded capabilities. They had completed Interphaser Version 2.5 barely a year ago.

Staring levelly at Lakesh, Grant said, "I think you have a personal stake in making this jump."

"Of course I do," Lakesh shot back just a trifle too defensively. "Access to Annunaki artifacts and weapons are of crucial—"

"No," Grant broke in harshly, "I think you're pretty sure there are no weapons of any worth in the pyramid. If there were, Enlil would have taken them when he shed the skin of Sam. I think your concerns are mainly tied up with those damned rings and your hope they can make people immortal."

Lakesh's eyes glinted with anger and he snapped defiantly, "Is that so difficult to understand? Why shouldn't we lay claim to as many Annunaki devices as we can find instead of allowing a Chinese warlord or worse, one of the Supreme Council, to abscond with them?"

"We just don't want you operating on your own agenda again," Kane declared darkly. "Like you've been known to do in the past."

Lakesh cast his gaze downward, either in shame or to hide the sudden rage in his eyes. He tended to blame himself for many things, and for a long time Kane gleefully helped him do so. As the project overseer for Cerberus, then as an adviser and even an architect of the Program of Unification, he had helped to bring about the tyranny of the nine barons.

Much later—far too late, as far as Kane was concerned—he turned against the barons, betraying them and even stealing from them to build his resistance movement.

"What are you proposing we do?" Brigid asked impatiently.

Inhaling a deep, calming breath, Lakesh gazed at her. "I am proposing that we take Seng Kao to China with us. He can act as our guide as we look for Erica. We can see for ourselves the extent of Wei Qiang's forces and if he poses a danger to us here."

Grant, Kane and Brigid exchanged swift glances. Kane ventured, "If it's the same Wei Qiang we've met, then he's definitely dangerous. He was a greedy and ruthless bastard, but I didn't get the impression he was interested in expanding his scope of operations."

"But he was an old man," Mariah interjected.

Brigid nodded. "If he's young again, then it stands to reason he'll be even more ruthless. It wasn't that long ago some of his tong scouted out New Edo. If he gets back into the conquering frame of mind again..." She trailed off, not finishing her thought. There was no need.

Making an angry rumbling sound deep in his chest, Grant snapped, "All right, Lakesh. You'll get your mission. When do we leave?"

Peeling back the cuff of his bodysuit, Lakesh consulted his wrist chron. "Ten hours. That will give us time to sleep and put together all the odds and ends we might need."

"Not to mention," Kane said with a sly smile, "time for you to make it up to Domi, particularly if you want her to go on the op with us."

Lakesh's response was terse. "I don't."

He nodded sharply to Mariah. "Thank you for your efforts, Dr. Falk."

Turning on his heel, Lakesh strode quickly from the workroom, leaving the four people to stare after him with mystified eyes.

"What the hell did he mean by that?" Grant asked. "You'd think he'd want Domi along."

Kane shrugged. "Maybe the bloom is off the rose, the honeymoon is over, the cap has been left off the toothpaste tube, the toilet seat not put down—"

"You've been watching too many old sitcoms,"

Brigid admonished him. "I think he's just scared to put her at risk."

Grant snorted and stepped toward the door. "But not us, I notice."

"If he was," Kane said dryly, "nothing would ever get done around here."

Chapter 12

Although he was fairly certain he would not find Domi there, Lakesh stopped in at the quarters he shared with the girl. As he expected, the room was empty but he saw she had been there—her web belt with its sheathed knife lay atop the small bureau.

Lakesh crossed the room and picked up the belt. Carefully, he slid the knife from the sheath, examining the nine-inch, wickedly serrated blade. He knew the weapon was Domi's only memento of the six months she'd spent as Guana Teague's sex slave in the Tartarus Pits of Cobaltville.

She had sold herself into slavery in an effort to get a piece of the good life available to ville dwellers, but she had never risen any further than Cobaltville's Tartarus Pits. Since baronial society was strictly class and caste based, the higher a citizen's standing, the higher he or she might live in one of the residential towers. At the bottom level of the villes was the servant class, who lived in abject squalor in consciously designed ghettos known as the Tartarus Pits, named after the abyss below Hell where Zeus confined the Titans.

Tartarus swarmed with a heterogeneous population

of serfs, cheap labor and slaves like Domi. She ended her period of slavery by cutting the monstrous Teague's throat with the blade, saving Grant's life in the same impulsive act.

Like so many others, Guana Teague had dismissed her as a semimindless outlander. The average life expectancy of an outlander was around forty, and the few who reached that age possessed both an animal's cunning and vitality. Domi was nowhere near that age, and in fact neither she nor Lakesh had a true idea of how old she actually was, but she possessed more than her share of both cunning and vitality.

Replacing the knife in the sheath, Lakesh caught a glimpse of himself in the mirror hanging over the bureau. As had become an almost daily habit over the past couple of years, he studied his reflection.

For almost three decades following his resurrection from cryostasis, he had experienced a moment of disoriented shock when he saw a wizened, cadaverous face gazing back at him. For the first few years after his awakening, he was always discomfited by the sight of blue eyes staring out at him from his own face.

The year before the nukecaust he had been diagnosed with incipient glaucoma, and although the advance of the disease had been halted during his century and a half in cryostasis, it had returned with a double vengeance upon his revival. An eye transplant was only the first of many reconstructive surgeries he underwent, first in the Anthill, then in the Dulce installation.

After his brown eyes were replaced with blue ones,

his leaky old heart exchanged for a sound new one and his lungs changed out, arthritic knee joints had been removed and traded with polyethylene. By the time all the surgeries were completed, the mental image he'd carried of his physical appearance no longer coincided with the reality. From a robust, youthful-looking man, he had become a liver-spotted scarecrow.

His glossy jet-black hair became a thin gray patina of ash that barely covered his head. The prolonged stasis process had killed the follicles of his facial hair, and he could never regrow the mustache he had once taken so much pride in. His once clear olive complexion had become leathery, crisscrossed with a network of deep seams and creases that bespoke the anguish of keeping two centuries' worth of secrets. For a long time, Lakesh could take consolation only in the fact that though he looked very old indeed, he was far older than he looked.

But now, although he looked far, far younger than his chronological age, he still felt a shock when he looked into the mirror, but it was different, stemming as it did from fear. At the temples of his thick, jet-black hair he saw a few gray threads, but his deep olive complexion was still unlined, holding few creases from either age or stress, although he certainly had a stockpile of both.

The vision in his blue eyes was still sharp. He glanced down with distaste at the pair of eyeglasses resting on top of the bureau. They were dark-rimmed with thick lenses and a hearing aid attached to the right earpiece. For the past decade he had worn them, knowing he resembled a myopic zombie. For the past year or so, they hadn't been necessary and he realized the prospect that they might be again shook him far more profoundly than he expected.

When he had first met Domi, his eyes had been covered by the thick lenses, the hearing aid inserted in one ear, and physically he most resembled a spindly old scarecrow who appeared to be fighting the grave for every hour he remained on the planet.

And then, not quite two years ago, Sam the imperator had laid his hands on Lakesh and miraculously restored his youth. He still remembered with vivid clarity how Sam, who resembled a ten-year-old boy, had accomplished the miracle by the simple laying on of hands. He would never forget how Sam laid his little hand against his midriff and how a tingling warmth seemed to seep from it. The warmth swiftly became searing heat, like liquid fire, rippling through his veins and arteries. His heartbeat picked up in tempo, seeming to spread the heat through the rest of his body, a pulsating web of energy suffusing every separate cell and organ.

He was aflame with a searing pain, the same kind of agony a man felt when circulation was suddenly restored to a numb limb. His entire metabolism seemed to awaken to furious life from a long slumber, as if it had been jump-started by a powerful battery.

He still remembered with awe that after the sensation of heat faded, he realized two things more or less simultaneously—he wasn't wearing his glasses but he could see his hand perfectly. And by that perfect vision, he saw the flesh of his hand was smooth, the prominent veins having sunk back into firm flesh. The liver spots faded away even as he watched.

Later, Sam claimed he had increased Lakesh's production of his antioxidant enzymes and boosted his alkyglycerol level to the point where the aging process was, for all intents and purposes, reversed. For the first few weeks following Sam's treatment, Lakesh's hair continued to darken and more and more of his wrinkles disappeared. For a time, he had felt he was living in the dream world of all old men—restored youth, vitality and enhanced sex drive, as Domi could attest.

But then the entire process reached a certain point and came to a halt. Lakesh estimated he had returned to a physical state approximating his late forties to early fifties.

Lakesh had assumed Sam possessed the ability to transfer his biological energy to other organic matter, which in turn stimulated the entire human cellular structure. He theorized the energy transfer might have rejuvenated the MHC in the six chromosomal structures, which resulted in turning back the hands of the metabolic clock, persuading the cells to reproduce and repair themselves.

He recalled the words of the extremely skeptical DeFore: "If aging is controlled by a kind of biological alarm clock, a sort of genetic switching system and the hands of yours were turned back, it stands to reason they'll start moving in the normal fashion again."

She went on to say, "Just as different kinds of clocks and watches are designed to run for different lengths of time after being wound, so different kinds of bodies are genetically designed to run for different periods. The mainspring of your body's clock could break at any time or it could go haywire. You could age ten years in ten seconds."

Comparing his body to a clock with a malfunctioning mainspring did nothing to ease Lakesh's fears, but it was actually a far more apt metaphor than he imagined at the time. Over the past year he learned the precise methodology at work—when he laid his hands on Lakesh, Sam had injected nanomachines into his body.

The nanites were programmed to recognize and destroy dangerous organisms, whether they were bacteria, cancer cells or viruses. Sam's nanites performed selective destruction on the genes of DNA cells, removing the part that caused aging. He had performed the same treatment on Erica van Sloan, whom he had convinced was his mother by dint of the fact he shared some of her DNA.

The nanites in Lakesh's body became inert after a time. He and DeFore feared that without the influence of the nanomachines, he would begin to age, but at an accelerated rate. But so far, that gloomy diagnosis had not come to pass. True, he was sporting new gray hairs and he noticed the return of old aches and pains, but so far, the aging process seemed normal. He was cautiously optimistic that he would not reprise the fate of the title character in *The Picture of Dorian Gray,* and he hoped Domi shared that optimism.

It had been a great source of joy to Lakesh when he learned Domi reciprocated his feelings and had no inhibitions about expressing them, regardless of the bitterness she still harbored over her unrequited love for Grant. In any event, he had broken a fifty-year streak of celibacy with her, and they repeated the actions of that first delirious night whenever the opportunity arose.

As Lakesh bleakly considered how those opportunities could be limited in the future, he removed the Hydra ring from his pocket. Cupping the massive piece of jewelry in his hands, he stared into the snarling dragon faces, the details dulled by its immense age. He felt his heart rate speed up, fancying he sensed the very fabric of time pulsing about him.

Time was the true enemy, his most mortal, implacable foe, not the overlords, not the diabolical Sindri or the seductive Erica. In the persona of Sam, Enlil had temporarily dammed the relentless river current of time, but eventually, sooner rather than later, he would yield to it, be washed away by it—unless he found another way to divert it.

As the concept registered in his consciousness, the nine malevolent dragon faces swelled in Lakesh's vision, like monsters dredged up from an almost but not quite forgotten nightmare from his childhood. For a moment he thought he heard, almost unimaginably distant, the rustle of leathery wings, the beat of a faraway drum—or a heart. The air of the room seemed to vibrate.

Straightening with a start, Lakesh held the ring at arm's length. He glimpsed the expression of sudden terror stamped on the face of his reflection and he whirled away from the mirror, jamming the ring back into a pocket on his bodysuit.

Lakesh stepped out into the corridor just as Wegmann strode past. He called out to him, "Have you seen Domi in the last few minutes?"

A balding, sharp-featured, slightly built man under medium height, with dark hair caught back in a ponytail, Wegmann served as the redoubt's engineer. He tended to the nuclear generators and the reactor buried deep within the stony bosom of the mountain. Normally taciturn while in the best of moods, he seemed even less inclined toward civility at the moment. As a response to Lakesh's question, he simply gestured with his thumb, pointing downward.

Lakesh wasn't offended by his manner—no one in Cerberus took Wegmann's misanthropic tendencies seriously. He had proved his courage and loyalty on more than one occasion in the past.

"Thank you," he called after him.

Wegmann only grunted and turned the corner.

Lakesh took the elevator down to the second level, strode along a short hallway and pushed through a set of swinging double doors into the exercise area. He walked past weight machines, stationary bikes, stair steppers and workout mats. None of it was in use, which he didn't find particularly surprising. Most of the Moon base émigrés were academics, after all. Exercise for the sake of exercise didn't appeal to them, and he could easily relate to that.

The small gym had been built to provide the original

inhabitants of Cerberus with a means of sweating off the stress of being confined for twenty-four hours a day in an isolated installation. After the nukecaust, just staying alive was as much exercise as they needed.

Lakesh stepped into the pool room. Circular and with curved walls like an upside-down bowl, the pool room was dimly illuminated by overhead track lighting. He heard the splashing of water and saw Domi floating on her back near the deep end, her small but perfectly shaped breasts pointing to the ceiling, her pale legs moving languidly beneath the surface. Her eyes were closed, the lashes looking like pine needles dusted with snow.

Standing at the edge of the pool, Lakesh said quietly, "Darlingest one, you and I need to talk."

Without opening her eyes, Domi murmured laconically, "You're about half-right."

Lakesh repressed a smile at Domi's studied nonchalance. He knew her wilderness-honed senses had informed her of his approach as soon as he got off the elevator.

Clearing his throat, he said, "I want to explain about my reaction when you mishandled the Hydra ring."

Domi's face remained as immobile as if it were sculpted from polished marble. She intoned flatly, "Who's stopping you?"

Lakesh sighed and removed the ring from his pocket. "Will you please look at me—and this—while I talk?"

Deliberately taking her time, Domi slowly turned over, then heaved herself out of the water and sat on the tiled lip of the pool, perfectly at ease in her nudity. Lakesh tried to keep his eyes from dwelling on her compact, perfectly proportioned body. Before arriving at the redoubt, the girl hadn't been accustomed to wearing clothes unless circumstances demanded them, and then only the skimpiest concessions to weather, not modesty.

Born a feral child of the Outlands, she was always relaxed being naked in the company of others and if those others didn't share that comfort zone, she could not care less. Despite the scars marring the pearly perfection of her skin, particularly the one shaped like a starburst on her right shoulder, Domi was beautiful in the way a wild mustang was beautiful.

Her body was a liquid, symmetrical flow of curving lines, with small porcelain breasts rising to sharp nipples, and a flat, hard-muscled stomach extending to the flared shape of her hips. With droplets of water sparkling on her arms and legs, her skin looked opaque, its luminosity heightened by an absence of color. Even her patch of pubic hair was white.

Domi's ruby eyes flicked casually toward the ring in Lakesh's hand. "Seen it already."

Lakesh squatted, grimacing as his artificial knee joints creaked. "But you don't know what it is, not really."

"Do you?" Domi challenged, crossing her exquisitely molded legs.

Lakesh nodded. "I'm pretty sure I do, and I'm sharing the knowledge with you alone. Do you remember how I became young again?"

Domi uttered a scoffing sound. "I'm not a jolt-brain. 'Course I do. The little nites Sam—Enlil—put in you."

"The nanites, yes." Lakesh revolved the ring between

thumb and forefinger, allowing the jeweled eyes of the Hydra heads to catch the light and glitter almost hypnotically. "I'm of the opinion the so-called Hydra rings possess the same capabilities to introduce nanomachines into the body. They reverse the cellular deterioration caused by age, and all of them working in tandem might very well render a human being immortal...for all intents and purposes."

Her attention captured at last, Domi eyes widened and she leaned forward to inspect the ring more closely. "Live forever?" she breathed incredulously.

"For all intents and purposes," Lakesh repeated. "So that makes the Hydra rings incredibly ancient and probably fragile. That's why I was so impatient with you when you were careless with it."

Comprehension shining in her eyes, Domi put her face very close to the ring. She breathed, "Wei Qiang has one ring, we have one and Erica has all the others. We're going to China after them, aren't we?"

She spoke eagerly, her body tensing like a bowstring. Not for the first time Domi reminded Lakesh of a sleek snow leopard straining at the scent of prey.

Lakesh stood up, saying quietly but firmly, "Like you said before, you're about half-right."

Domi cocked her head in puzzlement. "Don't getcha."

Lakesh weighed his next words carefully, but he couldn't come up with a way of soft-pedaling what he had to tell the girl. Flatly, he stated, "Friends Kane, Grant, dearest Brigid and myself will take Seng Kao to China. You will remain here, in Cerberus."

Domi gaped up at him in stunned silence for a long moment, then got to her feet in a angry rush, bosom heaving. "No!" she cried. "No fucking way! Can't keep me here!"

"Can," he retorted, steeling himself to receive a torrent of vituperation. "And will. This mission is exceptionally hazardous. Not only will we be making a dark-territory probe, we'll be putting ourselves between two enemies."

"Not a child," she snapped, eyes gleaming with barely repressed rage. "Been on plenty of dangerous missions before, more than you have!"

"And you've been seriously injured and nearly killed more than once."

"People die, that's the way of it," she shot back.

Lakesh nodded in acknowledgment of her straightforward pragmatism. "Sometimes, darlingest one, it's just as important what people die of and why…and how it could have been prevented."

"What the fuck that mean?" The girl's voice rose to hover on the edge of utter fury.

Lakesh wasn't quite certain what he meant, except he was consumed with fear of putting Domi at risk on such specious and personal reasons. At the beginning of their relationship, he had felt compelled to keep his affair with Domi a secret, and he wasn't sure why.

At first he tried to convince himself it was concern over raising Grant's ire, but he knew that was simply a feeble excuse. With Grant's heart more or less pledged to Shizuka, the big man was too preoccupied with his attempts to make a new life with her on New Edo to give the more covert—and intimate—activities among the redoubt personnel more than cursory attention.

When Domi accused him of being ashamed of their relationship, Lakesh had suddenly realized the true reasons he had kept their affair a secret—he feared she would be swept up in the same karmic backlash that he had long feared would shatter him. When the punishment had been averted—due, he felt, to Domi's devotion to him—he had made a rather noisy fanfare of announcing their relationship to one and all. Much to his chagrin, most of the people in the redoubt already knew about it.

Now he was consumed with new fear about the future of their relationship, and he did not know how to express it to the girl or even if he should.

"It means," Lakesh said grimly, "that I'm not going to debate you on this matter. With the four of us gone for God knows how long, you're next in line for command of the installation."

Domi gestured impatiently, as if she were swatting a swarm of bugs. "Bullshit. DeFore, Bry, Farrell—they all have more seniority than me."

"But they don't have the respect among the crew you do." He dropped his voice to a low, reassuring croon. "Darlingest one, I need you here more than I need you out in the field, risking your life in China in what very well may turn out to be a one-way trip."

She continued to glare at him, not in the least mollified. "Put self at risk in field lots of times."

Under stress, Domi reverted to the abbreviated mode of outlander speech.

"You've been lucky," he declared. "We all have. But no luck can be expected to last forever."

"Forever," Domi snapped. "That's what this is all about, isn't it?"

Lakesh felt as if a cold finger stroked his spine. "What do you mean?"

"Live forever. You get every one of the rings, you get to live forever, right?" She threw her arms out in frustration, let them slap against her naked flanks. "Crazy."

She is so much like a child, Lakesh reflected. The life force was incredibly strong within her small body, a vibrant urgency to experience it to the fullest and fueled by the heat of primeval passion.

"Not crazy," he whispered, reaching out for her. "Desperate perhaps, but not crazy. *Both* of us can live forever and perhaps all of our friends. But I won't put you at risk on such a big gamble as this."

Domi evaded his hands. "You put me at risk in other ways."

"I won't reconsider," he said sharply.

With eye-blurring speed, her white hand whipped up and smacked against his cheek. He staggered, red welts marking the impact of her fingers. As Lakesh regained his balance, Domi spun and stalked out of the pool area, not grabbing so much as a towel on her way out. He watched her stride away with a furious, hip-swinging gait.

Lakesh remained standing at the poolside, resisting

the urge to rub his stinging face. He couldn't help but wonder gloomily if the slap was the last time that he would ever feel the touch of Domi's hand.

Chapter 13

A few minutes after noon the next day, Kane, Brigid and Grant convened in the antechamber connected to the jump chamber. The three people strode in wearing high-necked, midnight-colored shadow suits that absorbed light the way a sponge absorbed water. Although the material of the formfitting garments resembled black doeskin, and didn't appear as if it would offer protection from fleabites, it was impervious to most wavelengths of radiation.

Ever since they had absconded with the suits from Redoubt Yankee on Thunder Isle, the garments had proved their worth and their superiority to Grant and Kane's polycarbonate Magistrate armor, if for no other reason than their internal subsystems.

Manufactured with a technique known in predark days as electrospin lacing, the electrically charged polymer particles formed a dense web of formfitting fibers. Composed of a compiled weave of spider silk, Monocrys and Spectra fabrics, the garments were essentially a single-crystal metallic microfiber, with a very dense molecular structure.

The outer Monocrys sheathing went opaque when

exposed to radiation, and the Kevlar and Spectra layers provided protection against blunt trauma. The spider silk allowed flexibility, but it traded protection from firearms for freedom of movement. The suits were climate controlled for environments up to highs of 150 degrees and lows as cold as minus ten degrees Fahrenheit. Flat, square ammo pouches were attached to the small of their backs by Velcro tabs. Long combat knives, the razor-keen blades forged of dark blued steel, hung from scabbards at their hips.

Grant and Kane carried war bags full of assorted items taken from the armory, some brought along due to their maximum destructive capabilities and others that served altogether different functions. They were experienced enough to know they could not plan for all contingencies and were always prepared to improvise.

Quickly, with the efficiency born of long practice, the three of them inventoried their ordnance and other equipment spread out on the table, the ready room's only furniture. They checked over the three abbreviated Copperhead subguns. Under two feet long, with a 700-round-per-minute rate of fire, the extended magazines held thirty-five 4.85 mm steel-jacketed rounds. The grip and trigger units were placed in front of the breech in the bullpup design, allowing for one-handed use.

Optical image intensifier scopes and laser autotargeters were mounted on the top of the frames. Low recoil allowed the Copperheads to be fired in long, devastating, full-auto bursts.

Kane and Grant shrugged into gren-laden combat

harnesses, hooked the subguns to them and shook out their ankle-length, black Kevlar-weave coats before slipping them on, a little uncomfortable as always with their weight. The Mag-issue coats offered a degree of protection against penetration weapons and they were insulated against all weathers, including acid rain showers. Trans-comm circuitry was sewn inside the lapels, terminating in tiny pin mikes connected to a thin wire pulley. If they were searched, the transceivers would pass a cursory inspection.

They made sure the Sin Eaters were secure in the rather bulky holsters strapped to their forearms. The Sin Eaters were big-bored automatic handblasters, less than fourteen inches in length at full extension, the magazines carrying twenty 9 mm rounds. When not in use, the stock folded over the top of the blaster, lying perpendicular to the frame, reducing its holstered length to ten inches.

When the weapons were needed, they tensed their wrist tendons. Sensitive actuators activated flexible cables within the holsters and snapped the pistols smoothly into their waiting hands, the butts unfolding in the same motion. Since the Sin Eaters had no trigger guards or safeties, the blasters fired immediately upon touching their crooked index fingers. The right sleeves of their coats were just a bit larger than the left to accommodate the Sin Eaters and power holsters.

Brigid slipped on a long black leather coat with voluminous pockets. Inside one pocket she placed a flat case containing emergency medical supplies, including hypodermics of pain suppressants, ampoules of stimulants and antibiotics. Snugged in another pocket was her side arm of choice, a TP-9 autoblaster. She clipped one of the Copperheads to her own combat webbing.

Almost all of the ordnance was supplied by the Cerberus armory, quite likely the best stocked and outfitted arsenal in postnuke America. Glass-fronted cases held racks of automatic assault rifles. There were many makes and models of subguns, as well as dozens of semiautomatic pistols and revolvers, complete with holsters and belts.

The armory also housed heavy-assault weaponry like bazookas, tripod-mounted 20 mm cannons, mortars and rocket launchers. All the ordnance had been laid down in hermetically sealed Continuity of Government installations before the nukecaust. Protected from the ravages of the outside environment, nearly every piece of munitions and hardware was as pristine as the day it was first manufactured.

Lakesh himself had put the arsenal together over several decades, envisioning it as the major supply depot for a rebel army. The army never materialized—at least not in the fashion Lakesh hoped it would. Therefore, Cerberus was blessed with a surplus of death-dealing equipment that would have turned the most militaristic overlord green with envy, or given the most pacifistic of them heart failure—if they indeed possessed hearts.

Philboyd strode in from the op center, carrying a square metal-and-leather case containing survival rations, such as concentrated foodstuffs and bottles of purified water. "Lakesh asked me to bring this," he said.

"Where is he?" Kane asked. "We're burning daylight."

"Not really," Brigid said. "It's a little after 1:00 a.m. in China. That's why Lakesh chose this time to embark."

"Exactly," Lakesh announced, striding in with Seng Kao.

Both men wore blue-gray tiger-striped camo utility uniforms, taken from Cerberus storage. A 1911 Colt automatic pistol was snugged in a military-style flapped holster on Lakesh's right hip. Usually very well groomed, Lakesh's hair was uncombed and he looked haggard, as if he had not gotten much sleep and the little he had was fitful.

He carried the interphaser with both hands, with the device's cushioned carrying case hanging from a strap over his right shoulder. The zippered, watertight compartments contained the device's support systems. Carefully he placed the pyramidion on the table. From the base protruded a small power unit and a miniature control keypad.

All of them knew the shape of the interphaser was not based on aesthetics. According to Lakesh, the energy generated by the machine progressed by four different routes, rejoining in a single conclusionary figure at the apex of the pyramid. The energy flowed in a helix spiral pattern exactly opposite and of equal frequency. The intensity on each side of the vortex at any given point triggered a quantum induction shift by vibrational resonance.

"The transit coordinates are locked for a vortex point

on a hilltop about a quarter of a mile east of the pyramid's outer perimeter," Lakesh declared. "The same one to which you were transported a couple of years ago."

Grant arched a doubtful eyebrow. "How safe will that be?"

Lakesh shrugged. "Who can say? The hour will be late and hopefully no pickets will have been posted in the vicinity. Ideally, only the area immediately around the pyramid will be secured. With Erica's forces either routed, dead or absorbed, we can only hope Wei Qiang's attention will be focused on the interior of the pyramid, not the exterior."

"Most of the time," Kane pointed out, "the circumstances we phase into are the exact *opposite* of ideal."

"I am aware of that," Lakesh retorted. "In that eventuality, I will expect you and friend Grant to do what you do best."

The scientist did not elaborate, nor was there a need for him to do so. Years before, Lakesh had recruited the pair of ex-Magistrates to act as the enforcement arm of Cerberus, to bring into play the killer instincts he thought he lacked. Although Kane's and Grant's abilities surpassed that simplistic evaluation, it was an undeniable fact that wherever the Cerberus team went, violence and death were only moments away.

Regardless of the planning, terrible and bloody events almost always occurred and the body count soared. In Moscow and Mongolia, England and Utah, Antarctica and Cambodia, it was always the same.

Brigid Baptiste had once opined that Kane and Grant

were avatars, catalysts, triggering eruptions of savagery that had simmered at a low boil for long time.

Savagery and bloodshed were nothing new to either of the ex-Magistrates. Old habits and customs died hard with the two men, particularly because of the rigorous discipline to which they had submitted themselves. Casting aside their identities as Mags and accepting new roles as rebels and exiles hadn't been easy for either Kane or Grant. Although they never admitted it to each other, both men sometimes yearned to return to the regimentation and routine of their former lives. If nothing else, the world had made more sense back then.

But by doing the work of Cerberus in tandem with Brigid, Domi and Lakesh, they had scored many victories, defeated many enemies and solved mysteries of the past that molded the present and impacted on the future. More importantly, they began to rekindle the spark of hope within the breasts of the disenfranchised fighting to survive in the Outlands.

Victory, if not within their grasp, at least no longer seemed an unattainable dream. But with the transformation of the barons into the overlords, Kane wondered if the war was now over—or if it had ever actually been waged at all. He was beginning to fear that everything he and his friends had experienced and endured so far had only been a series of minor skirmishes, a mere prologue to the true conflict yet to come.

"Did you bring the ring?" Grant asked Lakesh.

"Of course," the scientist retorted, his contemptuous

tone of voice suggesting that he found Grant's question more than a trifle absurd.

Before Grant could respond in kind, Brigid interjected, "Let's calibrate the audio pickups."

Pushing aside her fall of hair, she reached up and touched the Commtact, feeling for the flat curve of metal attached to her mastoid bone behind her right ear. Lakesh, Grant and Kane did as she said, adjusting their own Commtacts.

The little comm units fit tightly against the mastoid bones, attached to implanted steel pintles. The unit slid through the flesh and made contact with tiny input ports. Its sensor circuitry incorporated an analog-to-digital voice encoder that was subcutaneously embedded in the bone.

Once the device made full cranial contact, transmissions were picked up by the auditory canals. The dermal sensors transmitted the electronic signals directly through the skull casing. Even if someone went deaf, as long as they wore a Commtact, they would still have a form of hearing.

A burst of static filled their heads and Brigid subvocalized in a faint whisper, "Testing, one-two, testing."

When her companions heard her voice echoing clearly inside their skulls, they nodded in confirmation. "Then we're good to go," she announced.

Philboyd gave her a jittery, nervous smile. "I wish I could go with you."

Brigid returned the smile with a reassuring one of her own. "You're of more use here as both support and to lead a rescue if one is necessary."

Kane didn't even bother repressing a snort of derision at the idea of the astrophysicist charging across China with guns blazing. Most of the people who lived in the Cerberus redoubt acted in the capacity of support personnel, regardless of their specialized individual skills or training. They worked rotating shifts, eight hours a day, seven days a week.

Primarily, their work was the routine maintenance and monitoring of the installation's environmental systems, the satellite data feed and the security network. However, everyone was given at least a superficial understanding of all the redoubt's systems so they could pinch-hit in times of emergency. Fortunately, only once had such a time arrived in the wake of Maccan's murderous incursion. Afterward Lakesh felt completely justified in his insistence that everyone have a working knowledge of the inner systems so as to keep the redoubt operational.

Grant and Kane were exempt from this crosstraining, inasmuch as they served as the exploratory and enforcement arm of Cerberus and undertook far and away the lion's share of the risks. On their downtime between missions they made sure all the ordnance in the armory was in good condition and occasionally tuned up the vehicles in the depot.

Brigid Baptiste, due to her eidetic memory, was the most exemplary member of the redoubt's permanent staff, since she could step into any vacancy. However, her gifts were a two-edged sword, inasmuch as those selfsame polymathic skills made her an indispensable addition to away missions.

Because Brewster Philboyd viewed Brigid as something of an anchor in his new life on Earth, he grew nervous and insecure whenever she went into the field without him.

Lakesh kept glancing toward the door leading into the op center, but doing it in such an obviously surreptitious way he drew Kane's attention.

"What are you waiting for, a bon voyage fruit basket?" he asked the scientist, feigning innocence. "I just happened to notice that Domi isn't here to wish us luck."

Lakesh regarded him grimly but did not reply. Picking up the interphaser, he carried it into the gateway unit. When making phase transits from the redoubt, they always used the mat-trans chamber because it could be hermetically sealed. The interphaser's targeting computer had been programmed with the precise coordinates of the mat-trans unit as Destination Zero. A touch of a single key on the control board would automatically return the device to the jump chamber.

Lakesh placed the pyramidion on the floor and waited for his companions to join him. When everyone was assembled, Brigid climbed up onto the platform, pulling the brown-tinted armaglass door closed on its counterbalanced hinges. It shut with the solid *chock* of locking solenoids, triggering the phase-transition coils enclosed within the platform. A high-pitched drone rose from the floor plates. When the interphaser was activated in conjunction with the energy produced by the mat-trans unit, a different set of control protocols were engaged.

Several years before, Lakesh had linked a switching

station with the main gateway board to govern the temporal dilation of the experimental Omega Path program. Since the energy outputs of the Parallax Points and the temporal dilator were of similar frequencies, it hadn't been much of a task to put the system back into use.

As had been done during the Omega Path experiments, the mainframe computer network was reprogrammed with the logarithmic data of the Parallax Points. The program prolonged the quincunx effect produced by rematerialization, stretching it out in perfect balance between the phase and interphase inducers. Upon standard gateway activation, a million autoscanning elements committed to memory every feature of the jumpers' physical and mental composition, even, Bry supposed, down to the very subconscious. The data filtered through the system's built-in memory banks, correlating it with a variation range field.

Once the autoscanning sequence was complete, the translation program of the quincunx effect kicked in, a process by which lower dimensional space was translated, phased into a higher dimensional space along a quantum path. The jumpers traveled this path, existing for a nanosecond of time as digital duplicates of themselves, in a place between a relativistic *here* and a relativistic *there*.

Lakesh exchanged a long look with his four companions. "Are we set?"

Grant nodded. "Do it."

Glancing toward a wide-eyed Seng Kao, Lakesh said, "The effect produced by this device is different than that of the gateway itself, but it's just as safe...safer in some ways."

"Unless we end up at the bottom of the ocean or inside a mountain," Kane commented cheerfully.

Seng Kao stiffened, sudden fear radiating from him.

"Mr. Kane is joking," Lakesh said, glaring at him. "Such an eventuality has never happened and never will, and he knows it."

In fact, Kane did know it, although the possibility that the interphaser could conceivably materialize them either in a lake or an ocean or underground, was a concept he privately feared. He knew an analogical computer was built into the interphaser to automatically select a vortex point above solid ground.

When Interphaser Version 2.0 was completed, Kane, Grant and Brigid had endured weeks of tedious training in the use of the device on short hops, selecting vortex points near the redoubt—or at least, near in the sense that if they couldn't make the return trip through a quantum channel they could conceivably walk back to the installation.

Lakesh nodded to Brigid. "If you would do the honors."

Kneeling, Brigid touched the interphaser's inset activation toggles on the miniature keypad. As she stood up, a waxy, glowing funnel of light fanned up from the metal apex of the pyramidion. It looked like diffused veil of backlit fog, with tiny shimmering stars dancing within it.

Seng Kao stared in wonder, and as he stared the light expanded into a gushing borealis several feet wide, spreading out within the chamber. A thready pulse of vibration tickled their skin, and shadows crawled over the armaglass walls, moving in fitful jerks and leaps. A faint hint of a breeze brushed their faces and ruffled their hair.

A glowing, phosphorescent lotus blossom sprouted from the base of the interphaser. It stretched upward, the tip splashing against the hexagonal pattern of the ceiling. The petals of witch-fire opened amid cracklings and flares of miniature lightning.

"One at a time now," Brigid said matter-of-factly.

Seng Kao cringed. "One at a time what?"

Lakesh gestured to the shimmering fan of light. "Walk into that, over the top of the interphaser."

Seng Kao eyed it fearfully. "No."

Kane sighed. "I'll go first—you Dragon Mama's boy you."

He stepped toward the pyramid, sidling between the writhing petals of energy—and vanished.

Chapter 14

They tumbled through a writhing tunnel made of raving, shrieking energy. Everyone experienced an assault on their senses—sight, hearing, touch and taste. For a long, terrifying moment, they felt their bodies dissolve, with no sense of gravity or of up or down or any kind of control.

There was nothing to see but a raging torrent of light, wild plumes and whorling spindrifts of violet, of yellow, of blue and green and red. They swirled like a whirlpool, glowing filaments that congealed and stretched outward into the black gulfs of hyperdimensional space. They shot past coruscating clusters of stars, of glowing globules of planets.

Streaks of gray and dark blue became interspersed with the multicolored swirls. Bursts of light flared in garish displays on the tunnel walls. They felt themselves diving through an alternately brightly lit and shadow-shrouded abyss, an endless free fall into infinity. They were conscious of a half-instant of whirling vertigo as if they hurtled a vast distance at blinding speed.

Then the sensation of an uncontrolled plunge lessened. Slowly, as if veils were being drawn away one by one, the darker colors on the tunnel walls deepened and collected ahead of them into a pool of shimmering radiance.

Brigid, Kane, Grant and Lakesh stepped out of the energy field. Seng Kao staggered awkwardly, crying out in terror. He would have fallen if Grant hadn't snatched him by the collar of his field jacket and kept him upright.

They moved away from the interphaser as the cascade of light whirled and spun around it like a diminishing cyclone, shedding sparks and thread-thin static discharges. As quickly as it appeared, the glowing cone vanished, as if it had been sucked back into the apex of the pyramidion.

The five people stood on the brow of a grassy hill overlooking a thickly wooded valley. The starlit night was cool. Wind sighed in the willows on the hillside, and moonlight glimmered from the surface of the distant river. They stood atop what appeared to be a gigantic stone dining table.

The massive slab looked to be twelve feet across with a deeply engraved surface, precisely inscribed with Chinese ideographs and even a form of hieroglyphs to form a perfectly integrated geometric design. The complex pattern of symbols bent, twisted, swirled and intersected in the center where the interphaser rested.

"This is new," Brigid remarked, looking down at the stone.

"Or very old," Lakesh intoned. "It's an ancient geodetic marker. Sam—Enlil—must have found it and cleared away the turf and topsoil since the last time we were here."

All of them knew that some ancient civilizations were aware of symmetrical earth energies and constructed monuments over the vortex points in order to manipulate those energies. They had seen several similar markers in the past, in places such as Iraq, India and even Australia.

Seng Kao hugged himself, continuing to gasp in lungful after lungful of air. Grant released him and looked up at the blue-black tapestry of the sky.

"Are we sure this is the right place?" he asked quietly.

"Pretty sure," Kane said dryly, gesturing over his shoulder.

Slowly the big man turned, surveying his surroundings—not that there was much to see on the crest of the hill other than the round slab—and froze at the sight of the vast pyramid blotting out a substantial portion of the sky and the landscape. Overwhelmed by the staggering height and breadth of the structure, his breath caught in his throat.

Grant had never devoted much thought as to how ancient peoples had constructed massive megalithic structures. But once again, seeing the most enormous and perfectly engineered Terran structure still in existence awakened awe within him, even though the half-mile-high Danaan pyramid on Mars had dwarfed it.

Bright beams of light played over its surface, knifing out from spotlights set up around the pyramid's base. By the ambient glow, the people on the hill could see a moving mass of tiny specks and a couple of larger moving specks that they identified as men and vehicles.

As he had the first time he'd seen it, Kane tried to estimate the pyramid's size by using the men and vehicles as reference points. He could only hazard the most approximate of comparisons—the pyramid of Xian was like a fifty-story building rising from a twelve-acre base. The megalith was of such staggering proportions as to make its true distance from their position difficult to gauge. Even nearly a quarter of a mile away from it, the bulk of the structure completely filled their field of vision.

The flickers of cook fires blazed among the scattering of soldiers bivouacked around the base of the pyramid, and the breeze carried the faint odors of charcoal. Someone plucked at the strings of a *ch'in,* the Chinese zither.

"There doesn't seem to be anybody around up here," Lakesh commented.

"We should still keep low," Grant replied. "In case anybody looks this way."

Reflexively, the five people crouched, Kane and Grant dropping to one knee. As Lakesh busied himself disengaging the power pack from the interphaser and placing the device within the carrying case, Grant, Brigid and Kane crept to the rim of the hill and lay on their stomachs, looking down into the valley.

From his war bag, Kane removed a compact set of night-vision binoculars. He switched on the IR illuminator and peered through the eyepieces. Viewed through the specially coated lenses, which optimized the low light values, the valley seemed to be illuminated by a lambent, ghostly aura. Where only black had been before, his vision was lit by various shifting shades of gray and green.

Kane swept the binoculars over the encampment, careful not to focus on the cook fires because the IR optics would enhance the medium-size blazes to an almost intolerable brightness. He saw craters punched in the side of the pyramid, but they were tiny pock-marks, dimples in the vast expanse of the facade.

As before, the sight of the pyramid made him feel distinctly uneasy. Its antiquity was beyond guessing even to a man who had seen the ancient monuments of Mars and the citadel of the Annunaki on the Moon. But whether the pyramid had been erected as the tomb of the fabled Yellow Emperor or served as his fortress, not even Brigid wanted to speculate. As far as any of them knew, it could have been built by the race they had known as the Archons, but Kane seriously doubted it was.

Kane pushed the thoughts from his mind and concentrated on the immediate task of intel gathering. The soldiers were as Seng Kao had described, wearing yellow tunics and helmets. They sat around fires and outside tents passing bottles and bowls from hand to hand. They did not appear to be celebrating their victory over the Dragon Mother's forces, but then, a full day and night had passed since they had breached the pyramid.

"See anything unusual?" Grant asked. "Any sign of Wei Qiang?"

"Not so far," Kane answered absently, continuing to pass the binoculars over the camp. He swept them over a wheeled boxlike shape, paused, then came back to it. "What the hell is that?"

"What the hell is what?" Brigid inquired.

"I'm not sure." Kane squinted through the eyepieces, studying the vehicle that resembled a multiwheeled, slightly flattened and elongated cube. From a turret extended the ten-foot-long barrel of a 40 mm cannon. A pair of foremounted machine guns rose from the armored hull.

Impatiently, Grant reached for the binoculars. "Let me see."

Kane did not so much as hand the binoculars over as allow Grant to snatch them from his hands. Putting them to his eyes, he asked, "What am I looking for?"

"You tell me," Kane shot back. "Since you're so keen to have a look-see."

After a couple of seconds of silent staring, Grant stiffened. "I think I found it. That weird-looking tank, right?"

"Right," Kane answered. "Do you know anything about it?"

After another couple of seconds of silent staring, Grant said reluctantly, "No…but Lakesh might."

"Lakesh might what?" the scientist asked, creeping forward on his hands and knees, dragging the interphaser case with him. Seng Kao followed closely.

Grant handed Lakesh the binoculars and pointed down into the valley. "Have you ever seen a tank like that one? Before you were frozen?"

Lakesh sniffed as if offended. "I wasn't really frozen, you know…it was a different form of suspended animation entirely. Calling people like me 'freezies' is a misnomer."

"I stand corrected," Grant growled impatiently. "And I also stand not giving a shit. Just answer my question, will you?"

Holding the binoculars to his eyes, Lakesh followed Grant's pointing finger and said, "I never saw a tank exactly like it, not in action anyway, but I've seen FCS— Future Combat System—vehicles in storage, in the Anthill. They were never used in a ground war, however."

"It's pretty unusual looking," Kane commented.

"True," Lakesh agreed. "It was part of a new armored infantry program…all different types of vehicles were based on a common platform, sharing the same frame, chassis and drive trains."

Grant nodded. "Makes sense. A modular approach means that all the parts could be mass-produced and standardized for easy assembly."

Lakesh handed the binoculars back to Kane. "The base concept was one of increased efficiency. That particular FCS was called a Scorpinaut, as I recall. It has limited submersible capabilities. However, as far as I know only a handful of prototypes were built. I remember seeing them in the Anthill…although there could have been more housed in COG facilities elsewhere."

Grant, Kane and Brigid knew to what Lakesh referred. As many as fifty years before the nuclear holocaust, a long-range construction project was undertaken by a program known as the Continuity of Government. The COG program was perceived as the ultimate insurance policy against Armageddon. Hundreds of subterranean command posts were built in various regions of the country, quite a number of them inside national parks, hiding in plain sight. The size and complexity ranged from little more than warehouse units to immense, self-sustaining complexes.

"In that case," Brigid stated, "if the FCS vehicles were hidden in COG installations, how did Wei Qiang find them?"

Kane had a suspicion, but he didn't put it into words. He scanned the troop-filled valley again, finding five large tents, bigger than any he had seen earlier, arranged in a circle. In the center of the cluster rose an expansive pavilion of bright yellow fabric. The sides were decorated with red cross-hatched ideographs.

On both sides of the pavilion stood three long wooden poles, each one twelve feet tall. Red-and-yellow banners wrapped the shafts, the loose ends fluttering in the breeze. Affixed to the very tops of the poles were human heads, the necks severed cleanly. Though the sagging, swollen faces were crusted with dried blood, Kane knew they were the heads of men, not women.

He was surprised at his surge of relief when he realized Erica's head was not bobbing at the end of a pike. Although he certainly felt no affection or admiration for her, he would not have taken any genuine pleasure in her death, either.

Kane waved Seng Kao forward and passed him the binoculars, asking, "Are those faces familiar?"

In a surprisingly curt tone, the man retorted, "They are my officers. I ordered them to defend Tui Chui Jian's fortress to the death. They died with their honor secure. The Dragon Mother will take great pride in their devotion."

Seng Kao returned the binoculars to Kane, his face impassive. He crawled away from the crest of the hill. Resisting the impulse to comment unfavorably on Erica van Sloan's idea of pride, Kane scanned the area around the tents again.

Guards stood stiffly in front of the pavilion's triangular flap, black automatic rifles held across their chests. Kane quickly identified the subguns as Calico M-960s, each one carrying full extended magazines of fifty 9 mm rounds. He also remembered the last time he had seen such a model and make of weapon, and his stomach slipped sidewise. The suspicion he had not put into words became a cold certainty.

Hiking himself up to one knee, he handed the binoculars to Brigid. "Take a look at the blasters the soldiers are carrying...that might give you an idea of how Wei Qiang ended up with all these toys."

A line of puzzlement creasing her forehead, Brigid did as he said. Then, in a flat tone she declared, "Calicos. And the last time we saw anybody who carried those was inside Medicine Mountain in Wyoming."

Grant hissed in anger and disgust. "*Shit.* The Millennial Consortium. I really hate those guys."

"So you've said," Brigid replied.

Grimly, Lakesh said, "That makes sense. They're the only group we know of who has been actively seeking COG vaults. But what in the name of God would have motivated the consortium to supply the army of a tong crime lord?"

Still peering through the binoculars, Brigid commented, "Maybe they know something we don't. For example—the symbol on the big tent down there means monarch. Apparently that's where Wei Qiang hangs his hat. Those other tents are probably his officers' quarters."

Grant stood up, brushing off the tail of his coat. "Why don't we just mosey on down and simply ask the old darlin' just what the hell he's doing here?"

Kane eyed the big man skeptically. "I don't think we'll get the chance to ask Qiang anything if we just 'mosey on down'…except maybe to request that he put our heads higher on the pikes so we can see more of Xian Province."

"Well," Grant said with a studied indifference, "I'm sure you have another plan."

Kane smiled thinly. "Oh, I definitely do." He glanced toward Seng Kao and beckoned to him with a forefinger. "Come over here. Chop-chop."

Brigid rolled her eyes in weary exasperation. "And that's probably what Wei Qiang will end up doing to us."

Chapter 15

They encountered the first picket nestled within a rocky swale at the base of the slope. A yellow-uniformed trooper sat huddled on a small boulder, nodding over the Calico clutched to his breast like a child.

As had been agreed before making the descent from the hilltop, Seng Kao marched boldly up to the man, his feet making a constant swishing as he strode through the high grass. He was within six feet of the trooper before the man roused with a start. He blundered to his feet in an embarrassed rush, shouting at Seng Kao to halt. The man did as the soldier said, lifting his arms high.

Both men exchanged a confusing flurry of Chinese, the trooper snapping questions and orders with Seng Kao doing his best to answer while obeying the commands. He placed his hands behind his head, linking the fingers and related a tale of being an emissary dispatched from Lau Wun, one of the local lords who offered aid to the army of Wei Qiang.

While Seng Kao was trying to convince the trooper of his bona fides, Kane rose from the shadows and glided silently, walking heel to toe, up behind the soldier. He swiftly slid his right arm around the man's neck while clamping his left hand over his mouth. In the same instant, he jacked a knee into the man's kidney with a sound like a dull ax chopping into wood.

Kane felt the soldier's lips writhe against his hand in silent agony, his nervous system completely over-whelmed by the sudden, incapacitating pain. With deftness Kane didn't expect, Seng Kao lunged forward and wrested the subgun from the trooper's hands.

The soldier was small in stature, shorter and slighter even than Seng Kao, and Kane had no problem wres-tling him behind the boulder upon which he had been sitting. He slammed the man hard against the ground and held him there by the shoulders as Grant roughly wrenched off his helmet and tossed it to Seng Kao. As the man positioned it on his head, Kane lifted the trooper up so Grant could yank off his uniform tunic, heedless of the brass buttons that scattered in all directions.

Seng Kao quickly shouldered into the uniform, then sat atop the stone again, mimicking the trooper's slumped-over posture. The entire sequence of events took less than a minute. Both Kane and Grant were slightly surprised by Seng Kao's militaristic efficiency, but they assumed Erica hadn't chosen him as her chief lieutenant because of his witty conversation.

Wei Qiang's soldier stared up at the four people looming over him, wet lips peeled back over his teeth in a grimace, his wide black eyes reflecting both star-light and naked fear. In a sharp, autocratic tone, Lakesh snapped out questions in hard-edged Chinese.

After a few moments of hard breathing, the man

replied, speaking so quickly his words sounded like a blur of fluid gibberish to Kane and Grant.

When the soldier paused for breath, Kane asked Brigid, "Did you catch any of that?"

She shook her head in frustration. "Only a bit. His name is Ingok and he's scared to death."

"It took him that long just to get that across?" Grant rumbled suspiciously.

"Of course not," Lakesh retorted peevishly. "He related everything we need to know without being specifically asked."

"Very disciplined," Kane observed sarcastically.

"Ingok is not a soldier by trade," Lakesh said. "He is a farmer. He was more or less conscripted into the army as it passed through his village."

"More or less?" Brigid echoed.

"He talks of Wei Qiang, how most of his army's officers are made up of bandits, recruited from the provinces they marched through. The crops of Ingok's village failed and the men were made an offer—if they joined Wei Qiang's army for a period of time, then their families would be provided for."

"It doesn't seem like Wei Qiang wasted much time or effort on training," Grant commented.

"Men like Ingok are used for cannon fodder," Lakesh replied curtly. "To be sacrificed so the higher ranks can survive and share the plunder." He asked the soldier another question, and the man responded in a calmer, less frenetic tone.

"He claims that Wei Qiang is inside the pyramid,"

Brigid translated. "And has been since yesterday morning. He was searching for the Dragon Mother, although camp scuttlebutt has it she got away. Wei Qiang intends to embark at dawn to find her."

"Why?" Kane demanded, perplexed. "He has the pyramid. Why is Erica so important to him?"

Lakesh put the question to Ingok. His head shake and shrug required no translation, but he added a stream of words.

"From what he has overheard," Lakesh said, "it is believed that Erica stole something of great value that Wei Qiang wants very badly."

"A set of ugly snake rings, for instance?" Grant inquired.

"Ingok doesn't know," Lakesh answered. "No one does. Wei Qiang's only confidant is a scar-faced Westerner, a white man."

Brigid pursed her lips contemplatively. "If Erica managed to escape the army unnoticed, then that suggests she had a method and a route planned well in advance."

Kane nodded in agreement and called out to Seng Kao, still sitting slumped on the concealing boulder. "You said Erica—the Dragon Mother—was going where again?"

"Yichang," Seng Kao answered promptly.

"How far away is it?"

"Perhaps thirty miles downriver."

"How would the Dragon Mother get there?" Kane asked.

"Captain Sun Fan," the man responded.

"What the hell is that supposed to be?" Grant growled. "Or is it a who?"

"A businessman. He owns a riverboat and operates up and down this stretch of the Yarkand. He is what you would call a freelance transporter, stopping at all the villages along the way. He delivers almost all of our supplies here. There used to be many of his type here, but they all fell prey to pirates."

"Erica hitched a ride with this Captain Fan?" Lakesh asked skeptically. "How?"

"The captain makes ports of call on four villages along the river. The entire round trip requires ten hours. He would have most likely picked up the Dragon Mother about this time yesterday morning."

"Picked her up where?" Grant demanded.

"There is a transfer point perhaps three miles downriver…less than an hour's hike if we're lucky. I can take you there easily. The captain prefers to make this last leg of his route at night so as to avoid notice."

Tilting his head back, Seng Kao eyed the position of the stars. "He should be along within an hour, an hour and a half. If we can reach the jetty in time, we might able to signal Captain Fan's boat when he comes around the bend."

"Like they say in the song," Lakesh said dryly.

Kane looked at him blankly. "What song?"

Lakesh shook his head, not bothering to answer. He asked Seng Kao, "Does Captain Fan know you by sight?"

"As a cousin knows his cousin," Seng Kao replied smoothly.

"You're sure he'd help Erica?" Brigid inquired.

"Without the aid of the Dragon Mother," Seng Kao stated, "and the arms she provided, Captain Fan would have been overrun by the river pirates long ago. The Dragon Mother and he enjoyed a long trade contract."

Lakesh tugged at his nose thoughtfully. "It will be touch and go, avoiding the guards on the way down to the river."

Grant snorted, nodding toward Ingok. "Not if this guy is a representative sampling."

"Good point," Kane said. "And since we've only the one option, other than reintroducing ourselves to Wei Qiang, let's move on it." He eyed Ingok. "What should we do with our piece of cannon fodder here?"

Seng Kao cast a glance over his shoulder. "Kill him. He is our enemy."

"You were *our* enemy, not all that long ago," Brigid reminded him icily. "Now you're our ally and this man might be yours tomorrow, for all you know."

"You are a foolish woman, just like the Dragon Mother said," Seng Kao replied grimly.

"She's the one on the run, who sent you to whine for our help," Kane said contemptuously. "We'll do things our way."

From his war bag he withdrew two sets of nylon cuffs. "We'll tie him up and leave him. It's not so cold that he'll suffer much. Somebody ought to be along to relieve him around daybreak."

Expertly, Kane bound Ingok's hands and wrists with the binders and fashioned a serviceable gag from a bandanna he found stuffed in his pocket. Although he looked displeased by the decision to spare Ingok's life, Seng Kao kept further opinions to himself. Wearing the yellow helmet and tunic of Wei Qiang's forces, he led the four outlanders into the valley, hugging the shadows cast by hillocks and overhanging willow trees.

They skirted a hedge-rimmed garden, with Seng Kao guiding them carefully toward a collection of old outbuildings, a maze of half-crumbled walls and vine-grown pagodas. The walls and decorative columns were covered with carved figures. Statues of solemn Buddhas, their faces softened by centuries of wind and rain, rose from the ground.

They saw no sign of any pickets at first, and then after they had negotiated a quarter of the way through the shrines, they heard the tramp of feet, just around a turn in a wall. Everyone flattened against the shadow-shrouded side of a building, remaining motionless.

From around the corner marched six men, five of them wearing yellow uniforms and helmets. Calico subguns hung by straps from their shoulders, short swords clanked at their hips and pistol butts protruded from web belts. They were a scarred, hard-bitten and grizzled group, exuding the air of the professional warrior, as completely opposite from Ingok as it was possible to be.

Both Kane and Grant recognized their type instantly—vicious fighters, outlaws who constituted a class of their own. They guessed that the five Asians comprised Wei Qiang's unit commanders.

They escorted a heavyset Caucasian man of medium height wearing a zippered dun-colored coverall. His eyes were masked by dark glasses despite the gloom, and inflamed scars curved up from both corners of his mouth, giving him a permanent macabre smile. Kane's lips drew away from his teeth in a wolfish grin.

Although the man's drab garment was sufficient identification, Kane glimpsed a small brass button pinned to his collar. It depicted a familiar stylized representation of a featureless man holding a cornucopia in his left hand and a sword in his right. That was more than enough to brand him a representative of the Millennial Consortium.

Grant and Kane exchanged swift hand signals, a very brief and manual discussion about ambushing the group. Lakesh intervened, extending a hand, shaking his head violently in negation and mouthing "No!" several times.

After the men were out of earshot, Kane declared in an angry whisper, "If we'd put the arm on them, grabbed the millennialist, then we'd have a good idea of Wei Qiang's plan—not to mention find out if it's the same Wei Qiang as we know."

"You wouldn't have been able to accomplish that without shots being fired," Lakesh countered just as angrily. "We've only gotten this far by the element of surprise. I'm not willing to sacrifice both of those advantages so soon."

Kane locked eyes with Lakesh, but before the staring match could officially begin, Brigid whispered, "You know he's right, Kane."

In fact, Kane did know it, but he was loath to admit that Lakesh's strategies were sometimes sound. Instead, he turned toward Seng Kao and snapped in a low voice, "Let's move on."

The man nodded and began wending his way through the shrines again, taking the point. As he passed a weed-choked pagoda, a soldier stepped from around the rear wall. His attention was fixed on Seng Kao so he didn't immediately see the outlanders.

But when he did, he came to a clumsy halt, trying to unlimber his Calico, but the strap fouled in the collar of his tunic. He opened his mouth to shout an alarm. Grant rushed forward, swarming over the astonished man, his left hand cupping the soldier's chin while his right forearm came across the windpipe and hauled back.

Putting all of his considerable upper-body strength into a backward wrench, Grant heard the crunch of gristle and cartilage. The man uttered a small, aspirated gurgle, stiffened, spasmed and died. Seng Kao had whirled, his own appropriated Calico held at waist level. When he saw the soldier sagging lifelessly in Grant's arms, a small smile of approval creased his lips.

"Was that necessary?" Lakesh asked sourly.

Grant dropped the soldier face-first to the ground, taking his Calico and tossing it to Lakesh. "We'll never know."

Gathering a fistful of tunic in one hand, Grant dragged the corpse along the side of the pagoda and around the corner. He took no pleasure in killing men such as Wei Qiang's soldier, since he was only a grunt, one of the many interchangeable drones not much different than Grant and Kane had been during their years as Magistrates. But for people who threatened those he loved, he reserved no mercy. It was an area in which he gave no quarter. He hid the body in the murk, among some high weeds and rejoined his companions. No one, not even Brigid, commented on his swift, deadly action.

The five people continued on their way through the valley. The Yarkand River was only a glistening ribbon in the fold of the night. Seng Kao found the trail easily, leading westward from the valley and following the river. The path was like a tunnel cutting through the tall bamboo woods bordering the banks. No one could glimpse the sky. Fortunately, the Nighthawk microlights taken from their war bags illuminated their way. The world was a primeval, menacing green with night-blooming epiphytes and flowering creepers stretching down from the overhead branches.

Now and then they roused families of snub-nosed monkeys slumbering in the boughs and there was a brief, outraged chittering and rustling of leaves. Once they disturbed a broad-horned water buffalo that surged up out of a mudflat and stared at them with startled, uncomprehending eyes.

After they had been walking for half an hour, Seng Kao pointed out a hut perched on wooden stilts above the shallows. From it a splintery pier stretched for twenty-five feet out into the broad river. The five people walked through the empty hut and along creaking timbers to the end of the rickety dock. They looked under the slatted boards, then up and down the river.

The Yarkand meandered past rock-tumbled shoals pressed close to both banks. There was no sign of any watercraft. No lights glittered anywhere along the banks. Southward the land lifted and the river seemed to funnel between black towering cliffs.

"Think we missed Captain Fan?" Kane asked quietly.

Seng Kao didn't immediately reply, but he kept his eyes fixed on the northern course of the river. From one of the pilings he removed a lantern and shook it. Oil sloshed in the well, and Lakesh lit the wick with a wooden stick match taken from a pocket. Yellow light spilled from it in a shimmering halo.

"If I was a riverboat captain," Grant rumbled, "I don't think I'd want to ply my trade so close to an invading army. Maybe he decided to lay low for a while."

"The captain is not the low-laying type," Seng Kao replied. "He is very brazen and likes a little bit of attention."

Kane squinted upriver, looking in the same direction as Seng Kao. In the gloom he caught a brief, firefly flicker, then a shape that put him in mind of a jeweled water bug hove into view, swinging around the bend. A loud hooting whistle echoed and screeched up and down the concourse. The boat was a high-riding junk, but at first glance it reminded Kane of a floating gaudy house. Torches blazed all along the gunwales, and paper lanterns flared from the rigging.

"Likes a little bit of attention, does he?" Brigid murmured.

"A little bit," Seng Kao admitted.

Chapter 16

With a thud of diesel engines and the splash of backwash, the junk lumbered toward the end of the dock. Like most of the other junks they had seen, the ship had high poops and overhanging stems. It was made to appear top-heavy by the pair of tall pole masts and big sails with batten lines running entirely across the deck.

Over the bang, thump and creak of the ship's approach they heard the bleat of goats, the squeal of pigs and the clucking of chickens, as well as the skirl of panpipes and the wail of a lute. A thick odor of wet fur, manure and even the astringent scent of burning charcoal wafted from the deck and clogged their nostrils.

Seng Kao took off his helmet and held the lantern close to his face. A hoarse voice shouted from the boat's deck, and Seng Kao responded, apparently repeating the same words in some sort of arranged pass code.

The junk eased up against the piling, bumping gently, the wooden hull cushioned by old tires lashed to it by thick hawsers. The engine roar softened as it throttled down to an idle. The junk looked for all the world like a Noah's ark, but the manner in which it was illuminated made it look more like pictures of Christmas trees they had seen. The open deck was filled with people, bales of cargo, bleating lambs, cages of chickens and even a few pigs, but the boat itself was immaculate, the paint fresh and all the metal parts polished and oiled. The ribbed sailcloth looked as spotless as a linen tablecloth.

A loop of rope snaked out from the rail, and Seng Kao secured it to the piling. A wooden gangplank stretched from amidships and clattered down loudly on the end of the pier. A medium-sized man appeared at the rail. The outlanders knew without benefit of a formal introduction that he was Captain Sun Fan.

He looked to be in his forties, with the long head and flat-featured face of a northern Chinese and a body as solid as the statues of Buddha they had seen earlier. He wore a blue-crowned nautical cap, a sleeveless black shirt and white, baggy ducks. The knees bore dark stains. His bare, muscular arms were covered with red-and-gold tattoos—serpentine dragons coiled seductively around simpering, naked girls.

Sun Fan did not seem surprised to see the five people standing on the dock. He exchanged brief words in Mandarin with Seng Kao, then declared in surprisingly good but somewhat broken English, "Told to expect you. Good thing you show up—this be my last down-river trip until further notice. All other boats been took by Wei Qiang."

No one responded for a long, awkward moment of surprise. Then Lakesh ventured, "Who told you to expect us?"

Gesturing impatiently, Sun Fan retorted, "Who you

think? Come aboard, we behind schedule, got pirates to watch out for, too. This be their last chance at me so they be especially ambitious."

Without hesitation, Seng Kao strode up the gangplank, pausing long enough to clasp the captain's hand as he passed by. The outlanders did not move, and Sun Fan challenged loudly, "Well? Stay or go, no mind to me."

Kane, Brigid and Grant all exchanged questioning glances, then one by one they marched up the gangplank. Lakesh trailed after them, removing the rope from the piling. He moved slowly, almost reluctantly. When all of the outlanders stood on the quarterdeck, tattooed sailors wearing white headbands and pantaloons brought out long wooden poles and used them to push the junk away from the pier.

Turning to Sun Fan, Lakesh asked, "Your destination is Yichang?"

The captain nodded. "Of course. That where I dropped off Tui Chui Jian, yesterday at dawn."

Kane surveyed the crowded deck, noting that most of the people seemed to be peasant farmers and traders. Men and women alike wore conical straw hats and blue coolie jackets. "They're going there, too?"

Sun Fan smiled, but without mirth. "They got no choice but flow with the current, to let it carry them to end of the line where the Yarkand empties into the Yangtze. All of us, as you Americans say, am in same boat together."

The junk turned slightly to port, the ancient engines chugging louder. Captain Fan offered them cups of tea and told them to find places among the passengers to spend the rest of the voyage. Even as he spoke English as the congenial host, he interrupted himself to snap out orders in Chinese and his dark, darting eyes missed nothing that went on about the boat.

"Do you usually have so many passengers and so much cargo?" Grant asked, gesturing to the press of humanity and animals. A cow lowed somewhere aft.

"Trouble is brewing all over Xian," the captain replied. "Lots of talk driftin' downriver that Wei Qiang will conquer all of China, then Burma and Laos. Add to that, outbreaks of disease and crop failures, things aren't good. You sure you want to get off at Yichang?"

"We're not sure of anything, truth be told," Lakesh said frankly. "Is there trouble in that place?"

Sun Fan shrugged. "Smallpox, or so I've heard. Not an epidemic yet, but that could change."

"Are all these people going there?" Brigid asked.

"Yes. There is no village beyond. The Yarkand feeds directly into the Yangtze, and after Yichang it's too damned full of pirates for me. I can handle the river rats 'long this here stretch, but the Yangzte is like a sea. I'll unload what I have here, then settle down for while before I make a return trip. Mebbe you be coming back with me?"

A sailor approached, bearing a wicker tray holding clay cups of dark liquid. An unfamiliar odor floated up from the tea, and only Lakesh and Seng Kao took the cups.

"Maybe," Kane said uncertainly. "It depends on our business there."

"You mean if you find Tui Chui Jian or if Wei Qiang and his army ain't taken the place over already?" He chuckled, as if he were untroubled by the prospect. "Your heads be ones at risk, not mine."

"And why is that?" Grant challenged.

Sun Fan shrugged. "Wei Qiang knows I provide valuable service. He may want to put me under exclusive if he make Xian his home base, like the Dragon Mother did."

Lakesh's hand paused in lifting the tea cup to his lips. "That's rather mercenary, isn't it?"

The captain's eyebrows drew down. "Don't know what that means. I'm in a business that can only stay in business by doin' business. The Dragon Mother go 'way, no more contract. Wei Qiang be here now, mebbe-so give *new* contract."

Seng Kao, despite his devotion to Tui Chui Jian, did not criticize his cousin's policy.

Sun Fan excused himself and crossed the deck, climbing a short set of steps to the pilothouse atop an elevated superstructure placed amidships. Seng Kao joined him. Despite the captain's instructions to the outlanders to find a place to sit among the passengers, it was easier said than done.

Kane surveyed the crowded forward deck of the junk, watching the people curled up in every corner among the piles of cargo. It was truly a tumbled mass of humanity, moving like a sluggish tide, stirred by the urging to go somewhere and find a new place where life might be just a little bit better. Women and children gazed at them curiously, even a bit fearfully. The men's faces remained studiedly neutral.

Sun Fan's crew was a burly, rough-looking collection of men, reminiscent of the Mongol tribesmen they had encountered years ago in the Black Gobi. They were short and husky with swarthy faces and slitted eyes glittering with suspicion of the outlanders. Under the circumstances, Kane couldn't blame them.

Folding his arms over his chest, Grant gusted out a weary sigh. He rested his weight on the rail, ignoring how it creaked beneath him. "So far this trip to China has been about as rich and culturally rewarding as the last time we were here."

"Yeah," Kane agreed. "But at least we're getting to see more of it." With both arms he gestured expansively to the boat and the river. "Gee, I never dreamed of seeing or smelling anything as exotic as this—how about the rest of you?"

Lakesh ignored the sarcastic inquiry and scanned both banks, although there was little to see but a few dark and empty houses on their tall stilts above the river mud. "I wonder how serious a threat pirates actually pose along this waterway."

Brigid tossed back a strand of hair. "I'd say sailing into an outbreak of smallpox is a little more serious."

"The captain said it wasn't an epidemic," Grant pointed out.

"True," Brigid conceded, "but any place that's a hotbed of disease, especially one that could cause disfigurement, doesn't seem like Erica's first destination of choice."

She cast Lakesh a penetrating glance. "Does it?"

For a moment, Lakesh seemed unaware of both Brigid's gaze and the implications of her statement. Then he glared at her, forehead furrowed in angry confusion. "You're asking me?"

"I am."

"How should I know?" he demanded with asperity.

"You've known Erica a hell of a lot longer than we have," Kane reminded him. "Longer than we've been alive."

"I was acquainted with her," Lakesh stated. "I didn't really know her. Not until she..." His words trailed off.

"Until you let her and Sam—Enlil—gate into Cerberus?" Grant supplied.

Lakesh refused to be baited and turned his back on the big man, but his thoughts flew back to the first time he had glimpsed Erica van Sloan, in the cold corridors of the Anthill. He and the majority of Totality Concept scientists had been taken there days before the nuclear war. He barely remembered her, and wouldn't have paid any notice to her at all except for a couple of very distinctive characteristics—first was her statuesque beauty, surprising for a cyberneticist and the fact she had been attached not just to Operation Chronos but to the project overseer, Dr. Torrence Silas Burr.

Like Lakesh, she had been revived when the Program of Unification had reached a certain stage. She was only one of several preholocaust humans, known in the vernacular as "freezies," resurrected to serve the baronies. When he saw her again, well over a century later during a council of the nine barons, she was a withered old hag hunched over in a wheelchair, looking nothing like the tall, vibrant, superbly built beauty he had seen striding through the Anthill.

After delving into the Cerberus database, he learned that Erica van Sloan was of half Latino and half British extraction, possessing both a 200 point IQ and a beautiful singing voice. At eighteen years of age, the haughty, beautiful and more than a trifle arrogant Erica earned her Ph.D. in cybernetics and computer science. She wanted to pursue a singing career, but within days of her graduation from Cal Tech she went to work for a major Silicon Valley hardware producer as a models and systems analyst.

Eight months later, she left her six-figure salary to accept a position with a government-sponsored ultra-top-secret undertaking known as Overproject Whisper. In the vast installation beneath the Archuleta Mesa in Dulce, New Mexico, she served as the subordinate, lover and occasional victim of a man who made her own officious personality seem mousy and shy by comparison.

Torrence Silas Burr was brilliant, stylish, waspish and nasty. He excelled at using his enormous intellect and equally enormous ego to fuel his cruel sense of humor. The word *love* had never been part of Erica's emotional vocabulary, so she substituted for it the word *submission* and Burr took full advantage of her devotion. He delighted in belittling and degrading not just her, but the other scientists assigned to Overproject Whisper.

The one scientist he could not deride was Lakesh,

who was responsible for the final technological breakthrough of Project Cerberus, which permitted Operation Chronos to finally make some headway.

Although the Totality Concept projects were rarely coordinated, the techs of Operation Chronos used Lakesh's mat-trans discoveries to spin off their own innovations, and achieve their own successes. Operation Chronos dealt in the mechanics of time travel, forcing temporal breaches in the chronon structure. Its essential purpose was to find a way to enter "probability gaps" between one interval of time and another. Inasmuch as Project Cerberus utilized quantum events to reduce organic and inorganic material to digital information and transmit it through hyperdimensional space, Chronos built on that same principle to peep into other time-lines and even "trawl" living matter from the past and perhaps even the future.

Although more than one hapless human being was snatched from a past line and brought forward into the present, Burr had only one proved success with a trawling subject, who arrived in the twentieth century sane in mind and sound of body.

But on the eve of the nuclear conflagration, Burr vanished, leaving both the Anthill and a disconsolate Erica to try to fill the vacuum. She coped with the desertion of her lover by volunteering to enter a stasis canister for a period of time, to be resurrected at some future date when the sun shone again and the world was secure.

When Erica awakened from her long slumber, the Anthill installation suffered near catastrophic damage and a number of stasis units had malfunctioned. Her canister was one of them. Due to that malfunction she was revived as a cripple.

Like Lakesh and several other predark humans, Erica was resuscitated to serve the baronies and to use her technological skills to contribute to the furtherance of baronial rule.

Then Enlil, in the guise of the childlike Sam, restored her youth by the same method he later used on Lakesh—through the introduction of nanomachines into her body.

A surprised murmur from Kane commanded his attention and drew him back from the past. He turned around as the man fumbled in his war bag. "What is it?"

Kane stared at the open water beyond the junk's stern. "I thought I saw something."

"Besides black?" Brigid asked.

Squinting, Kane caught a fleck of white on the broad surface of the Yarkand. Bringing up the binoculars, he flicked on the IR illuminator and put them to his eyes.

"Well?" Grant asked gruffly.

Kane didn't respond for a moment, concentrating on locating the speck again. It was a low-slung, single-sailed sampan about fifty yards behind the junk. A tiny straw-plaited cabin humped up from amidships. The boat was not outfitted with running lights, but he glimpsed ghostly shapes clustered astern. He counted three men.

The sampan's prow cleaved straight and smooth through the water so Kane figured the boat was powered by an outboard motor, even though he couldn't hear it over the racket of the junk's twin diesels.

"We're being followed," Kane announced, handing the binoculars to Brigid.

"I don't doubt it," she replied wryly, peering through the eyepieces. "This ship could be followed from deep space."

After gazing at the sampan for a few seconds, she passed the binoculars to Grant, commenting, "Three men aren't much of a danger."

"Assuming those three are all we have to worry about," Grant muttered as he swept the lenses back and forth over the river's surface.

"You think there may be more?" Lakesh asked tensely.

"Could be," Grant said negligently.

Lakesh frowned, then cupped his hands around his mouth and called for Sun Fan. The captain came down from the pilothouse and crossed the deck to join them, stepping over several sleeping children with an aggravated grimace.

After surveying the sampan through the binoculars and exclaiming incredulously over their ability to turn night into a gray-green equivalent of dusk, he declared matter-of-factly, "River rats working for old Chien Ho's crew."

"Who is old Chien Ho?" Kane wanted to know.

"The main pirate hereabouts. Those three are just keeping tabs on us—make sure we don't put ashore someplace and screw up Chien's plan."

"What plan is that?" Brigid asked, her tone troubled.

Sun Fan handed her the binoculars. "Most likely an ambush downriver, afore we get to Yichang."

"You don't seem too worried about the prospect,"

Grant observed sourly. "You've got the welfare of your passengers to think about."

Seng Kao spit over the side, then waved to the mass of people huddled on the deck. "It always like this," he stated wearily. "Farmers and traders go back and forth, up and down river anytime things get bad where they live. They be a superstitious bunch, never learn anything new. Soon they wake up and light their damned charcoal cook fires on my clean wooden deck, and I'll have to kick some asses, maybe throw a few overboard."

"That seems rather a harsh penalty," Brigid opined.

Seng Kao eyed her haughtily. "You ever have smelly farmers with their stinkin' pigs come your house and set fires on your floor, you not think so."

The captain sighed and rubbed the back of his neck. "The river gets narrower 'tween here and Yichang, waters more shallow. But we make it there okay. After that..."

He shrugged and returned to the pilothouse, picking his way over slumbering people and animals.

Grant gazed after him in angry surprise. "What the hell is *this*—" he heaved his shoulders in an exaggerated imitation of Sun Fan's shrug "—supposed to mean?"

The corner of Kane's mouth quirked in a dour, humorless smile. He raised his right arm, bending it at the elbow. A tiny electric motor whined as he flexed his wrist tendons and the Sin Eater snapped out from the sleeve of his coat firmly into his hand. "I'm going to interpret it as a suggestion that we check over our weapons."

Chapter 17

Kane awakened instantly, his upper body snapping erect and dislodging Brigid's head from his shoulder. For a split second, he wasn't certain what had woken him, then he realized the steady throb of the diesel engines had dropped in volume, the rhythm slowing. The change in the sound had penetrated his sleeping mind.

Kane peered around at his surroundings as Brigid rubbed her eyes with the heels of her hands. She and Kane were half-prone, leaning up against a burlap-wrapped bale of fabric. He saw Grant sitting nearby, lifting his head with a startled jerk. There was no sign of Lakesh.

"What's going on?" Brigid asked drowsily. "Are we there yet?"

Kane glanced up at the sky. There was no sun. Gray clouds tumbled overhead, a pale sunlight peeping through them. He consulted his wrist chron and for a couple of seconds didn't believe what the glowing LCD told him. Then he remembered it was still set on Montana time and he performed quick calculations in his head.

"It's about 5:30 a.m.," he said.

Brigid pushed herself to her feet, grimacing as she

kneaded her lower back. "Then we should be arriving at Yichang."

Kane felt stiff and sore, rusty and bad-tempered as he always did after sleeping in his clothes. He stood up and affected not to notice the slight difficulty Grant experienced as he used the corner of a crate to heave himself upright. The big man stumbled unsteadily to his feet, wincing in pain. More than a year ago he had suffered an injury that resulted in partial paralysis, and occasionally he experienced trouble with his left leg.

A thin mist floated above the surface of the river, blotting out details of the western bank as the junk's whistle shrieked a greeting. The dim outline of a village slowly emerged from the fog. No one on the deck spoke, even though most of the passengers were awake and stirring. A blanket of tension lay over them. Their expressions were solemn and anxious as they looked out at Yichang, still a hundred yards beyond the ship's bow.

A teenaged girl, a straw hat hanging from a cord about her throat, cast an apprehensive glance over her shoulder at Kane. Her black hair was cut in a straight line across her forehead, and the expression on her round face was one of a silent plea—she wanted to be reassured that everything was all right in Yichang.

The village sprawled in a bizarre jumble of architectural styles. On the waterfront there were thatch-roofed huts, several with upturned eaves supported by stilts. A number of tin-roofed sheds spread out over the landing, on either side of a single pier that thrust out like a gnarled finger into the river.

As Sun Fan had said, the Yarkand was definitely narrower here, the current much faster. Foam floated along the surface. A flotilla of fishing boats, most of them skifflike sampans, were tied up along the bank and to the dock itself, but no one seemed to be around them. Kane looked out at the flowing river, listening to the creak of the rigging and the throb of the engines.

Then his sixth sense, what he referred to as his point man's sense, raised the hairs at his nape. The skin between his shoulder blades seemed to tighten, and he shivered as with a chill. His point man's sense was really a combined manifestation of the five he had trained to the epitome of keenness. Usually some small, almost unidentifiable stimulus triggered the mental alarm, but he saw nothing overtly threatening.

As if to confirm his point man's assessment, Brigid murmured, "At this time of day, fishermen should already be out on the river. The whole waterfront should be jumping."

"Just what I was thinking," Grant said curtly. Nodding to the silently staring passengers, he added, "And so do they."

Kane looked up toward the pilothouse. Through the open door he saw Lakesh standing beside Captain Sun Fan at the big wheel while the man guided the junk expertly toward the long pier of Yichang. Both men stared intently ahead.

Swiftly, Kane went across the deck and climbed the steps. As he entered the pilothouse, Sun Fan cast him a worried glance and said, "I don't like it."

"Neither do I," Lakesh said. "For a fishing village, Yichang seems to be singularly empty."

"Water very shallow here," Sun Fan commented worriedly. "Sandbars, rocky bottom, tricky to maneuver. All the marker buoys gone."

The sun suddenly lifted over the eastern ridges, and the river mist thinned, then vanished. Dawn turned the surface of the river an unearthly shade of gold and green.

The captain leaned out of the pilothouse and shouted instructions to a crewman on the deck. The sailor repeated the call, and within moments Kane felt the vibrations of the junk as the engines were slowed even more.

Looking beyond the waterfront into the village proper, Kane glimpsed no children in the streets or women doing marketing. He saw a few water buffalo splashing and grunting in the shallows, giving the tied-up sampans a wide berth. His point man's sense howled an alarm.

"Captain," he said sharply, "I think we should sheer off."

Sun Fan cast him a surprised glance. "Why? You see something?"

"It's what I *don't* see. Veer away before we get any closer."

When the captain hesitated, Kane shouldered him aside, seizing the wheel and spinning it to starboard, hoping to turn the bow off the approaching pier and present a broadside to the fleet of sampans. The junk lurched and Sun Fan snarled in anger, stumbling against Lakesh.

In a reproachful tone, Lakesh began, "Friend Kane, you are being too—"

The stutter of an automatic rifle broke the quiet of the cool postdawn air. Glass shattered and flew from the pilothouse windows. Sun Fan's angry snarl turned into a squawk of fear, and he threw himself to the deck behind the wheel. Lakesh and Kane joined him there. Kane's gren-laden combat harness and Copperhead pressed painfully against his ribs.

Screams of terror and panic erupted from the deck as the passengers and crew alike began stampeding to cover and dropping flat. Reaching up behind his right ear, Kane activated the Commtact. "Grant, Baptiste— are you able to spot the shooters?"

"Hell, no," came Grant's lionlike roar of outrage. "We hit the deck just like everybody else."

Brigid's tense, breathless voice whispered inside his head. "You're in a better position to take a look than we are, Kane."

More rifles opened up, bullets slamming against the pilothouse walls. Wood splinters flew through the air. More glass jangled and ricochets went keening away. Both Lakesh and Sun Fan shielded their faces from fragments of glass and wood.

Kane crawled through the narrow door and pulled himself around the corner of the pilothouse to a point where he could see the waterfront. He saw dark-clad men racing down the dock, all of them armed. The sampans were pushing away from the bank, and from the little cabins muzzle-flashes stabbed like clusters of mad fireflies. Autofire rattled and bullets sent water fountaining up all around the junk. A hailstorm of slugs thudded into the hull, just above the waterline. Kane recognized the distinctive rattle of AK-47s.

He grasped the mechanics of the trap in an instant—the pirates had hidden in plain sight within the sampans, waiting until the junk had entered the narrow, shallow strait flowing past Yichang. Rather than mount an attack where Sun Fan's ship had more maneuvering room and could outrun them without fear of striking a submerged obstacle, the pirates had removed the warning buoys and waited until the junk slowed.

Kane cast a glance back in the direction from which they had sailed. As he expected, he saw three sampans closing in on them fast, water purling around their prows. The drone of the outboard motors was very audible now.

Speaking rapidly, Kane relayed to Brigid and Grant the situation. "I'm not sure if we're outnumbered yet," he concluded grimly, "but we're sure as hell inconvenienced."

"Why doesn't Sun Fan do something?" Grant demanded angrily.

As if on cue, the captain leaned out of the wheelhouse and began shouting orders, and his words were repeated among the sailors and passengers. Rising to a crouch, Sun Fan spun the wheel and the junk continued its starboard turn toward the opposite bank just as a concentrated volley of gunfire blazed from boulders and thickets that edged it.

Kane lowered his head, glimpsing spear points of flame flickering from almost every foot of the embankment. Steel-jacketed bullets sped from both sides of the river and sang through the rigging and sails. The pirates were not expert marksmen, and many miniature waterspouts sprayed up just before the junk's bow, but it was only a matter of seconds before the junk was trapped in the apex of the triangulated cross fire. Kane felt an instant of grudging admiration for Chien Ho's grasp of tactics, but then his mind turned to defense.

Sun Fan turned the wheel away from the bank, trying to maintain a position in the center of the river. The current slowly pushed the junk in a clockwise circle, and a stream of bullets raked the vessel, chewing through sails, rope and wood. Holes appeared in the sailcloth, giving them the likeness of giant lace doilies. One of the crewmen doubled up and fell overboard, tumbling headfirst into the water. Sun Fan howled in wordless fury.

"Time for us to do something," Kane snapped, wrestling to detach his Copperhead from the combat harness.

"I concur," Lakesh said, duckwalking over to him, his autopistol in hand.

"I wasn't talking to you," Kane countered. "But as long as you're here, lay down some cover fire."

"Fire where?"

"Anywhere on the river," Kane said impatiently, hiking himself up on one knee and bracing the butt of the Copperhead against his shoulder. "Doesn't Sun Fan have any weapons on board that his crew can use?"

Before Lakesh could reply, half a dozen sailors rose up at the starboard rail, heavy automatic pistols in their hands. They poured a hail of fire onto the decks of the sampans. Lakesh joined in, squeezing the trigger of his Colt deliberately and carefully, spacing his shots.

One of the sampans slowed and a man stood up, bringing his AK-47 to his shoulder, and he squeezed off a protracted burst, the bullets chopping flinders from the rail. A sailor cried out and flailed backward, grabbing convulsively at his chest.

Kane squinted into the Copperhead's scope, targeted the sampan's outboard motor and squeezed the trigger, holding it down. The subgun tore off a series of reports so fast they resembled the sound of coarse canvas tearing. The bullets punched through the motor's housing and internal fuel tank, splashing the contents over the deck of the boat. Kane continued to fire at the engine, striking sparks from the metal with a sound like a hammer pounding repeatedly on an anvil.

A pirate yelled at the man with the autorifle and he hastily adjusted his aim, lifting the barrel toward Kane. A swath of bullets hammered at the pilothouse, bullets clawing finger-long chunks of wood from the corner. Kane registered the heat of a bullet passing close to his face, but he continued firing at the outboard.

A shaved sliver of a second later, the sparks ignited the spilled gasoline. To Kane's surprise, an explosion erupted from the stern of the boat, throwing it high into the air, surrounded by a red-and-yellow ball of flame. Apparently the sampan had a larger fuel reservoir than was normal, with a direct feed line from a hidden tank to the motor.

The pirates fell or jumped overboard and began

swimming frantically through the layer of burning fuel on the surface toward the other boats.

"Stylishly cold-blooded, Kane," Lakesh remarked. "And effective."

Not sure if the scientist was being sarcastic or offering genuine praise, Kane demanded, "You hit anything yet?"

"No," Lakesh answered, squeezing off another shot.

A man on the deck of a sampan staggered, dropping his AK-47 so he could clap both hands around the blood-spurting hole that appeared in his belly.

"Yes," Lakesh intoned.

From the deck below and behind him, Kane heard the stuttering of Grant's Sin Eater and the door-slamming bang of Brigid's TP-9. Twisting his head, he saw them using crates of cargo as bulwarks as they returned the fire from the pirates on the opposite bank. Almost all of the passengers lay flat on the deck. They cried out in terror as they clutched at family members and animals. Pigs squealed, goats bleated and the chickens went into a cackling frenzy. The cacophony was maddening.

The sound of the sampans' engines rose in pitch, and four of the craft surged forward simultaneously, circling the junk like blood-crazed sharks. The bone-rattling chatter of the AK-47s drowned out the staccato hammering of Grant's Sin Eater. He ducked as bullets gouged the rail, stinging his face with splinters.

"I'm getting sick of this shit," he grated to no one in particular, although his three companions heard him perfectly.

Reaching under his coat, Grant detached a small, apple-shaped metal orb from his harness. The Cerberus redoubt had a seemingly inexhaustible supply of V-60 minigrenades, and rarely did he go into the field without bringing a few along. Craning his neck to see over the rail, he glimpsed a sampan sliding alongside the junk. As its gunwale rasped against the hull, Grant unpinned the grenade with his left hand and his right arm swung up and out in a looping overhand.

With unerring accuracy, the small sphere bounced from the sampan's bow and rolled across its deck. A blast of orange flame blossomed with an eardrum-compressing concussion. Fragments of wood rose into the air. The screaming pirates catapulted over the side, wreathed in cocoons of fire. The boat sank almost immediately.

On the starboard side, more sampans plowed through the waters of the Yarkand, steady fusillades of autofire scorching a path before them. The sails of the junk acquired more ragged holes. Fragments of wood flew from the deck rail and two more of the crew dropped, writhing around bullet wounds.

Three sampans drew alongside the junk, and coils of knotted rope licked out, the grappling hooks catching fast on the starboard side forward. Voicing shrill, fierce cries, the pirates swarmed up the ropes and leaped aboard the junk.

Nothing was calm and organized about the boarding. Both Kane and Lakesh fired steadily and the first wave of attackers folded over, some falling into the river or thudding back onto the decks of the sampans. Kane burned through the rest of the Copperhead's clip, blazing rounds across the deck, spent rounds tinkling down around him in a glinting rain. He scattered shots among the surviving boarders, driving them to cover behind the crates and bales of cargo. Then the subgun's bolt snapped open on an empty chamber, and the sudden silence of the Copperhead was at once noticeable among attacker and defender alike.

More boats pulled close. Sun Fan cried out commands, but his crew didn't hear them over the cacophony of screams. They backed away from the rail, intimidated by the ferocious appearances of the attackers who came boiling over the side in a howling horde.

The pirates were stocky, saffron-skinned men. Their faces were broad and flat, their hair black and coarse. Their limbs were decorated by elaborate and luridly colored tattoos, and they were dressed in a random assortment of rags and headgear, from red scarves and white turbans to fur caps. They were armed with autorifles, hatchets and curved *dao* swords. All of them had the bearing and feral expressions of rabid animals.

Kane absently noted that none of them had daggers clamped between their jaws, which indicated they had a degree of common sense, at least. The passengers scrambled desperately to the far side of the junk, hemming in Brigid and Grant and obstructing their field of fire.

The defense put up by Sun Fan's crew was disorganized and sporadic. They retreated toward the quarterdeck, fighting a rearguard action without watching one another's backs or even taking the time to aim their pistols properly. More pirates hauled themselves over the rail until Kane estimated nearly a score was assembled on the deck, struggling with the crew and a handful of the more courageous passengers.

Kane heard Sun Fan voicing another shouted harangue to rally his sailors, but it terminated in a choked cry. Quickly, he back-crawled into the pilot-house. The captain sagged over the wheel, wheezing, blowing droplets of blood from his slack lips. A wet stain spread across his shirt. Judging by the pink froth on his lips, Sun Fan had taken a bullet in a lung.

Kane pulled him away from the wheel and sat him down, propping him against the wall. Looking out the window, he saw that the junk had almost drifted past the village's dock. He came to a swift decision. Gripping the wheel, he shouted, "Brace yourselves!" and gave it a hard spin.

"Why?" Brigid asked, voice tight with tension.

The vessel heeled over to port so sharply that men on the deck went sprawling. Some stayed on their feet by clutching the rail while a number of the pirates tumbled down into the Yarkand.

The armed men on the dock fired at the approaching ship, bullets punching dimples in the hull. They realized standing their ground was futile, so they turned and began running. Amid a tumult of screams and gunfire, the junk crashed against the corner of the pier, splintering planks in explosions of broken, flying timbers.

Holding on to the wheel tightly, Kane bit out, "That's why."

Chapter 18

The impact bowled almost half of the pirates off their feet as the echoes of the shuddering crash filled Kane's ears. Interwoven with the deafening cracks of rupturing, splintering wood were cries of shock, pain and anger from animal and human throat alike.

The junk jolted to such a violent halt, Kane nearly pitched headlong from the pilothouse. The entire ship tilted sharply to port. Loose boxes and crates slid over the boards and toppled onto people cowering on the deck. Pigs escaped from their owners and raced in a squealing, panic-stricken stampede all over the boat.

Kane stepped out of the pilothouse, jerking away from Sun Fan's grasp on the tail of his coat. "My boat—" the captain gasped. "You bastard, wreck my boat—"

Kane gazed down at the disarray on the deck and saw Brigid and Grant climbing to their feet, angrily pushing and kicking aside boxes and bales that had fallen on them. A freed chicken flapped past Grant's face, leaving a flurry of feathers in its wake. Impatiently, he waved them away. Glancing up at Kane he demanded, "Are we finally going to put a stop to this?"

"That's the plan, Duke," Kane replied.

To Lakesh he said, "Cover us."

Before the man could lodge an objection, Kane leaped down from the superstructure to join his two friends. On his way he casually stomped a pirate between the shoulder blades as he attempted to rise, driving him face-first against the deck.

The yelling pirates, in the process of making a concerted rush, stumbled to a surprised, clumsy halt when they caught sight of the three black-clad strangers standing in their path. Their cries died in their throats, their eyes flicking from the gun barrels to the grim faces of the people holding them. They stared in wild-eyed amazement and fear.

For a long tick of time the tableau held frozen. Then one of the pirates, his face deeply scarred, uttered a piercing shriek and plunged forward. After a second, his companions kicked themselves into motion after him.

Veterans of dozens of battles, the Cerberus warriors rushed across the deck in a wedge formation to meet them. Kane took the point of the V, the rapid drumming of his Sin Eater hurling the pirates back. Grant and Brigid assumed positions on either side of him. When they fired, it was without haste or mistake. At every shot a pirate either tumbled overboard or spun, grabbing at a wound.

Kane bounded forward, the Sin Eater in his fist blazing on full-auto, cutting a swath through the men, stitching their chests, ripping holes in arms and legs. Several of the pirates returned fire with AK-47s, but hampered by their companions, they hit nothing but wood and air. Still, they pelted forward in a bellowing mob.

Inspired by the example of the outlanders, Sun Fan's crew made a crazed, desperate countercharge against the invaders. For a few very long minutes, it was a confused, brutal, bloody battle on the decks. The sailors armed themselves with flat, curved swords and boat hooks.

Kane glimpsed Seng Kao wielding a sword, slicing halfway through the neck of a pirate. Blood spouted from the severed carotid artery, a scarlet fountain that splashed across the deck and slicked the boards. The other crewmen followed his lead, surging forward to engage the enemy breast to breast, blade to blade.

The pirates had not expected an easy fight, but they had not dreamed it would be like this, either. The presence of the three outlanders could not have been anticipated by the keenest tactical mind. The pale-eyed man moved with a speed that almost defied the eye. Sword slashes either sliced empty air or did not penetrate his coat. The flame-haired woman moved almost as swiftly, avoiding all the hands that clutched for her.

A toothless, shaved-headed man with great brass earrings hanging from the stretched-out lobes of his ears grabbed Brigid by the collar of her leather coat, yanking it down to pinion her arms against her sides. A microsecond later the side of the man's head shattered, blowing gray and crimson over the face of a pirate trying to get into position behind Grant.

Temporarily blinded by blood and flying brain matter, the man paused to clear his vision. Brigid twisted around and squeezed off a single shot, the bullet snapping his head back and sending blood misting over the people behind him.

Panting, Brigid looked around and saw Lakesh crouched beside the pilothouse, his Colt autopistol held in a two-handed grip. Brigid acknowledged his life-saving shot by saluting him with the barrel of her own weapon as she shrugged back into her coat.

The field of combat wasn't designed for mutual advantage. There were only winners and losers, the living and the dead. It was the code by which the pirates and Kane and Grant lived, how they had been trained as Magistrates. The pirates and the crew battled without order or plan, massed in a straining, screaming, hacking mob. Swords clashed and clanged with gonglike chimes. The chopping through flesh and bone was like the sound of a very busy butcher's shop.

Bodies slammed into Kane, nearly knocking him off his feet, fetching him up hard against the base of the main mast. He couldn't fire his Sin Eater safely without hitting his allies or noncombatants, so he used it as a bludgeon, clubbing away hands and blades menacing him.

With a semimusical clang, the barrel of the pistol impacted against a sword blade and knocked it from a man's grip. He snatched it out of the air by the ivory grip and flicked out the blade, the tip dragging across his attacker's throat. The man stumbled back, a hand clapped to side of his neck. A bright arterial jet spurted from between his fingers.

Another pirate loomed up in front of him, and he glimpsed the glint of steel driving toward him. Kane tried to sidestep, but his movements were restricted by the press of bodies and the mast at his back. He felt the dull impact of the sword point as the man stabbed at him, trying for his heart. The tough fabric of his coat resisted the steel tip, and though he was pushed off balance, Kane returned the thrust with his own weapon.

The two-foot-long blade struck the pirate at an upward angle, sliding between his ribs, grating on bone. The man coughed and convulsed in a death spasm, folding over the sword and wrenching it from Kane's hand. He didn't bother trying to withdraw it. Instead he lunged away from the mast.

The pirates, divided into broken groups, were hewn down or driven over the sides. Some closed ranks and fought back with their swords, but they were overwhelmed by the infuriated sailors and an equal number of the passengers converging on them, flailing away with farm implements. Hoes and rakes didn't inflict lethal wounds, but they were most definitely incapacitating.

Shouting in fear and confused anger, their morale broken, the surviving pirates fought their way back to the gunwales and dived overboard. The ones who could struck out swimming for the bank opposite Yichang. Others clambered aboard the sampans. Calmly, Grant picked off a pair of the swimming men, drilling them with a single shot apiece to their backs. They splashed and floundered, then sank amid spreading red stains.

The teenaged girl Kane had noticed earlier stood at the side, emptying a glass hurricane lamp full of clear fluid over the rail. A boy a few years younger than her followed the fall of liquid by dropping a makeshift torch made of twisted strands of smoldering hemp.

The straw cabin of the sampan went up in a whooshing billow of yellow flame. There were screams and splashes as the men dived for safety into the river. The pandemonium ebbed by degrees. The passengers moved cautiously along the deck, gazing after the pirates as they turned their sampans upriver or crossed over to the opposite bank. When the people realized their attackers were thoroughly routed, they broke into ragged cheers, pumping victorious fists into the air.

Aware of the presence of Brigid, Grant and Kane on the blood-washed deck, the smiling Chinese people milled around them, patting their shoulders, clutching at their hands, speaking loudly and rapidly.

"Old Chien Ho didn't expect this kind of reception," Grant commented, toggling home a fresh magazine in his Sin Eater.

"Speaking of whom," Brigid said, "was he part of the boarding party?"

"No," Sun Fan said from behind them.

They turned to see the captain sagging between Lakesh and Seng Kao. A makeshift bandage had been crammed under his shirt, but blood crawled down his torso and soaked into the waistband of his pants.

Between clenched teeth, Sun Fan said, "Old Ho stayed in the village and watched…he and his men probably took a few elders hostage so nobody would raise an alarm." His slanted eyes considered Kane angrily. "You piled up my ship, damn you."

"To save her, I had to pile her," Kane retorted with a studied nonchalance. "If I hadn't, your ship, the crew, the cargo and the passengers would be in the hands of your old Ho right now."

"You'll understand if I check her over for damage afore I kiss your ass in gratitude." The captain coughed and pink foam flecked his lips.

"You've been hit in a lung," Brigid observed. "You're not checking anything over. We don't appear to be taking on water, so I think you can rest easy."

Lakesh handed Sun Fan over to a sailor. "We need to go ashore and try to get a line on Erica. Seng Kao, will you act as our guide?"

Seng Kao spoke softly, questioningly in Chinese to Sun Fan, and the captain waved him toward the village, coughing again. "Go. Any of you see that old Ho, kill him for me."

"We don't know what that old Ho looks like," Grant remarked.

Seng Kao stated tersely, "I do. His family is from here. I'm very familiar with the Hos."

"We *are* talking about a man, right?" Kane ventured doubtfully.

The five people retrieved their belongings and hoisted themselves over the rail of the junk, dropping the few feet to the dock. Nearly half of the pier was warped out of shape, knocked out of true, with planks shattered like matchwood and pilings broken off below the waterline. However, the hull of the junk, although deeply scored and scraped, had not caved in at the point of impact.

Looking toward Yichang, they saw people slowly, timidly emerging from houses and peering down toward the riverfront. Men, women, children crept out onto the street and cautiously approached the pier. Dogs began to bark, tremulously at first, then with growing enthusiasm.

The passengers of the ship jumped onto the dock and set up a relay system to pass down possessions, children and bleating goats to the people who had already disembarked. Villagers came out to greet them, studiously ignoring the outlanders.

Once out of the waterfront area and into the village, the Cerberus warriors were surprised by how quickly flies, people, cattle and chickens started clogging the streets in stark contrast to how deserted Yichang had appeared barely half an hour earlier.

Seng Kao stopped a gray-haired man wearing the dark blue tunic and threadbare trousers of a peasant and questioned him. Although he answered the man's questions, he did not make eye contact with the outlanders.

"Like Sun Fan figured," Seng Kao stated, "old Ho came here last night and took the entire village council and their families hostage, threatening to kill them if anybody interfered with his plan."

"Where is he now?" Lakesh asked.

Seng Kao shrugged and gestured vaguely toward the countryside. "He fled. Nobody wanted to pursue him."

Grant scowled. "Why the hell not? Ho could just regroup and try this again."

"They are a poor people here...they have more than

their share of worries...too many to go tracking down a pirate chief who they all fear."

"Don't they have enough men to fight?" Brigid asked.

"Yichang is much like my own village. They have fought against bandits and warlords before and paid for it with dead children, women who were raped and babies whose heads were smashed against trees." The man smiled sadly. "I know you people of the West think that death is better than slavery, but to people like these who have only rice and fish and family, slavery can seem like a luxury."

Kane glanced around uneasily. "What about the smallpox outbreak?"

"Only a few people are ill. They are quarantined in houses at the edge of the village."

Brigid patted the medical kit hanging from her shoulder. "Perhaps we can be of some help."

"Perhaps," Lakesh said uneasily. "But we have our own agenda."

The five people strode into the village, finding it a fermenting cauldron of people, noise, color and stink. The smells of fish, rice and cinnamon, as well as poor sewage drainage, filled the air as the morning brightened. Most of the houses were made of woven bamboo with thatched roofs and the classic upturned eaves of Oriental architecture. There was a small marketplace with food stalls and little apothecary shops. The odor of roasting fish reminded them all of how long it had been since they had last eaten.

Noticing Grant eyeing a steaming dish of vegetables

and meat, Kane warned, "I'd be careful about what I choose to eat around here."

"It's been a long time since I've had fish or fowl," Grant retorted.

"Who says that's fish or fowl? Instead of glub-glub or quack-quack it could be bowwow or even meow."

Brigid shot him an irritated glance. "Thinking that way about foreign food is one of the first misconceptions about different cultures, Kane. I thought you knew better by now."

He shrugged negligently. "I don't know what would have given you that idea."

At the sound of shrill, atonal pipes, mingling with the shiver of reverberating gongs, Seng Kao led them toward a big pagoda that dominated the village square. The ornate structure looked almost absurdly out of place among the humble shacks and huts. Four wide stone steps worn shallow by centuries of worshipers ascended to an open, central hall.

Between the support columns stretched silk tapestries bearing colorful images of votaries in hundreds of prayerful moods—standing with bowed heads before a weeping willow, kneeling, reading scrolls, or sitting in a lotus position. One of the images depicted a man with his eyes concealed by a strip of cloth pulling back on a bowstring, an arrow nocked and ready.

"A Buddhist temple," Brigid said.

"Shaolin, actually," Lakesh replied.

"What's the difference?" Grant asked.

"Buddhism is a relatively new religion to China,"

Lakesh answered. "Over a thousand years ago, during the reign of Emperor Liangwuti, an Indian monk named Bodhidharma came to China to preach Buddhism. After he had been received in audience by the emperor, he went to the Shaolin Temple of Mount Shung and meditated there for nine consecutive years. During his stay in the temple, he taught the monks the special, almost mystical art of making every finger a dagger, each arm a spear and the open hand a sword."

"And shooting arrows while blindfolded?" Kane asked.

Lakesh nodded. "Among other things."

From within the temple trudged four saffron-robed, shaved-headed priests. They strode down the steps in single file and moved in a shuffling, almost gliding dance step toward the riverfront area. They walked past the outlanders apparently without seeing them.

The last monk in line paused and regarded them with a grave, over-the-shoulder glance. Middle-aged and medium-sized, he whispered briefly to one of his companions, then approached. He wore round gold-rimmed spectacles over smiling, slanted eyes. Steepling his fingers beneath his chin, he inclined his head in a bow and Lakesh followed suit.

"You are outlanders," he said in surprisingly good English.

"Obviously," Lakesh replied.

"My name is Tai Mi. And you, I understand, are Mohandas Lakesh Singh."

Surprise widened Lakesh's eyes. "You understand that from whom?"

Tai Mi did not answer the question. "You have come to this village at a difficult and dangerous time. Our lives are confused, in turmoil. There is illness and there is fear."

"So we can see," Lakesh replied respectfully. "But we are here with a very definite purpose in mind."

"Yes, I know. However—"

"Who told you about us?" Kane broke in bluntly.

"Word has reached us about all of you. It does not matter how, but—"

"It fucking well *does* matter," Kane interrupted again, a steel edge to his voice. "Tell us."

"Ease up, Kane," Brigid whispered reproachfully. Diplomacy, turning potential enemies into allies against the spreading reign of the overlords, had become the paramount tactic of Cerberus over the past year. Lessons in how to deal with foreign cultures and religions took the place of weapons instruction and other training, but Kane's impatience often led him to forget what he had learned.

Still, over the past three years, Brigid Baptiste, Grant and Kane had tramped through jungles, ruined cities, over mountains, across deserts and they found strange cultures everywhere, often bizarre re-creations of societies that had vanished long before the nukecaust. The village of Yichang was a utopia compared to some places they had visited.

Tai Mi eyed Kane impassively. In soft, gentle tone, the monk said, "I beg your pardon, but you are strangers here and uninvited ones at that. I suggest your search for Tui Chui Jian is, at this point in time, futile."

"So you *do* know who we're looking for," Kane challenged. "Where is she?"

The monk shook his head. "I cannot help you."

"Why not?" Grant demanded harshly.

"Because I can only try to save your lives."

Lakesh frowned. "From what? The smallpox?"

The monk turned his dark eyes toward him and answered wearily, "No, from something far worse... from Wei Qiang. He is on his way and will be here before the day is out."

Chapter 19

The house to which they were escorted was a long, two-story bungalow situated on the outskirts of the village. It was a peasant's farm, built in the old provincial style with a tiled roof and a walled court. The farm animals ran loose, with grunting pigs, clucking chickens and honking geese chasing one another around the compound. The backyard was heaped with debris.

Beside the gate that opened into the courtyard a little jade image of Kuan Yin, the goddess of mercy, stood upon a pedestal. A placard covered with bold Chinese characters was nailed to the wooden slats above it. Brigid and Lakesh gazed at ideographs, their lips moving as they tried to read them.

Kane turned toward Seng Kao. "You know what that says, right?"

Seng Kao nodded. "Yes. It is a warning that smallpox is in this house."

Grant whirled on the monk, face contorted in incredulous anger. "What the hell are you pulling here, Mai Tai?"

"Tai Mi," the man corrected. "And I'm not trying to pull anything but to save your lives."

"By quartering us in a house full of disease?" Kane challenged.

Lakesh chuckled, but it sounded forced. "Can you think of a better place in which to hide?" He cut his eyes over to the monk. "This *is* a ruse, right?"

Tai Mi smiled slightly and nodded. "Of course. An old woman whose son deserted her lives here, and though she is very advanced in years, she does not suffer from the smallpox."

"What does she have?" Brigid asked, hefting the medical kit. "Perhaps I can be of some help to her."

The monk nodded again. "Perhaps you may." He gestured toward the gate. "Please go in and stay within the walls. I will let it be known throughout the village that you have not been seen."

"We haven't?" Grant inquired skeptically. "How can you be so sure of that, especially if money is offered?"

"Yeah," Kane said in a voice heavy with suspicion. "What if somebody spills their guts the second Wei Qiang shows up?"

"Wei Qiang is a terrible man," the Shaolin priest stated with no inflection in his tone, as if by rote. "But do you think he is the first terrible man who has come this way? Yichang has seen many of them, since ancient times. We have survived while they have perished. You should take some solace in that."

"Will your priesthood resist Wei Qiang?" Brigid asked.

Tai Mi sighed. "We are forbidden by our creed to use ax or knife or club."

He turned away. "Make yourselves as comfortable as

you can. We will send someone with food and information before much longer."

They watched Tai Mi trudge back toward the village.
"What the hell did he mean by taking solace in that?"
Grant demanded impatiently.

Brigid smiled wanly. "I interpreted it to mean that
Yichang has survived encounters with warlords and
conquerors in the past because everyone cooperated
with one another and was of one mind to survive."

Grant eyed her bleakly. "That's a nice spin on it.
For everybody's sake, I hope your interpretation is the
right one."

"Me too," Brigid murmured fervently.

The interior of the house was dusty and musty, full
of shadows and cobwebs. It was built with a very open
floor plan, basically only one huge room that seemed
large enough to accommodate the Cerberus armory. An
old kerosene stove sat in a corner, an iron pot of rice still
warm there.

A big bed with a gilt-edged headboard dominated
one side of the room, and it was draped by a fall of
gauzy mosquito netting, hanging from a ceiling hook.
A three-paneled dressing screen partitioned a corner.
They could barely make out the shape of a woman re-
clining, half-submerged in a mass of pillows and
blankets. A stout middle-aged woman in a high-collared
tunic with baggy trousers and black cotton shoes sat on
a stool at the right-hand bedside. When the outlanders
entered she rose swiftly, bowed and scuttled through the
nearest door.

"She didn't seem to want to get acquainted," Kane observed sourly.

"Does she expect us to take care of her patient?" Grant demanded, voice thick with angry impatience.

"We at least ought to introduce ourselves," Brigid said. "The Chinese place a lot of emphasis on etiquette."

She and Lakesh cautiously stepped up to the foot of the bed and a low moan of terror greeted them. "Hello," Lakesh said quietly in Mandarin. "We will not hurt you. Do not be afraid. Perhaps we can help you."

Because of the mosquito netting and the shadows, they couldn't see the woman's face clearly, but they received the impression she was old and wrinkled, with white hair tied back. Brigid started to push aside the netting but the old woman cringed, clutching at the sheets and drawing them up to her chin.

Lakesh laid a restraining hand on Brigid's arm. "Perhaps we should leave her alone until she becomes accustomed to our presence."

Brigid nodded and they joined their companions on the far side of the room. They opened an equipment case and passed around ration packs and bottles of water. Seng Kao abstained, lighting a joss stick before a stone good-luck tiger-dog placed upon a tiny altar. He murmured a few words of prayer, then went to stand near an open window. He stared resolutely out, his hands clasped behind his back.

"Disappointed that Erica—the Dragon Mother— wasn't here to give you a big hug with her scaly arms?" Kane asked him.

Seng Kao did not answer.

"Well, now, don't be too upset," Kane continued blandly, uncapping a bottle of water. "She's never been what I'd call trustworthy. I wouldn't have been too surprised to find her married to old Chien Ho. She'd make a good Ho."

Seng Kao's shoulders stiffened and even in the dim light, they saw a red flush working its way up his neck.

Wearily, Brigid said, "You don't need to bait him, Kane. There are better ways to pass the time."

"You'd think so, wouldn't you?" he inquired sarcastically. "But if we can't find Erica, this has been one hell of a wasted trip. I suppose I can pass the time figuring out a way to get us past Wei Qiang's army so we can return to the vortex point in Xian and go home."

"You're being a bit premature," Lakesh said sternly. "Obviously Erica told Tai Mi to expect us."

"Yeah," Grant grunted. "But why, if she's not around and he's not going to take us to her?"

Lakesh shrugged. "I'm sure both of them have their reasons."

"Yeah," Grant said sourly. "Too bad neither of them are around to explain them."

Kane began pacing the big room in agitation. "It looks like we're stopped before we start."

"Take it easy," Brigid told him with an encouraging smile. "There's nothing to be done now but wait. You shouldn't stress."

"I don't stress," he snapped.

"Yes, you do," she replied with calm detachment. "Big-time."

Kane knew she spoke the truth, but it still rankled him. He knew he shouldn't feel worried, not in the company of Grant and Brigid Baptiste. Lakesh had once suggested that the trinity they formed when they worked in tandem seemed to exert an almost supernatural influence on the scales of chance, usually tipping them in their favor.

The notion had amused Kane, since he was too pragmatic to accept such an esoteric concept, but he couldn't deny that he and his two friends seemed to lead exceptionally charmed lives, particularly he and Brigid.

Kane shied away from examining the bond he shared with Brigid. On the surface, there was no bond, but they seemed linked to each other and the same destiny. He recalled another name he had for Brigid Baptiste: *anam-chara*. In the ancient Gaelic tongue it meant "soul friend."

From the very first time he met her he was affected by the energy Brigid radiated, a force intangible, yet one that triggered a melancholy longing in his soul. That strange, sad longing only deepened after a bout of jump sickness both of them suffered during the mat-trans jump to Russia. The main symptoms of jump sickness were vivid, almost real hallucinations.

He and Brigid had shared the same hallucination, but both knew on a visceral, primal level it hadn't been gateway-transit-triggered delirium, but a revelation that they were joined by chains of fate, their destinies linked. The idea that he and Brigid had existed at other times in other lives had seemed preposterous at first. Perhaps it still would have if he hadn't experienced the same jump dreams as her, which symbolized the chain of fate connecting her soul to his.

It had required nearly a year before the two very different people achieved a synthesis of attitudes and styles where they could function smoothly as parts of a team, extending to the other professional courtesies and respect.

Although they never spoke of it, though Kane often wondered if that spiritual bond was the primary reason he had sacrificed everything he had attained as a Magistrate to save her from execution. The possibility confused him, made him feel defensive and insecure. That insecurity was one reason he always addressed her as "Baptiste," almost never by her first name, so as to maintain a certain formal distance between them. But that distance shrank every day.

During the op to the British Isles, when Kane had protested to Morrigan that there was nothing between him and Brigid, the Irish telepath had laughed at him. She said, "Oh, yes, there is. Between you two, there is much to forgive, much to understand. Much to live through. Always together…she is your *anam-chara*."

He wasn't sure if believed that, but he knew he always felt comfortable with Brigid Baptiste, despite their many quarrels. He was at ease with her in a way that was similar, yet markedly different than his relationship with Grant. He found her intelligence, her iron resolve, her well-spring of compassion and the way she had always refused to be intimidated by him not just stimulating but inspiring. She was a complete person, her heart, mind and spirit balanced and demanding of respect.

Brigid Baptiste was one of the toughest human beings he had ever met. For a woman who had been trained to be an academic, an archivist and had never strayed more than ten miles from the sheltering walls of Cobaltville, her resiliency and resourcefulness never failed to impress him. Over the past few years, she had left her tracks in the most distant and alien of climes and breasted very deep, very dangerous waters.

Kane found the thought of losing that person too horrifying to contemplate, not just because of the vacuum she would leave in the Cerberus personnel, but because of the void her absence would leave in his soul.

An hour passed. The heat of the day built quickly, and the big room turned stifling. Kane shucked out of his heavy coat, although the thermal controls of the shadow suit kept him comfortable. Still, the scent of the incense irritated Kane's sinuses. Grant, whose sense of smell was impaired due to having his nose broken three times in the past, sat down in a papa-san chair and appeared to nod off. Seng Kao continued to stand at the window and stare, as if he were utterly entranced by a scene only he could see.

Desperate for a breath of fresh air, Kane went out into the courtyard and carefully peered over the top of the gate. Once again the village seemed almost deserted, and he wondered if the Chinese observed an Oriental version of the siesta, even though it was still early in the day.

He debated their next move, but he couldn't come up

with anything reasonable. He felt trapped by the wait, but there was nothing he could do about it unless he decided to embark on a door-to-door search for Erica. Intellectually he understood waiting was part of the life he had chosen to lead—you hurried up so you could wait, just like in the Mags. He swore explosively and fetched the gate a frustrated kick.

A little gray kitten came waddling out of an overturned wooden bucket, yowling in annoyance that its nap had been interrupted. It stumbled up to Kane's boot and for lack of anything better to do, he picked up the small cat, absently stroking the top of its head with his thumb. Almost immediately, it began to purr, eyes closed in bliss, tiny mouth curved in a smile.

"How'd you manage to stay out of the stew pot?" he asked it softly. "Or is that just one of the cultural misconceptions Baptiste talks about?"

For the next few minutes, Kane occupied himself with petting the little animal and checking it over for fleas and ticks. The kitten cooperated with the grooming, twisting this way and that within his hands.

He was so engrossed that at first he paid no attention to the distant roar of engines, hovering at the very edge of audibility. Then he recalled he had seen no vehicles anywhere in or around the village, and his uneasiness exploded into a raging alarm. The noise grew louder and he spun, rushing back into the house, slamming the door open with a shoulder, still carrying the kitten.

Everyone looked up at him, startled. "I think Wei Qiang has just arrived," he announced grimly.

Lakesh made a studiedly casual show of consulting his wrist chron. "He made good time."

"Why the hell wouldn't he?" Grant growled, pushing himself to his feet. "It's not like he's been delayed by fighting river pirates."

Brigid's emerald eyes flitted back and forth from Kane to Lakesh to Grant. "Do we just sit tight and hope Wei Qiang will be put off by a notice from the local board of health?"

"If he's here at all, that means he wants Erica badly. A sign on a gate won't be much of a deterrent." Kane glanced toward Seng Kao, who had slowly turned away from the window. Even though the man's face was its usual immobile mask, he sensed a change in him.

Seng Kao swallowed and said reluctantly, "I must agree, Tui Chui Jian."

"I'm afraid I must, as well," a melodic female voice declared from behind them. "You have served me splendidly, Seng Kao."

The four outlanders recognized the vibrant tones of the voice, as well as the subtle note of autocratic authority underscoring it.

Kane's head swiveled on his neck so sharply that his neck tendons twinged in pain. He saw the figure thrusting aside the mosquito netting, pulling away the white, lank-haired wig to reveal black, lustrous hair piled up like a crown atop her head. With her other hand she peeled away the layer of painted rice paper adhering to her face.

She stood much taller than most Chinese women, long legged and statuesque with endowments the white silk smock could not conceal. Her violet eyes gleamed with a strange, dark luminosity.

Seng Kao rushed to her and dropped to one knee, bowing his head. In an adoring, reverent whisper, he said, "I live only to serve you, Tui Chui Jian."

Chapter 20

Astonished into speechlessness, they stared at Erica van Sloan, who stood with her shoulders square and proud. Her sculpted features, devoid of cosmetics, looked like an ivory mask, serene, confident and just the slightest bit smug. Dropping the wig and the rice-paper disguise to the floor, she said, "I hope you've not been too uncomfortable here."

Kane's lips peeled back from his teeth in a silent snarl. He took a menacing step forward. "Not half as uncomfortable as we're going to make it for you."

Erica made a motion with both hands as if she were smoothing the smock over her hips. A small, utilitarian pistol, a Makarov, seemed to pop into her fist. Kane froze in midstep.

"Don't move, please. It would be unfortunate for you and your little friend." The pistol didn't waver in her grip.

The kitten mewed an interrogative, and Kane carefully set the animal on the floor. "You take a lot of stupid chances, Erica."

"A lot fewer than you do," she countered coldly. "What was the remark about me making a good Ho?"

"Oh, that." The snarl on Kane's face molded itself

into a somewhat abashed grin. "I kid the Dragon Mother...I kid."

Erica sighed, her bosom straining at the fabric of the smock. "In the interests of an alliance—" She tossed the gun behind her onto the bed. Every movement was a careful and practiced gesture.

"Was it very difficult finding me?" she asked.

Seng Kao took it upon himself to answer. "No, Dragon Mother."

Erica touched him gently on the head and he rose, turning to face the outlanders with an imitation of Erica's smug smile ghosting over his lips.

"You knew she was here all the time," Grant snapped accusingly.

Seng Kao shook his head. "No, but I realized the old lady was the Dragon Mother as we came in."

"How?" Brigid asked, green eyes glinting with suspicion.

Erica unpinned her hair and shook it loose. It tumbled down to hang like twin black curtains on either side of her face. "My followers and I share a special bond."

"The SQUIDs interface," Lakesh intoned. "It's nothing more special than that."

"So the monk lied to us," Grant said darkly. "So much for piety."

One corner of Lakesh's mouth lifted in a smile. "Not really, friend Grant. Tai Mi said an old woman whose son had deserted her lived here. That's basically the truth, even if neither Erica nor I look our ages."

Waving an immaculately manicured hand, Erica replied, "None of that matters, Mohandas. In a short time, Wei Qiang will dispatch his soldiers on a door-to-door search, and I'd prefer not to be here."

She stepped behind the dressing screen as Kane said sharply, "I notice you haven't asked about the Hydra's ring."

"Is there a reason I should?" She slid out of the smock and peered at him over the wooden frame.

"Aren't you the least bit interested whether I brought it with us?" Lakesh asked.

"No…because you wouldn't be here otherwise."

Kane opened his mouth to voice a profane question when a machine gun began to hammer in the distance. Everyone jumped, turning to look out the window.

"I guess it's safe to assume that Wei Qiang is announcing himself," Brigid said quietly.

Erica stepped out from behind the screen, adjusting the satiny midnight-blue-and-red uniform tunic, carrying stilt-heeled boots with her. Sitting down on the edge of the bed, she began tugging them on. "We need to get out of here as quickly as possible."

"And go where?" Grant demanded impatiently.

"The Tomb of the Three Sovereigns," she answered without hesitation.

Lakesh blinked at her in confusion. "Why would we go there?"

She favored him with a small, careful smile. "Because that's where we'll find the mausoleum of Shi Huangdi…and the Armor of Immortality."

BRIGID FROWNED thoughtfully. "So you think that's Wei Qiang's objective...the Armor of Immortality?"

Erica grimaced as she worked her foot into the boot. "It's the obvious conclusion to reach, isn't it?"

"Not to me," Grant declared. "Who the hell is Shi Huangdi?" He stumbled a bit over the pronunciation.

"He was allegedly one of the Yellow Emperor's direct descendants, a grandson," Brigid replied. "Also known as Ren Wen Chu Zu, which means 'founder of civilization.'"

"Yes," Erica said dryly, stamping her foot on the floor. "He ascended to the Chinese throne at the age of thirteen, over three thousand years ago, and he immediately began construction of his mausoleum, which was completed thirty-six years later."

"What was so special about him?" Kane asked.

Brigid answered, "Shi Huangdi was remembered as the ruler who united the seven warring clans of ancient China in 221 BCE, and his reign was marked with great advances in all sections of society—from the construction of roads and canals to the connection of the various border walls of his kingdom into the one Great Wall.

"He also standardized the systems of writing, of weights and measures, and of currency in order to simplify communication and record-keeping. He abolished feudalism, forcing the nobles to reside under his thumb in the capital city, and divided the rest of China into thirty-six separately governed provinces, each with its own bureaucracy and defensive military. He also fostered religion, sacrificing to the gods in thanks for his military and diplomatic successes in finally uniting

China and completing the work his grandfather, the Yellow Emperor, had begun."

"He sounds like a great man," Lakesh commented.

Brigid smiled wanly. "Shi Huangdi was also a tyrannical despot and ruled with an iron hand for many years, implementing draconian laws and levying large tax rates to oppress the commoners of ancient China and maintain and solidify his tenuous grasp on the monarchy. He ordered that all books of a nontechnical nature be burned, in an attempt to eliminate the teachings of Confucius and the education system that accompanied Confucianism.

"In his final years, Shi Huangdi became quite withdrawn and mystical, much like the Yellow Emperor. He surrounded himself with magicians and alchemists, providing them only one task—to find or create an immortality formula. Shi Huangdi became increasingly maniacal near his death, and wanted a means that would allow him to rule as a divine emperor forever, to continue the work of his ancestor. But he died—broken, insane and alone—after a trip to Japan in search of his essential elixir of life in 210 BCE."

Kane squinted in confusion. "If the man died, then why do you think he would have the Armor of Immortality in his damned tomb?"

Erica stood up, sweeping him with a scornful stare. "You're just not getting this, are you, Kane? I think Wei Qiang, Huang-ti and Shi Huangdi are the same man."

"And you believe he faked his death as Shi Huangdi?" Lakesh asked.

"I believe he faked his death many, many times over

the centuries," Erica answered matter-of-factly. "I thought that would have occurred to one of you by now."

"For the sake of argument," Brigid said icily, "let's assume your hypothesis is correct. Why would Wei Qiang need the Hydra's rings and the Armor of Immortality if he's already immortal?"

A woman screamed in the distance, a high, sustained note of terror that was abruptly cut off. Grant and Kane went to the front window and looked out. The sporadic crackle of gunfire reached them, sounding closer.

"We'd better find another place for hypothesizing," Grant stated grimly, turning to eye Erica. "I hope you have one in mind."

"Not much of one." Erica lifted the corner of the mattress and removed a carved wooden box from beneath it. "A small cove down on the river where I have a boat prepared."

Lakesh stepped forward, eyes on the box. "What's in that?"

Smiling slyly, she shook it. Objects rattled within. "Seven very old and very ugly rings...do you have one you'd like to add to the collection?"

His hand went reflexively to his chest. "Not at the moment."

Kane shrugged back into his coat. Brigid picked up the equipment cases and handed the one containing the interphaser to Lakesh. Impatiently she said, "Lead on, Dragon Mama."

The group of people left the house by the front door, but eased out of the compound through a rear gate. The sun was just past its zenith in the blue sky, starting its downward arc toward afternoon. Looking toward the village, they saw yellow-uniformed soldiers advancing along the road, running and crouching as if they expected an ambush to be mounted from the houses along the way. They watched as the troopers crept cautiously up to the doors of the homes and kicked them in.

"They're not taking any chances," Brigid said.

"From what I've seen of Wei Qiang," Erica replied, "he's a thorough man."

"That wasn't the impression we got," Kane commented.

Erica's eyes widened, then narrowed. "You've *met* him?"

"Yeah," Grant answered casually. "Over three years ago, on the island of Autarkic. He's a tong warlord, and he looked like he had both feet and his legs in the grave back then."

Lines of consternation appeared on Erica's smooth forehead. "It doesn't sound like the same man at all."

From the waterfront area came the sudden crumping swish of an artillery piece, and over the roofline they saw a great fountain of water erupting into the sky, mixed in with scraps of wood.

"Wei Qiang is sinking boats," Seng Kao said flatly. "Cutting off escape routes."

Erica whirled. "Let's get moving before our own is cut off."

The six people sprinted through a maze of gardens and fields, following a circuitous route to the river. The sound of combat and screaming people floated to them from the village. Subguns chattered, the characteristic rattle of Calicos. Kane's jaw muscles bunched. The people were apparently fighting back, but he didn't understand why. He struggled with the urge to turn and join them.

Directly ahead of them lay paddies and a pattern of irrigation ditches. After splashing their way through a marshlike paddy, they came in sight of the Yarkand. The river beyond the village's landing was broad and shallow with rocky banks and white rapids that made small rainbow flashes in the slanting sunlight. Kane looked south and saw how mountains pressed in to pinch the water course between sheer cliffs and high hills.

Erica led them across a ridgeline, then down a rock-littered slope. A long sampan was tied to a rickety old dock within a small cove, essentially invisible unless someone knew it was there or had exceptionally keen eyesight. Instead of feeling relief, Kane felt his uneasiness grow.

The people crossed the dock and boarded the boat. Although the craft was equipped with an outboard, Seng Kao pushed away from the dock with a long pole he picked up from the bottom. As the sampan drifted toward the mouth of the cove, less than a hundred feet off the port bow, Kane's sense of danger clamored for attention in the back of his mind. Exchanging a swift glance with Grant, he could tell by the set of his jaw that the big man sensed a trap. He looked at Erica van Sloan's determined, poised profile as she stared at the swiftly flowing Yarkand beyond the mouth of the cove.

Driving the pole into the water and propelling the

boat forward, Seng Kao said, "We will hug the shore-line and drift down until it is safe to start the motor."

A subgun suddenly hammered from behind them, and splinters flew from the side of the sampan in a stinging spray. Erica screamed, clutching at her left shoulder. She toppled backward, over the side into the water. Seng Kao bleated an anguished cry and dropped the pole, preparing to leap overboard, but blood sprang from the right side of his head and he collapsed, falling atop Lakesh in a limb-twisted tangle.

Grant and Brigid opened up with their weapons, hosing bullets with their Copperheads set on full-auto toward the sheltering rock walls of the cove behind them. It wasn't something either person did without extreme provocation. Men in yellow helmets and tunics raced along the top of the cove walls, firing as they came.

Brigid swung her Copperhead toward them, raking the boulders with a jackhammering ferocity. Geysers of dust and stone shards flew in all directions as the bullets chiseled dust-spurting notches in the stone.

Kane's gaze passed over the water, and he came to a swift decision. Struggling out of his coat, he snapped to Brigid and Grant, "Cover me!"

"*Cover* you?" Grant echoed incredulously.

Brigid twisted, eyes wide. "Don't—!"

Sucking in a lungful of air, Kane vaulted over the side, splashing feetfirst into the water. Helped by the weight of his Sin Eater, he sank quickly, his ears registering the muffled, multiple thumps of bullets striking the water around the boat. He swam beneath the sampan, back toward the dock. The water was not very deep, perhaps only fifteen feet, but it was dark, cloudy with silt. He came up under the pier, beside one of the slime-coated pilings, and saw Erica's head breaking the surface.

Gasping, she clawed away the long black hair clinging to her face. Her uniform tunic had been torn open at the shoulder, and she widened the rip so she could examine the abraded flesh and the sprouting of wooden splinters. She ignored a blood-oozing scratch on her right cheek. Her eyes were wide, but shining more with anger than fright or pain.

"Are you all right?" he whispered.

"I've been betrayed!" she declared.

"Big surprise," he muttered. "Think you can make it back to the boat?"

She nodded, then swung her head up and around as boots pounded on the dock overhead. Clutching her hand, Kane inhaled a deep breath and dived. Erica went under the surface with him, and they crawled along the reedy bottom toward the sampan.

They both noted the comet streaks of bubbles marking the trail of bullets plowing into and beneath the surface. The pair continued stroking, past the paths of the slugs punching into the river around them.

Kane and Erica came up under the bow of the sampan. Grant and Brigid were still firing, and they heard soldiers shouting to one another on the banks. Clearing his water-occluded vision with a swipe of a hand, Kane glimpsed several men running along the top of the cove wall, meaning to cut them off at the mouth. From nearby came the roaring of an engine, but his soaked hair hung in his eyes and he couldn't spot the source.

Grasping the side of the boat, Kane heaved Erica out of the water. Lakesh grabbed her as she fell over the gunwale, crying out in pain. The sampan rocked dangerously when Kane pulled himself aboard. He reached for the pull cord of the outboard motor, but Lakesh said quietly, "Never mind, friend Kane. Never mind."

As he turned to look at Lakesh, opening his mouth to voice a profane demand, Kane's words clogged in his throat. Blocking the narrow channel that led out into the river, water streaming from its metal hide, rose the dark shape of a Scorpinaut. The turret revolved with a whine of electric gimbels and the bore of the cannon fixed directly on the sampan, like the stare of a hollow, cyclopean eye.

"This would probably be an excellent time to put up our hands," Brigid said dispassionately.

Chapter 21

A dozen soldiers lock-stepped the six people along the dock to the bank of the cove. When Erica tried to reach up to twitch away the splinters protruding from the flesh of her left shoulder, two troopers grabbed her arms, wrenching them up behind her back in hammerlocks. She was unable to completely repress a cry of pain, but she tried to keep her head held high.

All of them had been disarmed, even the wounded Seng Kao, who had suffered a superficial bullet graze to his temple. The wound was crudely bandaged with a strip of none-too-clean cloth, which served more as a sponge to soak up the blood rather than stopping the hemorrhaging at the source.

Brigid received a great deal of attention from the soldiers as they stripped off her coat, patted her down and fingered her distinctly un-Oriental hair. The troopers seemed enchanted by both its color and texture.

Brigid tolerated the manhandling expressionlessly. Due to her many years as an archivist in the Cobaltville Historical Division, Brigid had worked hard at perfecting a poker face. Since archivists were always watched, probably more than anyone else working in the other divisions, they developed a persona of cool calm, unflappable and immutable.

Kane by nature wasn't so restrained, but due to all the missions he had shared with Brigid, he had absorbed some of her stoicism. Still, it required a great effort to keep from laying about him with his feet and hands when he saw the attention the soldiers directed toward her.

She caught his eye, shook her head slightly, and he tamped down his rage. Brigid presented the facade of being calm and in control even with gun barrels pointed at her. She was definitely frightened, but over the past few years she had come to accept risk as a part of her way of life, taking chances so that others might find the ground beneath their feet a little more secure. She considered her attitude inspired less by idealism than by simple pragmatism. If she had learned anything from her association with Kane, Grant and Domi, it was to regard death as a part of the challenge of existence, a fact that every man and woman had to face eventually.

She would accept it without humiliating herself if it came as a result of her efforts to remove the yoke of the baronies from the collective neck of humanity. She had never spoken of it, certainly not to the cynical Kane, but she had privately vowed to make the future a better, cleaner place than either the past or the present.

The Scorpinaut lumbered out of the cove and up the side of the slope, the massively treaded tires crushing rocks and tearing deep gouges in the earth. Kane and Grant eyed it closely as it chugged past, noting that it was plated with a lightweight ceramic-composite armor.

The long-dead FCS designers had exchanged protection for speed and mobility.

Once the six people were off on the dock, the soldiers marched them heedlessly through weeds and over loose rocks to the ridgeline that overlooked the cove. The Scorpinaut sat nearby, its engine idling. When it fell silent, the troopers jerked them to a halt.

From around the machine's rear strode a tall, color-fully clad man. His hands were clasped behind his back. He wore a black silk tunic decorated with dragons worked in golden thread. A fur-trimmed cloak of yellow fell from his shoulders to the backs of his ankles. He was obviously Chinese but taller than the soldiers, with a deep chest and broad shoulders.

He wore a thin black felt skullcap, the forepart curving toward the bridge of his nose like an elongated widow's peak. His mustached face was grotesquely masklike, with the flesh drawn tightly over the bones. Bowing deeply, the soldiers dropped all their gear at his feet. He paid no attention to it.

A heavyset man wearing sunglasses and a khaki coverall stood behind him, hands on his knees. He strug-gled to catch his breath, his respiration as labored as if he had just run all the way from the village. Kane figured he had—he was the same man wearing the insignia of the Millennial Consortium they had spied the night before.

The tall man's dark gaze flitted over the faces of the Cerberus warriors. There was some force swimming in them that raised the fine hairs on Kane's nape. It was a spark of fanaticism, a single-minded dedication to achieving an inexplicable objective.

A trooper offered the man the wooden box Erica had carried. When he took it, sunlight glinted from the gold-wire fingernail protector capping his left thumb. A nine-headed Hydra ring encircled the middle finger of the same hand. He lifted the lid and inspected the contents.

The man in sunglasses peered over his shoulder and exclaimed in a nasal, reedy voice, "One is missing!"

The tall man's expression did not change. Closing the lid of the box, he eyed the people meditatively. Addressing Lakesh and Brigid, he said in flat, uninflected English, "I don't know you."

"I am Dr. Mohandas Lakesh Singh. This is Brigid Baptiste."

Wei Qiang did not respond. Instead, he nodded to Erica. "You I have seen, but not formally met, Tui Chui Jian."

As his gaze fell upon Grant and Kane, he said in a sibilant whisper, "You two I remember. Your arrogance made an indelible impression on me."

Grant and Kane were surprised into speechlessness, but Brigid challenged, "You *are* Wei Qiang?"

The man smiled in an odd, cold way. "I have been called that, yes."

"But you were first called the Yellow Emperor, weren't you?" The tone of Brigid's voice was heavy with irony, as if she dared the man to confirm her accusation.

"You're not the same Wei Qiang we met on Autarkic," Kane said faintly. He sounded doubtful, however.

The man's smile widened. "I told you both that we

might yet have a chance to do business together, and here we are."

Brigid cast Kane a questioning glance and he nodded, his face paling. "That's what he said to us, yes. Only the real Wei Qiang would know that."

"You look quite a bit different," Grant said.

Qiang smiled pridefully, almost preening. "Younger, more vital, yes."

"Not really, no," Grant replied disinterestedly. "Just different."

Wei Qiang drew himself up haughtily. "What are you doing here?"

None of the Cerberus personnel responded. Qiang stepped closer to them. "Nothing to say, Mr. Kane? Nor you, Mr. Grant?'

The millennialist edged forward, still breathing hard. "Kane and Grant?" Lowering his sunglasses, he peered intently over the rims at Brigid. "And Brigid Baptiste. Of course, I should have realized. You three have interfered with consortium operations in the past."

"And you are?" Lakesh inquired politely.

"My name is Werner Musgrave, a representative of the Millennial Consortium."

Grant nodded to him in acknowledgment, saying almost apologetically, "I hate you guys."

"What are you doing here in China?" Kane demanded. "According to that fat bastard Benedict Snow, the consortium's mission is to dig out the United States."

Wei Qiang's lipless mouth twitched in annoyance.

"None of you are in any position to ask questions of us, Kane."

In a mild tone, Lakesh ventured, "Then perhaps we may reach an accord of communication rather than confront each other as adversaries. We are all reasonable people."

Wei Qiang smiled slightly and intoned, "'The reasonable man is a shining light under the Eye of Heaven. A man who uses his mind is not a beast of the field or a creature of the sea; he is touched with the divine.'"

"Lao Tzu?"

"It is the philosophy of Cao Zhi," Qiang answered. "Sixth century. I've always found his poetry exquisite, even when he was just a child."

"I see. What about my proposal?"

Wei Qiang scrutinized him silently for a long, silent moment, then announced, "Yes, we should indeed communicate."

Turning to Erica he asked, "Where is it?"

Erica met his stare with one of wide, violet-eyed innocence. "Where is what?"

Wei Qiang snapped out a few words in Mandarin. Instantly a trooper stepped up beside Erica and closed a hand over her bare left shoulder. He squeezed, bearing down. Erica swallowed a scream of agony as the wooden splinters were driven deeper into her flesh. She sank to one knee, eyes brimming with unshed tears of pain. Seng Kao started to lunge forward, but the butt of a Calico slammed into the pit of his stomach bent him double.

At another word from Wei Qiang, the soldier released

Erica and stepped away. The tall Chinese asked again in a calm, unperturbed manner, "Where is the ninth ring, Tui Chui Jian?"

Between clenched teeth, Erica inquired, "How did you know where to find me, find my boat?"

"Your nurse," Qiang answered. "She has a familial relationship with the pirate, Chien Ho."

"Not his mom?" Kane blurted.

Wei Qiang eyed him imperiously. "A sister. She believed that she could earn favor for both herself and her wayward brother if she betrayed Tui Chui Jian to me."

Grant cast Brigid a sour glance and whispered, "Figures."

Wei Qiang returned his attention to the kneeling Erica. "Where is the ninth ring? I shan't ask again."

In a voice tight with effort of controlling pain, Erica inquired, "Would you believe me if I told you?"

Qiang nodded toward the trooper, who squeezed her splinter-filled shoulder again. "A woman always speaks the truth under pain."

This time Erica did not cry out, setting her teeth and squeezing her eyes shut. When the soldier released her, she exhaled a shuddery breath. "Not always."

"That is because you are not aware of my methods."

Despite himself, Kane felt a surge of admiration for the surprisingly strong-willed woman. Out of the corner of his eye, he glimpsed Lakesh's right hand steal toward his shirtfront, a movement that he quickly checked.

In a low, dispassionate tone, Wei Qiang stated, "You, Tui Chui Jian, have been living a soft life of utter decadence in a place not meant for you. It is time you faced the realities of your situation."

He stabbed a finger toward Seng Kao, who was forced erect and dragged forward, arms twisted up between his shoulder blades. With a foot, Wei Qiang prodded thoughtfully at the bundle of Sin Eaters, coats, combat harnesses and Copperheads, then bent over and detached one of the small V-60 grenades. Holding it between thumb and forefinger, he eyeballed it closely like a shopper studying an egg at a market, then he spoke quietly in Mandarin.

A yellow-uniformed soldier roughly whipped the blood-wet bandage from Seng Kao's head, and another trooper clamped his hands on the hinges of the man's jaw, forcing his mouth open. Seng Kao struggled, trying to pull away.

Stepping forward, Wei Qiang pinched the man's nostrils shut. As Seng Kao reflexively opened his mouth to gasp for breath, Wei Qiang used his free hand to cram the grenade into it, leaving only the lever safety ring protruding from between his lips.

A trooper took the strip of bloody cloth, ran it under Seng Kao's chin and knotted the ends tightly at the crown of his head, lending him the ludicrous aspect of wearing floppy rabbit ears. However, no humor showed in the man's eyes—as understanding dawned, only sheer terror gleamed there as his hands were bound tightly at the small of his back.

Erica made an effort to rise but Seng Kao shook his head and uttered a muffled imprecation. Kane felt sweat forming at his hairline. Inserting the conical tip of the fingernail protector into the grenade's ring, Wei Qiang stared unblinkingly at Erica. "Where is the ninth ring, Tui Chui Jian?"

She shook her head, her black tresses screening her face. "I don't know."

Wei Qiang swept the Cerberus personnel with his cold eyes. "Do any of you know?"

Lakesh took a breath and husked out, "I do."

Wei Qiang did not move. "And where is it?"

"Let that man go," Lakesh replied, "and I'll tell you."

"Ah." Wei Qiang nodded as if he expected the answer and was now satisfied that he had received it. "And you had led me to hope you were a reasonable man, Dr. Singh."

With one swift, short movement, Qiang jerked away the grenade's ring and the lever clattered to the ground. He voiced a sharp command and two soldiers, their slanted eyes suddenly wide with fear, latched on to Seng Kao's arms and dogtrotted him swiftly toward the lip of the ridge overlooking the cove.

"Stop!" Lakesh shouted, fumbling beneath his shirt. "I'll tell you—"

The troopers pitched Seng Kao headlong over the edge of the ridgeline and then dropped flat to the ground, burying their faces in their arms.

Kane spun toward his friends. "Duck and cover—"

A thunderclap blast slammed his words back into his throat. For a second, tongues of flame billowed upward. The detonation of the grenade hurled rocks, scraps of cloth and other items less identifiable high into the air.

Everyone recoiled, flinching from the ridgeline as a fine rain of sand, pulverized pebbles and droplets of blood drizzled down. Nausea roiled in Kane's belly when he heard the slippery slap of body parts raining down around him.

The echoes of the explosion continued to quiver in the air, as of a musical note refusing to fade. A mushroom of black smoke floated up from beneath the ridge.

Lakesh whirled on Wei Qiang, teeth bared in fury. "You psychotic bastard! There was no need for that!"

Wei Qiang arched an eyebrow. "Really, Dr. Singh? I thought we needed to communicate with each other. First I administered a lesson…let no insult go unavenged. I trust I made my point?"

Lakesh balled his fists, struggling to rein in his anger, eyes flicking from the gun barrels trained in his direction. Behind him, Grant murmured, "Easy."

"Where is the ninth ring, Dr. Singh?" Qiang asked, a note of impatience entering his voice.

"Why should I tell you anything?"

"You will talk or you will die. All of you will die. Which do you prefer?"

Lakesh turned toward Musgrave. "Is your organization working with this homicidal madman or for him?"

Musgrave's right hand almost automatically went up to touch the scars on his face. "How is that relevant?"

"Because the consortium might find it more profitable to make a bargain with Cerberus."

For an instant, Musgrave seemed interested in the possibility, but after a sideways glare from Wei Qiang, he said sullenly, "Cerberus has cost my organization a great deal of time and matériel. There can be no bargain. The Millennial Consortium is not to be trifled with. Our goals are above the limited perspective of individuals. You need to be taught our solid technocratic values before any kind of agreement can be reached between us."

"Enough," Wei Qiang snapped. He gestured imperiously to Erica. The troopers looked at her with eyes gleaming like rabid animals and hauled her to feet, dragging her forward.

Qiang silently surveyed her as if she were a mildly interesting insect he had found scuttling in his garden. Moving with slow deliberation, he wrested away the golden cone from his thumb, revealing a three-inch-long nail, its edges beveled and curved like the blade of a scimitar, the surface coated heavily with glossy lacquer.

Lightly he dragged the edge across Erica's left cheek, leaving a vertical line shining pinkly against the smooth alabaster of her complexion. She recoiled, but tried to maintain a composed, defiant expression. In a soft, almost intimate voice, Wei Qiang asked, "Why did you steal my property? Why did you take the rings?"

"The rings are not your property," Erica retorted coldly.

"No?" Qiang's tone acquired a mocking lilt. "And how would you know?"

"I'll tell you what you want to know, Qiang," Lakesh said sharply.

Without taking his eyes from Erica's face, he replied calmly, "Yes…yes, you will."

Wei Qiang slashed with his thumbnail in a swift figure-eight motion. The scream that burst from Erica's lips was ear-shattering. She flailed backward, hand clapped over the raw, bleeding mass of her right eye. A grinning trooper caught her up in her arms, embracing her tightly as she twisted and convulsed in agony and shock.

Brigid murmured wordlessly in horror, her face draining of all color. Kane and Grant remained motionless, their bodies as tense as drawn bowstrings. Reaching under his shirt, Lakesh snatched away the Hydra ring that had been hanging from his neck by a thin chain.

"Here!" he shouted, his voice a strangulated blend of fury and disgust. He tossed it to the ground at Wei Qiang's feet. "Take it! And let her go!"

Wei Qiang favored him with a pitying smile, then he inspected the wet crimson glistening on the razored edge of his thumbnail. The tip of his tongue came out, touched the blood and he turned his head and spit. "Sour...just like I expected."

He took a step toward the struggling Erica, lifting his left hand. Kane prepared himself to leap on the soldier covering him and Grant. Then he caught a brief, almost subliminal blur of movement streaking overhead. With a resonant, meaty thud, a long arrow drove into and through the neck of the trooper standing on Grant's right.

Chapter 22

Kane's battle-trained muscles, tested and refined in a hundred situations where a fraction of a second gave him all the edge he needed in a life-or-death struggle, exploded in a perfect coordination of mind, reflexes and skill.

Before the arrow-impaled man had fallen, Kane hurled himself forward, shoulder rolling between Brigid and Lakesh. He caught a fragmented glimpse of fearful desperation crossing the face of the soldier when the man realized what his captive was doing.

He tried to bring his subgun to bear, but Kane rose smoothly to his feet right in front of him, his right hand slapping aside the barrel of the Calico and his left hand stabbing out with a thumb and forefinger at the larynx. There was a mushy snap, as of a stick of wet wood breaking, as his windpipe collapsed, and the yellow-helmeted trooper dropped to his knees, a little spurt of blood spilling form his lips. Kane snatched the subgun from his hands, pivoting on the balls of his feet.

At the same instant, Brigid fell flat, balancing herself on her right hand. Using it as an axis, she spun, slamming a reverse heel kick into the back of a trooper's ankles and sweeping his legs out from under him. As he went down, Grant delivered the steel-reinforced toe of his left boot to the underside of his jaw. The crack of bone was loud and ugly.

Wei Qiang lifted his voice in an outraged shout, and the trooper holding Erica van Sloan twisted her, then flung her away as he tried to unlimber his subgun. Erica went in the direction of the throw, somersaulting backward against the legs of two soldiers behind her. She knocked one of them off his feet, causing another to trip over him and sprawl facedown, dropping his Calico in the process.

Lakesh sprang for the fallen subgun, deftly plucking it from the ground by its short barrel and whipping it around to slam the butt against a trooper's jaw. A soldier snapped up his own weapon, centering the sights on the scientist. Another feathered shaft sped through the air and struck the man in the sternum with a grisly crunch.

The point drove between the bands of Kevlar on the tunic and penetrated the man's chest, bursting out between his shoulder blades. Screaming like a wounded beast, he toppled onto his back, clutching at the arrow, blood fountaining from his open mouth.

Lakesh fumbled with the unfamiliar Calico for a long, panicky second, then directed a staccato burst in the general direction of Wei Qiang and Werner Musgrave. The two men scrambled behind the bulwark of the Scorpinaut, trying to stay ahead of the stream of poorly aimed lead. Dirt fountains erupted at their heels, little slivers of stone pelting their legs.

Brigid rolled across the ground, snatched up a pair

of Copperheads from their bundle of gear in midtumble and bounced to her feet. She fired both weapons at the soldiers who hunkered down within the wheel wells of the FCS, shooting back hastily, without aiming.

Brigid didn't really aim, either—her objective was to keep the soldiers pinned down and seeking cover. Brass arced in a glittering rain from the Copperheads' ejector ports. The racket was deafening, nerve-racking. The rattling bursts of autofire, the sledgehammer pounding of rounds crashing against the exterior of the Scorpinaut and the high-pitched whines of ricochets all combined to make a hellish cacophony.

Two troopers recovered enough of their emotional equilibrium to return the fire with their handguns. Shots cracked and boomed. A bullet hissed past Brigid's ear and another tugged at her long hair. She maintained pressure on the triggers of the Copperheads. Three bullets took a trooper's right ear off, bit into his neck and hammered him between the eyes, blowing out the back of his skull in a gouting slop of blood, bone chips and brain matter.

One of the troopers Erica had bowled over struggled to his feet, raising his subgun just as an arrow struck him in the right thigh, piercing it completely. The man staggered, shrieking, clutching convulsively at the shaft.

Kane turned his appropriated Calico on him, stitching his midriff with a zipper of slugs. The trooper went down heavily, a wild stuttering burst from his weapon striking sparks from the hide of the Scorpinaut.

Lakesh, seemingly oblivious to the carnage about

him, lunged forward and snatched the Hydra's ring from the ground. He examined it closely for damage, blowing dirt from its jeweled eyes.

A trio of soldiers regrouped, firing in the direction of Grant, Brigid and Kane, their weapons chattering, muzzles flashing with little twinkles of dancing flame. Three shots from Kane's subgun drilled holes through the lower face of one of them, punching him backward with such force his head struck the ground first.

Brigid framed the trooper next to him in her sights and fired a two-second burst that opened up his throat, propelling him backward in a crimson mist. The man was dead before his body fully settled, but he kept his finger on the trigger even as he fell, the wild fusillade striking his companion in the legs.

On the prow of the Scorpinaut, the front-mounted, box-fed .50-caliber machine guns suddenly rose on their armatures, swiveling and locking in a position to catch everyone, outlander and soldier alike, in a triangulated cross fire.

"Down!" Grant bellowed. "Everybody get down!"

He flung himself full-length, rolling frantically toward the front of the vehicle. Flickering tongues of flame lapped out in rotating circles as rattling roars pressed against his ear drums. He saw his friends following his example, dropping flat and crawling forward as fast as they could. However, the soldiers evidently believed they were immune from gunfire and they kept to their feet. A storm of .50-caliber bullets pounded into a pair of troopers, breaking their chests and heads open amid flying ribbons of blood. Great gouts of earth exploded all around them.

As Grant rolled across the pile of their gear, his hands groped blindly over the combat harnesses until his fingers came in contact with the familiar canister shape of an M-33 fragmentation grenade. Taking a deep breath and holding it, he jerked the grenade away from the vest, leaving the safety ring still connected to the spring clip.

Lunging to his feet between the pair of jackhammering machine guns, he reached up with his left arm to grasp the barrel of the cannon. He chinned himself up by one arm, wriggled around, his thumb flipping away the priming lever. He jammed the grenade into the bore, smacking it with the palm of his hand to push it on its way.

Grant dropped, falling flat and yelling, "Fire in the hole!"

The detonation of the grenade was like a distant thunderclap. For a microsecond, the bore of the cannon was haloed in a red flash. Then flying tongues of flame billowed outward. The outlanders felt the concussion in their bones. The entire vehicle jumped. The barrel of the cannon bulged out at the juncture where it joined with the turret. Smoke spouted from splits in the alloy. Both machine guns fell silent in the same instant.

The topside turret hatch swung open, and amid billows of gray-white vapor, a blood-streaked man clawed his way out and tumbled gracelessly onto the chassis of the FCS. Coughing, he waved his arms as if to signal he wished to surrender, but an arrow impaled him from back to front and he fell from the Scorpinaut to the ground, writhing only briefly before ceasing to move altogether.

"Where'd you come up with that strategy?" Kane asked Grant.

"I improvised," the big man replied hoarsely and retrieved his Sin Eater, still snugged within its power holster, from their bundle of belongings.

Wei Qiang's voice bellowed commands and warnings in Mandarin.

Kane eased around the front of the Scorpinaut. "Who is he yelling at?"

As he did so, he glimpsed four yellow-robed, shaved-headed men emerging from thickets and shrubbery. All of them wielded long bows and carried wooden quivers full of arrows.

Tai Mi, his face bruised, blood trickling from a laceration in his scalp, shouted in English, "Flee, you fools!"

He pointed an arrow in the direction of the village. They followed the barbed point and saw at least a score of helmeted men approaching at a run, chanting, *"Jun Zhu! Jun Zhu!"* Behind them rolled a Scorpinaut, engine roaring.

Kane helped Erica van Sloan to her feet. Although she kept her right eye covered by bloody fingers, she shook loose from his grasp. "I'm only half-blind, Kane."

"Suit yourself," he replied, bending to collect their gear.

"You haven't much time!" Tai Mi shouted, a note of angry desperation entering his voice. "Flee!"

"Flee where?" Lakesh demanded.

Tai Mi pointed with the arrow again, indicating the cove. "There!"

Brigid cast a worried glance at the approaching soldiers, barely one hundred yards distant. "We won't be able to get out of range of their guns in that sampan!"

Grant gusted out a short chuckle. "We won't have to...look."

Turning, Brigid saw the high masts of Captain Sun Fan's junk as it hove into view at the opening to the river.

"Go!" the monk shouted, nocking the arrow. "My brothers and I will give you time to reach the ship."

"What of you?" Lakesh called.

"Our temple was set afire," he answered flatly, hefting the bow. "This is all we have left."

"The priests are forbidden by their creed to use ax or club...but not arrows," Kane murmured.

"Convenient loophole," Grant grunted, jogging toward the ridgeline. "It just might save our asses, if we're lucky."

The five of them ran, sliding and stumbling down the face of the slope. Erica had a difficult time maintaining her footing because of the hand she kept pressed to the right side of her face, but she did not ask for help. She passed the maimed, headless corpse of Seng Kao without a word or a backward glance.

They dashed down the short dock to where the sampan was moored and scrambled aboard. Erica sat with her back against the tiny cabin wall amidships. Her clenched teeth gleamed between her full lips as if she were struggling to bottle up a groan or a scream.

Lakesh pulled the rope off the piling and Grant yanked the starter cord of the outboard motor just as the first of Wei Qiang's soldiers appeared on the crest of the ridge. Several of them fired in haste, a couple of bullets splashing the surface of the water only feet from the boat's stern. Others hit the dock, sending splinters flying like confetti.

The outboard caught on the first try and the sampan lunged away from the pier, foaming ripples spreading out in a V beside the prow. More slugs punched little fountains in the water around them. Kane slammed his appropriated Calico into full-auto and squeezed the trigger. The weapon bucked in his hand as he sprayed the ridgeline. Grant crouched, sinking his head between the wide yoke of his shoulders.

Brigid squeezed off several rounds from her TP-9 and glimpsed a yellow-tunicked body rolling down the slope, breaking a few shrubs and dislodging a number of rocks before it sprawled loose-limbed and lifeless in the mud of the cove.

When the bolt of the Calico snapped loudly open on an empty chamber, Kane dropped it and grabbed a Copperhead, firing steadily. Most of the soldiers were too worried about catching a bullet to risk exposing themselves to return the fire, so when Grant gunned the outboard to its highest rpm, no more bullets came their way.

Kane got up and walked to the bow of the sampan, balancing himself against the rocking of the light boat. He stepped over Lakesh, who was attending to Erica. The scientist asked, "Is everyone all right?"

"So far," Kane replied. "That could change."

Erica snorted, hand still over her eye. "Tell me about it."

"We'll treat you as soon as we can," Lakesh told her sympathetically.

As the craft passed between the bastions of rock into the river, Kane waved toward the crew of the junk assembled at the side. They shouted in response and gesticulated wildly, pointing back toward the cove.

Twisting, belly slipping sideways, he saw a Scorpinaut lurch to the lip of the ridge. Wei Qiang stood atop the turret. Before Kane could shout a warning, the bore of the 40 mm cannon erupted thunder and smoke. The shell splashed into the water of the cove only a few feet to port. Scarcely had the ripples begun to spread when a column of water boiled up in an explosive geyser. The sampan rocked from the concussion. Foaming spray cascaded over the sampan and drenched everyone on the deck.

"Can't this thing go any faster?" Brigid shouted, tossing wet hair from her eyes.

Wiping water from his face, Grant snapped, "We could always swim."

He steered the boat clear of the cove and turned it almost immediately to port so the tumble of weed-choked rocks would provide cover from the cannon. With its diesel engines throbbing, the junk hove to on an intercept course, its exhaust funnels giving off oppressive fumes.

Kane glanced back, but couldn't see the Scorpinaut. He couldn't be sure, but he doubted Wei Qiang would be so angry as to lay down a blind firing pattern in the hope of sinking them or the junk. After half a minute, when no more cannon rounds came their way, he realized his assessment had been correct, but he did not feel relief. Wei Qiang knew their destination.

The junk came alongside in a rush of foam, and ropes came looping down to make the sampan fast. Sun Fan's face appeared at the rail, pale and drawn, but creased in a sardonic grin. Touching the brim of his cap with a forefinger, he said, "Looks like we am still in same boat together."

Chapter 23

The Yangtze was tremendous, a vast flow of silt-laden water so broad that it was almost an inland sea. Far, far off to port Kane saw a few twinkling lights ashore, four miles or more away. To starboard there was nothing but the purple-hued tapestry of the Chinese twilight and a sense of timelessness. The Yangtze's volume equaled that of all the rivers in Asia, and at almost four thousand miles in length, it had been rightfully termed the "long river."

Not only the longest river on the Asian continent, it was also the third-longest in the world after the Amazon and the Nile. The Yangtze began in the Tibetan Plateau and, fed by the snow and ice melt from the surrounding mountains, it emptied out into the South China Sea near Shanghai.

The concourse was cut through with countless webs of channels and tributaries, filled with the traffic of barges, fishing boats, transports, launches, junks and sampans. According to Brigid, before the nukecaust about 350 million people lived on the banks of the Yangtze and its seven hundred tributaries. For many thousands of years, the fortunes of the Chinese living near the river were affected in some way by the rise and fall of the Yangtze.

The engines thumped and the rigging creaked as the wind filled the main sail. Kane leaned on the railing of the quarter deck, feeling the hull vibrate slightly as the junk's twin diesels pushed it southward. The deck rocked gently as the prow cleaved a foaming path through calm waters of the river.

Although night had not fallen completely, ahead he could see only a gray emptiness of waters stretching to a deeper gray of the horizon. The setting sun was a faint orange smudge in the western sky. Here and there the junk passed small boats with lanterns in their bows, where men caught whatever swam by night.

At the sound of footfalls behind him, Kane turned as Brigid approached, cleaning her hands with a square of blood-damp fabric. The medical kit hung from her right shoulder.

"How is she?" Kane asked.

"Better than I expected," Brigid answered with a hint of bewilderment in her voice. "I removed all of the splinters and patched up her shoulder. I don't think there's much chance of infection."

"And her eye?"

Brigid sighed. "I'm afraid she's going to lose it. I doubt even Reba could do anything to save it at this point."

"You did the best you could," Kane said reassuringly. "Reba trained you, so Erica was in good hands. The field medicine Grant and I know is down and dirty, stitch and go. If she only had the two of us to treat her, she would have probably lost both eyes."

Brigid didn't smile. "At least I didn't have to extract a bullet from Sun Fan."

Kane smiled thinly. "That's something."

Upon boarding the junk nearly three hours earlier, they learned that Captain Sun Fan's bullet wound wasn't as serious as they initially figured. A fragment of a ricochet had nicked his lung when it bounced from a rib and then passed on through his body. Although the injury had been treated and bandaged, he had experienced a great deal of pain, which Brigid helped alleviate with analgesics from the medical kit. Sun Fan's emotional pain wasn't as simple to ease when he learned the details of Seng Kao's murder at the hands of Wei Qiang.

Kane half expected the man to hold Erica van Sloan responsible and to greet her arrival with a torrent of vituperation. Instead, his reaction to the wounded Tui Chui Jian was solicitous in the extreme, even reverent. The high degree of respect that bordered on devotion shown to the foreign-born woman was both a puzzle and an irritant.

Erica asked Sun Fan to set a course to a region known as the Sanxia, and the captain agreed without question. He offered her the use of his stateroom beneath the pilothouse. Brigid and Lakesh accompanied her below in order to treat her injuries.

As the junk set sail toward the shadowy loom of cliffs extending up from the horizon, Grant and Kane kept a watchful eye astern for signs of pursuit from Wei Qiang. By the time the ship navigated the narrow strait between the cliffs and entered the Yangtze proper, Wei Qiang still had not made himself visible.

Both men gloomily agreed that Qiang was aware of their destination and probably had already made his own travel plans. Grant asked Sun Fan about Sanxia.

The captain smiled wanly. "It means the Three Gorges—the Qutang, the Wuxia and the Xiling Gorge. Past them, the Yangtze plunges off the roof of the world."

Grant eyed him uneasily. "We're not going that far, are we?"

Sun Fan shrugged, then winced. "Don't know. Better ask Tui Chui Jian. I'm only the captain."

He briefly explained that by the time Wei Qiang appeared in Yichang, he had already pushed the junk away from the damaged dock and was sailing away from the waterfront area, so his ship wasn't present when Qiang's forces began destroying boats. He had sent word to the Shaolin Temple that his ship stood ready to serve the Dragon Mother.

As the afternoon slipped into early evening, Grant found a place on the aft deck to lie down and catch a nap. Accustomed to going long periods without sleep, both he and Kane had been trained by the Magistrates to sleep whenever the opportunity presented itself, so as to build up a backlog. Kane knew he should be doing the same thing, but he was too keyed-up, Mag conditioning notwithstanding.

Nearly a century before, the Magistrate Divisions had been formed as a complex police machine that demanded instant obedience to its edicts and to which there was no possible protest. Magistrates themselves were a highly conservative, duty-bound group. The customs of enforcing the law and obeying orders without question were ingrained almost from birth.

The Magistrates submitted themselves to a grim and unyielding discipline because they believed it was necessary to reverse the floodtide of chaos and restore order to postnuke America. As Magistrates, the courses their lives followed had been charted before their births. They had exchanged personal hopes, dreams and desires for a life of service. They were destined to live, fight and die, usually violently.

All Magistrates followed a patrilineal tradition, assuming the duties and positions of their fathers. They did not have given names, each taking the surname of the father, as though the first Magistrate to bear the name was the same man as the last.

The originators of the Magistrate Divisions had believed that only surnames, family names, engendered a sense of obligation to the duties of their ancestors' office, insuring that subsequent generations never lost touch with their hereditary roles as enforcers. Last names became badges of social distinction, almost titles.

As Magistrates, Grant and Kane had served together for a dozen years and as Cerberus warriors they had fought shoulder to shoulder in battles around half the planet, and even off the planet. At one time, both men enjoyed the lure of danger, courting death to deal death. But now it was no longer enough for them to wish for a glorious death as a payoff for all their struggles. They had finally accepted a fact they had known for years but never admitted to themselves—when death came, it was usually unexpected and almost never glorious.

Kane returned his attention to Brigid, trying to shake off the sense of dread that had settled over him like a cloak. "Is Lakesh still with Erica?"

"He's gone to fetch her something to eat," Brigid answered.

Kane snorted. "I wonder what Domi would say or do if she saw him acting as the Dragon Mama's nursemaid."

Brigid acknowledged the comment with a distracted smile. "I think we may have misjudged her, Kane. She's a lot stronger and braver than I ever gave her credit for."

"I think you're just feeling the physician's empathy for a patient, Baptiste."

"I'm not a doctor," Brigid retorted stiffly, "despite what some people have said. I'm only saying that Erica is a very tough woman."

"Not to mention self-serving and treacherous," Kane interjected flatly. "Don't forget those delightful personality traits."

"She was only treacherous when she was duped by Enlil, used as his pawn."

"And now?"

Brigid blew out a frustrated, weary breath. "I wish I knew. But I think Lakesh may have been right when he insisted she would make a valuable ally."

"Could be," Kane admitted after a moment of thoughtful silence. "But where is she taking us?"

"The region of the Three Gorges...they're famous for

their natural wonders. The walls of the gorges are steep and can reach as high as three thousand feet."

"And that's where we'll find the tomb of Shi Huangdi?"

Brigid shrugged. "Or the tomb of the Yellow Emperor. Or both, since I suspect they were the same man."

"And," Kane ventured, "Wei Qiang is both of them?"

Before Brigid could reply, Lakesh approached, carrying a covered ceramic dish. A spicy aroma floated from it. Brow furrowed with worry, he asked, "Have either of you seen Erica?"

Brigid's eyes widened with surprise. "No...she's not in the cabin?"

Lakesh shook his head. "I just came from there. She's gone. I would've thought she would've been in too much pain to move around much."

"I gave her a couple of heavy-duty painkillers," Brigid said. "They weren't strong enough to knock her out, but she should be disinclined to do anything other than sit or lie down."

Kane grimaced in aggravation, glancing around the darkened deck of the junk. Out of fear of drawing the notice of pirates, Sun Fan had opted to sail the Yangtze with only a minimum of lighting.

"Let's split up and look for her," he declared. "There are only so many places she can go."

Lakesh went forward, wending his away among the bales of cargo, stumbling slightly as the junk chugged and nosed through a dark tangle of driftwood floating down the current from thousands of miles upstream. He paused at the starboard rail to take an awed look at the enormous river spreading as far as the eye could see under the dark China sky, the rolling surface dimly reflecting the pinpoint flecks of the emerging stars.

Suddenly, a voice barely above a whisper spoke to him from a crevice formed by the intersecting corners of two crates. "Go away."

Lakesh turned and was barely able to make out the form of Erica van Sloan huddled on the deck between the pair of crates. He was astonished to see she was crying, her face glistening with tears. He stood looking down at her, at a complete loss of anything to say. Finally he asked, "Are you all right?"

She chuckled mirthlessly and whispered, "Please leave me alone, Mohandas."

"What is it?" he asked gently. "I want to help. Are you hungry? I've brought you something to eat."

She looked up at him, her beauty made grotesque by the padded bandage covering the right side of her face. Her raven's-wing hair was pinned up at the back of her head. "You always make me feel so petty and malicious, do you know that? Not even Silas made me feel that way."

He cleared his throat self-consciously. "I don't mean to, Erica."

"What do you feel about me? Do you hate me?"

"No, of course not. We may have been enemies in the past, but even then I didn't hate you."

"Do you feel sorry for me, then? I think you do."

He placed the covered dish atop a crate and slowly sat down beside her. The air was cool so close to the flowing waters. Erica's tear-damp face was earnest, and her violet eye searched his when he said, "I don't feel any sorrier for you than myself or the others who were forced into the big sleep of the centuries."

"Except I tried to make myself a queen when I woke up from the sleep, and that made you resentful," she replied flatly.

An iron edge in his voice, he retorted, "I resented that you tried to make yourself a queen by using me while you were being used by Enlil."

"You don't know what it was like for me." Her voice was low and quaking with barely repressed fury. "The things I had to do just to survive—" She broke off and laughed bitterly. "Before the skydark, I was young and beautiful. Men desired me. I wanted nothing—clothes, jewelry, cars. Then I went into stasis and when I woke up I was all alone, ugly, old and crippled. No man wanted to come near me...the exact opposite of Sleeping Beauty. And then Sam—Enlil—made me young and beautiful and powerful again. And now here I am."

She closed her eye and intoned, "Here I am, half-blind, floating around in China, trying to make myself immortal. I must be insane."

"No more insane than I," he said softly. "I have the same goal."

"So you've figured out that the Hydra's rings are of Annunaki technology...and more than likely, with the Armor of Immortality, they infuse the body with repair nanomachines?"

He nodded. "Yes. It's the most logical explanation."

Erica sighed. "We're very alike, Mohandas. Both of

us are scientists, survivors, cast adrift in a nightmare world not of our making, full of savages that we must live among. But you can't trust anybody and neither can I. You're as lonely as I am."

Lakesh smiled sourly. "Sometimes I'm lonely because of the reasons you cite. But there are people I trust."

"You don't trust *me*."

"No, I don't," he replied frankly. "But I would like to. That's why I've made overtures to you over the last year, to enter into an alliance with Cerberus."

"I know, but you..." She trailed off and bit her lower lip, drawing her legs up to her chest and hugging her knees. They heard the water purling softly past the keel. Then, she nodded as if she had come to a decision, then reached up and quickly undid her hair, letting it tumble down over her shoulders.

She smiled at Lakesh, as if suddenly shy. "You're the only person I know from the old world and I don't understand you at all. It's as if you refuse to give up or be satisfied with the status quo, in spite of all the things that have nearly destroyed you. Enlil tried to destroy you—he used me to try to destroy you. But that only gave you more strength to fight back, didn't it?"

Lakesh didn't answer immediately. Then, thoughtfully, he said, "I've not given it much thought, Erica. But you're stronger than I."

She laughed, but it held no mirth. "You're wrong, Mohandas. I'm very weak. I'm attracted to power, to the very concept of ruling over others. That was the whole point behind the development of the SQUID implants, you know. I have these feelings, contradictory ones. I want to build and I want to destroy. I want to pull down the world that men like you and the barons made and build a new one so I can control it myself."

She chuckled again. "Maybe the SQUIDs have made me bipolar."

"No," he said. "You're just conflicted and hurt and angry. I understand all of those feelings. We both want to make sure the world doesn't come under the yoke of the Annunaki again."

"Is that why you do what you do? Do you think being immortal will help you keep that from happening?"

"Yes," he answered without hesitation.

She turned to face him, her lips parted. "Do you still think I'm beautiful?"

"Yes," he said, again without hesitation.

"Do you want me?"

He could think of nothing to say. Erica leaned closer to him. "Most men in my life wanted me. It was a strange thing. I had contempt for them if they wanted me, but I hated them if they didn't. Isn't that schizophrenic?"

"Not really."

"You don't think so? Maybe I wouldn't hate you, Mohandas, if we—"

"No," he broke in more harshly than he intended.

"We have time." Her voice dropped to a silky whisper. "We're alone here. Your friends won't know."

Erica pulled at her tunic and shrugged out of it. In the

starlight, her body looked smooth and sleek, full of pride and simmering sexuality, despite or perhaps because of the bandage taped to her left shoulder. "You want me."

"You *are* very beautiful," he admitted. "But nothing is going to happen between us. I'm already committed to someone."

Her lips curled in a sneer. "Who? That little albino bitch? Do you think she's faithful to you, an animal like that?"

"I know she is," he replied stolidly. "Is that all you have to say?"

Taking his hands, she placed them on her full breasts. Beneath the thin covering of her brassiere, Lakesh could feel her nipples taut with desire and he felt a stirring in his loins.

"Go on," she whispered. "Make love to me. Fuck me. Do what you want."

"Stop it, Erica," he said grimly, trying to pulling his hands away.

"I want you to do it with me. I want to know if you're really different from all the other men in my life, like Silas."

"Why is that so important to you?"

"It just is, that's all. Here we are, in this strange world, on a mission to find a way to live forever if we aren't killed first. This might be my—*our*—last chance."

Lakesh disengaged himself and stood up, turning away. "I'm sorry, Erica."

She rose swiftly to block his way. Her posture was at once seductive and a challenge.

He stared at her unblinkingly, making sure to keep his face expressionless. "Get out of my way."

"Oh, you son of a bitch," she hissed in a voice sibilant with spite. "You think you're too good for me, is that it?"

"You're being ridiculous."

"Am I?" Her voice lifted abruptly. "I repulse you now, don't I? Next you'll say you turned me down for my own good."

"I did," he said coldly. "Maybe one day your arrogance will permit you to understand that."

Erica tried to slap him, but Lakesh caught her wrist and spun her. She was stronger than he thought and she turned into the spin. He kicked her at the back of the knee and as her leg buckled, she dragged him down with her to the deck. Instantly, her arms locked around him and her lips pressed against his, her body moving beneath his with wanton abandon.

He forced her arms away, and although he felt like three different varieties of bastard for doing so, he squeezed her injured shoulder. She cried out sharply and released him. He rose swiftly to his feet, staring down at her, mind awash with a torrent of conflicting emotions.

For a long moment, Erica van Sloan lay gasping on the deck, one hand cupping her bandaged shoulder, gazing up at him with fury that slowly yielded to puzzlement then to shame. She looked down at herself and hastily closed up her tunic.

"You think I'm a whore," she whispered. "You wouldn't be the first man to think that. I suppose I was. That's what Silas thought, that's what Enlil thought, that's even what Baroness Beausoleil thought and they were right. I'll never be anything different, even if I do become immortal. I whore myself for power."

"Get up, Erica," Lakesh said wearily. He extended a hand and after a moment's hesitation she took it and allowed him to help her to her feet. He didn't release her hand. Instead, he squeezed it tightly, drawing her close.

In a low voice, tone packed with conviction, he said, "You're not a whore. You're a brilliant, brave, exceptionally resilient and resourceful woman. But you're also a spoiled, narcissistic bitch who never learned how to channel her base impulses into something more constructive than finding new ways to be worshiped."

His grip tightened around her hand and her one eye squinted in pain. "There is much to admire about you, Dr. van Sloan," he continued, "and much to despise. I'd prefer to admire you than despise you—but that's completely of your choosing."

Lakesh released her hand, flinging it away in sudden anger. "Before we reach our destination you had best make your choice so my friends and I will know how to deal with you. I can promise you one thing—it will be the most important decision of your life."

Chapter 24

The early-morning sun rose above the flat blue horizon like a fiery jewel, as if it had been disgorged from the depths of the Yangtze. The open river at dawn was beautiful with the reflected sunrise shimmering on the surface.

Kane, Brigid, Grant and Lakesh gathered on the aft deck, using a bale of cargo as a makeshift table and a collection of small barrels and kegs as chairs. The Cerberus warriors had slept in hammocks in the crew's quarters and been awakened at dawn by the odor of hot food. Breakfast was a mixture of white rice mixed in with bits of fish, slices of orange and thick gravy. The four of them brought plates up to the deck and tried to eat with chopsticks.

Unsurprisingly, only Lakesh and Brigid showed any facility with the wooden utensils. After dropping more food on their laps and on the deck than in their mouths, Grant and Kane ended up scooping it out of the plates with their fingers. They glared at Brigid and Lakesh in the process, silently daring to them to criticize. Wisely, both people elected to discuss other topics than table manners.

"Has anyone seen Erica this morning?" Brigid asked.

"The great lady has yet to emerge from her boudoir," Kane replied dryly. "She's probably waiting for someone to draw her a bath of milk and honey."

Lakesh frowned at him in disapproval. "I don't think you understand the extent of physical and emotional trauma inflicted upon her. She's wounded in both body and spirit."

Grant eyed him suspiciously. "Do you have some inside knowledge about that?"

"I don't need any to realize Erica requires our understanding and time to heal. I doubt we'll see her for hours, if at all."

As if on cue, Erica van Sloan chose that moment to make her entrance topside. They were all surprised into momentary speechlessness by her appearance.

Instead of the disheveled and pain-racked creature they had seen the night before, Erica was stunning in a red silk blouse embroidered with heavy golden thread depicting coiling dragon forms. The high collar did not detract from the long, slender column of her throat.

Her black hair was smooth and sleekly brushed, framing the calm, sculptured beauty of her face. If not for the scratch marring the alabaster perfection of her cheek and the black patch covering her right eye, none of them would have guessed she had incurred so much as a stubbed toe the day before. A square of white gauze was barely visible at the edges of the patch. Only the dark fires glinting in her left eye denoted any emotion.

Erica strode across the deck, taking long measured

strides, not responding to the deferential bows and whispers of "Tui Chui Jian" directed toward her by the sailors she passed.

When she reached the makeshift table, she nodded regally. "Good morning, my friends. I trust you slept well."

Kane extended the middle of his right hand to which a clump of stewed fish clung. "Care to join your friends at breakfast?"

Erica did not respond to the sarcastic query. "The captain informs me we'll reach our destination by late afternoon, so it's best we discuss how to proceed."

"Just what destination is that?" Brigid asked.

"A temple in the Wuxia Gorge region. But that's only where we will disembark. The next leg of our journey is overland."

"Do tell," Grant said gruffly, pushing a keg toward her with foot. "Take a pew and start talking."

Annoyance at the big man's casual tone flashed in Erica's eye but as she sat down she asked, "Do you have the ring on you, Mohandas?"

Lakesh produced it from a pocket of his field jacket, holding it out to her on the palm of his hand for inspection. She reached for it, but he closed his fingers around it.

"I'll keep hold of the only ring Wei Qiang doesn't yet have in his possession, if you don't mind," he said.

Her shoulders stiffened at his tone, edged as it was with recrimination. "It's my property."

"The hell it is," Kane said. "God knows who it originally belonged to, but nothing in that pyramid is yours. You didn't even inherit it."

"More than likely," Brigid stated, "Huang-ti was the original owner. And if Wei Qiang is really the Yellow Emperor, he's only reclaiming what is rightfully his."

"Perhaps so," Erica retorted coldly. "But I don't think he can activate the Kai Bu Xiu with only eight of them."

"Activate?" Grant echoed. "So you think the Armor of Immortality, if it really exists, is some sort of machine?"

"Of some sort," Erica said dryly. "A machine of the Annunaki, I'm betting. It's either a version of or the template for various magic cauldrons that figure in ancient legends."

Kane frowned. "What are you talking about?"

"The Cauldron of Daghda provided food for everyone," Brigid said, "and the Cauldron of Bran the Blessed conferred rebirth. In Greek mythology the priestess Medea restored people to youth in a magic cauldron."

"In the case of the Cauldron of Bran," Erica interposed, "it could only restore the dead to life as long as the Nine Rings of Eternal Return were worn upon the fingers."

"Are we going to look for a cauldron or a suit of armor?" Grant growled impatiently.

"Both, maybe," Lakesh said.

Erica nodded, her manner becoming a bit less formal. "During my time in the pyramid, I tried to catalog all the relics and artifacts stored in the vault, indexing them in the correct cultural and chronological order. It wasn't easy because so much of it was derived from Annunaki and Danaan technology."

A rueful smile creased her lips. "Imagine trying to put together a huge jigsaw puzzle, with all the pieces manufactured in different epochs, different lands and different societies and none of them having more than the most general idea of the final picture."

Lakesh chuckled. "The confusion was probably engendered deliberately, you know. That way mere humans couldn't put the artifacts to use for their own purposes or benefit."

"Probably," Erica agreed. "But all of us here know that the Annunaki selected certain humans, certain genotypes in extended family groups for eugenics experiments. Over many generations, over a period of centuries, they sampled, reordered and realigned their DNA in tiny details. They isolated particularly desirable genes and spliced them with others. They preselected the makeup of the entire genetic blueprint. The individuals subjected to this process passed on this set of precisely planned characteristics."

"And those individuals became the first god-kings, the Annunaki intermediaries," Brigid declared. "So you postulate that Huang-ti was one of those?"

Erica nodded. "One of the first in this part of the world. I think Enlil took a special interest in him."

Grant narrowed his eyes. "Why do you think that?"

She favored him with a smug smile. "Firsthand experience, Grant. Only Sam knew the nature of all the artifacts within the vault in the pyramid. And since Sam was Enlil—"

"And Enlil was Changhuan, the Yellow Emperor's guardian dragon," Brigid blurted in sudden excitement.

"Exactly," Erica said matter-of-factly. "I'm positive Enlil is responsible for sending Wei Qiang to oust me from the pyramid, using the rings and the promise of restored youth as an inducement."

She cut her eyes sideways over to Lakesh and added lowly, "And some of us know how powerful an inducement that can be."

Grant's expression was indefinable, but his tone was heavy with irony when he asked, "And you expect us to believe that Enlil all of a sudden decided to evict you and he raised an army for Wei Qiang so he could do it?"

"Why not?" Erica asked crisply.

Kane said, "If Enlil is behind this, he depended on the Millennial Consortium to do all the hard stuff…the fact that the soldiers are armed with Calicos proves that much."

Lakesh tugged at his nose contemplatively. "Assuming that's the case, why is he using Wei Qiang for this? Why not do it himself?"

Kane and Grant exchanged glances, then looked expectantly over at Brigid. "That's a good question, Baptiste," Kane said. "What do you think?"

Slowly Brigid said, "I think—and I'm only speculating—that Enlil wants control of China again, but he's too overextended to embark on a war of conquest with his own forces. Who knows, he may not want the other members of the Supreme Council to know what he's doing. Therefore, he's using Wei Qiang to do the conquering for him, like he did in the old days, but the Millennial Consortium is supplying the army. Enlil is manipulating them both."

Grant blew out a disgusted breath, shaking his head. "Goddamned arrogant snake faces. They're sneakier now than they were as barons."

No one disagreed. For the past three-plus years, Lakesh, Kane, Brigid and the movement had struggled to dismantle the machine of baronial tyranny in America. They had devoted themselves to the work of Cerberus, and victory over the barons, if not precisely within their grasp, did not seem a completely unreachable goal—and then unexpectedly, a little over a year before, the entire dynamic of the struggle against the nine barons changed.

The Cerberus warriors learned that the fragile hybrid barons, despite being close to a century old, were only in a larval or chrysalis stage of their development. Overnight, the barons changed. When that happened, the war against the baronies themselves ended, but a new one, far greater in scope, began.

The baronies had not fallen in the conventional sense through attrition, war or coups d'état. No organized revolts had been raised to usurp the hybrid lords from the seats of power, nor had insurrectionists met in cellars to conspire against them.

The barons had simply walked away from their villes, their territories and their subjects. When they reached the final stage in their development, they saw no need for the trappings of semidivinity, nor were they content to rule such minor kingdoms. When they evolved into their true forms, incarnations of the ancient Annunaki overlords, their avaricious scope expanded to encompass the entire world and every thinking creature on it.

The Cerberus warriors had hoped the overweening ambition and ego of the reborn overlords would spark bloody internecine struggles, but in the months since their advent, no intelligence indicating such actions had reached them.

Of course, the overlords were engaged in reclaiming their ancient ancestral kingdoms in Mesopotamia. They had yet to cast their covetous gaze back to the North American continent, but it was only a matter of time.

Before that occurred, Cerberus was determined to build some sort of unified resistance against them, but the undertaking proved far more difficult and frustrating than even the cynical Kane or the impatient Grant had imagined. Even long months after the disappearance of the barons, the villes were still in states of anarchy, with various factions warring for control on a day-by-day basis.

"Let me get this straight," Kane said. "Enlil wants to take possession of China again, but he wants Wei Qiang to be his puppet on the throne?"

Brigid nibbled her underlip reflectively. "Apparently, that was the same deal he cut with Huang-ti and all of his other alter egos down through the centuries. At some point, he and Huang-ti must have had a falling out. At the very least, he no longer had access to the Nine Rings of

Eternal Return and the Armor of Immortality and so he began to age...apparently very slowly, but age he did."

"Which strongly suggests," Lakesh said, "that periodic treatments are required to maintain a relative level of youth and vitality. Apparently, when both the armor and the rings work in tandem, it makes the human organism immune to disease or breakdown of the cellular structure."

Kane narrowed, then widened his eyes as he tried to comprehend all the implications. "Are you saying Huang-ti can never die?"

"Oh, he could have his throat slit," Erica stated, "or be clubbed to death in his bed. That may be the source of the tales of Shi Huangdi's paranoia about assassination. But if he didn't suffer any accidents, and chance worked in his favor, he could conceivably live for what seems like forever."

"Why didn't Huang-ti retrieve the rings and armor before now?" Grant demanded.

Erica shrugged, then winced, gingerly massaging her injured shoulder. "He may not have known where the rings were...or if he did, how to retrieve them. And of course, the armor is useless without the rings."

"With only one of them," Kane pointed out, "the armor is useless to us, too."

The corner of Brigid's mouth lifted in a smile. "Even with all nine rings in our possession, the armor won't do us any good, either. I'm certain it's programmed to interface only with Huang-ti's genetic structure."

Grant's brows drew down, turning his face into a ferocious mask. Angrily, he snapped, "Then why the hell are we on the opposite side of the world trying to lay claim to the damned thing?"

"So we won't have to contend with an immortal plenipotentiary of Enlil," Lakesh shot back impatiently. "Besides, the less Annunaki technology floating around free, the better it is for us—for humanity."

Brigid's eyes suddenly acquired a hard emerald sheen as if a notion had just occurred to her. "Better for you personally, too."

"What do you mean?" Lakesh asked tersely.

Brigid gestured to Erica and to Lakesh. "You two are probably the most brilliant human scientific brains currently alive. Erica is an expert on nanotechnology and you know more about quantum physics, both theoretical and practical, than anyone in the last two hundred years."

"So?" Kane wanted to know.

Brigid's slight smile widened, but it didn't soften the hard gleam of suspicion in her eyes. "They think they can reprogram the rings and the armor to work on them."

Kane glared first at Erica, then at Lakesh, barely able to restrain himself from grabbing the man by the throat. All the pent-up anger, the old resentments he still harbored toward Lakesh and the man's conspiratorial tactics, came fountaining up within him.

Shortly after his resurrection from stasis, Lakesh had rifled genetic records to find the qualifications he deemed the most desirable to breed into potential warriors in his cause. Kane's family line possessed those qualities—high intelligence, superior adaptive traits and a resistance to disease. Kane wasn't a superhuman, but he was a superior one, one of the top candidates of the Purity Control program.

A few years before, Lakesh had arranged for Beth-Li Rouch to be brought into the redoubt to mate with Kane, to insure that his superior abilities were passed on to offspring.

From a clinical point of view, Lakesh's plan to turn Cerberus from a sanctuary into a colony made sense. To insure that Kane's superior qualities were passed on, mating him with a woman who met the standards of Purity Control was the most logical course of action. Without access to the ectogenesis techniques of fetal development outside the womb, the conventional means of procreation was the only option. And that meant sex and passion and ultimately, the fury of a woman scorned.

Kane had refused to cooperate for a variety of reasons, primarily because he felt the plan was a continuation of sinister elements that had brought about the nukecaust and the tyranny of the villes.

"Is that true?" he demanded in a voice made guttural by fury. "You two are in cahoots to make yourselves immortal?"

Lakesh calmly met Kane's enraged glare, unintimidated. "Don't be an ass, Kane." He swept Brigid and Grant with the same stare. "And that goes for you two. Erica and I are not in cahoots, but by working together it is possible we can change the system around so it will work on everyone."

"When were you going to tell us this was the plan?" Brigid snapped.

Erica sighed. "It's not a plan, Baptiste. Mohandas and I have not discussed it, but both of us had the same goal in mind. Who wouldn't?"

"That's a damned good question," Grant said darkly. "Because the answer would include the entire Supreme Council, not just Enlil...and it's still only supposition that he has a claw in this particular pie, if at all."

"I agree," Kane stated. "It seems more like a consortium operation to me."

"I don't know anything about this Millennial Consortium of yours," Erica bit out. "But I know how Enlil's mind works...deception and diversion."

"Yeah, you ought to know all about that," Grant drawled. "He tricked you into thinking you were his mom."

Erica's lips peeled back over her teeth in a hard, humorless grin. "You're on my turf now, Grant. So watch your mouth."

Kane heard a faint, faraway whine and stiffened. "I hear something."

"Like what?" Brigid asked, puzzled.

Kane didn't answer at first, tilting his head back to scan the blue, cloud-flecked sky. "I've heard it before. We all have."

Brigid turned her head this way and that, like a foxhound casting for a scent. Quietly, she said, "You're right."

They stood up, shielding their eyes with their hands

as they looked from east to west, north to south. A couple of crewmen stared at them in puzzlement, then they heard the whining drone. With a sudden shimmering, a section of the eastern sky rippled, like water sluicing over a pane of dusty glass and revealing an image behind it.

A glinting silver orb appeared an eighth of a mile away, a featureless disk of molten silver twenty feet in diameter. Perfectly centered on the disk's underside bulged a half dome, like the boss of a shield.

"Shit," Grant hissed. "They had their LOC working. They could have been following us since the second we arrived at Xian."

His friends knew he referred to the sky ship's low observability camouflage screen. Microcomputers within the smart metal hulls sensed the color and shade of the background and exactly mirrored the background image.

The disk shot forward on a direct course with the junk, skimming over the river surface like a discus tossed by an athlete. The water parted before it in a wide V, a foaming rooster tail following in its wake. The sailors howled in fear and ran in a crazed panic from starboard to port and back. From the wheelhouse, Sun Fan shouted orders to which no one paid any heed.

When the disk was less than half a second away from colliding with the junk broadside, it executed a vertical L maneuver and shot straight up, missing the tall mainmast by a matter of inches, not feet. The downdraft hit, and the ship rocked violently, the rigging swaying, the sails belling out.

The silver disk ship swooped upward, then curved in a parabolic course to the south. In between one heartbeat and another, it vanished from sight.

After a long moment of staring at the sky, Lakesh said flatly, "Friend Grant, I believe you were mentioning something about Enlil's involvement being only supposition."

Grant refused to be baited, but Kane inquired, half to himself, "If that was really Enlil in the ship, why didn't he just scuttle us?"

Erica voiced a low, bitter chuckle. "The reason is obvious…isn't it, Mohandas?"

Lakesh nodded and turned, holding up the Hydra's ring between thumb and forefinger. "We still have the one ring. Enlil can't take the chance of losing it at the bottom of the Yangtze."

Chapter 25

The wind blew harder and curtains of rain blurred the view. The heavy sail had been rigged to keep the junk heading into the wind, but still she drifted toward the mouth of the gorge. The vessel creaked and the taut sail-cloth boomed, intercut with the humming vibration of rigging as strong gusts sang through it.

Sun Fan muttered, "Traveling the Wuxia Gorge is as difficult as climbing up to the sky." He grinned sourly at Grant, Kane, Lakesh and Brigid. "That's what Li Bai said anyhow."

"Who's that?" Kane asked, lowering the binoculars and cleaning the lenses of water droplets. "Your helmsman?"

Lakesh shook his head in exasperation. "Li Bai was a poet of the Tang Dynasty. He was known for his lamentations."

"Yeah, well," Kane retorted dismissively. "So are you."

He returned his attention to the castellated cliffs looming at least a thousand feet above on both sides of the Yangtze. Through his binoculars, he studied the high ramparts, then swept the lenses over the river as it flowed between the walls of the gorge, waves crashing and breaking on the bare stone, foaming spray flying in all directions.

The slate-green water heaved, capped with white. Small inlets and estuaries drawing away from the main waterway split the rock formations. On the narrow shoals at the foot of the cliffs lay the remains of wrecked boats, heaps of splintered timbers and flapping, ragged sails.

"Damned rough water ahead," Grant commented gruffly. He tugged up the collar of his Mag coat. "How do we propose we get through it?"

Sun Fan turned away from the bow. "Very carefully."

Shouting orders to the crew on the deck, the captain climbed up to the pilothouse and took the wheel. The sailors scrambled to various points around the junk, furling the mainsail. For the past few hours, the river had gradually narrowed to the point where both banks were visible, as well as a number of channels running around muddy islands, little more than dark fingers of rock thrusting up from the surface.

They passed fishing villages, collections of small huts propped up on stilts, and they saw more boat traffic. The junk stayed with the main channel, keeping as far away as possible from the other craft, and none of them paid the bigger boat much attention.

The four outlanders remained standing in the bow. In the distance beyond the sheer cliffs rising from the water, they saw a long line of ridges and peaks still capped in snow shouldering up from the hazy horizon. The sudden spring storm, which howled down from the mountains, carried with it a touch of the lingering winter at the higher altitudes.

The junk eased past an upthrust of black rock that jutted fifteen feet above the surface of the river. One side of it was quarried smooth and several ideograms were chiseled deep into it. Squinting at them, Brigid intoned, "'Wuxia's peaks rise higher and higher.'"

"Is that a warning," Grant asked, "or just a fairly obvious observation?"

Brigid shrugged, pointing to the inscriptions. "The character 'Wu' refers to a shaman. This gorge was named after an imperial physician called Wu Xian who lived during the time of Yu the Great. According to fable, the goddess Yao Ji and her eleven sisters quelled some unruly river dragons and then turned themselves into mountains, thoughtfully positioned to help guide ships downriver."

The deck shuddered underfoot and Lakesh stated nervously, "I think we'll need all the help we can get."

Sun Fan worked the wheel as the ship was caught by a current that swept it toward a cleft between the cliffs. Carried by the current racing more swiftly than the river itself, the junk picked up speed. The dark walls seemed to plunge toward them.

Studying the precipices towering high above, Kane glimpsed four oblong shapes dangling over a stone crag on the right by thick hawsers and commented, "It looks like coffins up there."

Shading her eyes with her hands, Brigid replied, "They are. It was a burial custom of the Ba people, dating back over two thousand years."

Grant grunted. "What kind of custom is that?"

"No historian is sure. However the Ba people—who were dwarves—had reputations for perverse behavior, such as that of protesting against heaven for their small statures. One such protest, for example, took the form of wearing too many clothes in summer and too few in winter."

"Yeah, that would get heaven's sympathy, all right," Kane replied sarcastically.

"In ancient Chinese lore," Brigid went on, "they were reputed to be gatekeepers at the Pillars of Heaven, since they refused to enter themselves."

"What does that mean?" Grant asked.

Brigid shook her head. "I don't know."

The Yangtze rose and fell under the boat as Sun Fan steered it closer to the gorge mouth. The gap widened and became a gushing channel swirling around broken rocks, spray rising like smoke. The rumbling sound ahead increased steadily until it became a constant roar.

The junk quivered, then sprang like a wild animal into the heart of the churning, turbulent strait. Mist and spray swirled past the prow. The river beyond the bow disappeared in a cloud of vapor as it flowed into a stretch of white-water rapids. Lakesh, Grant, Brigid and Kane backed away, taking up position amidship, clutching at the crisscross of rigging. Although he didn't say so, Kane was envious of Erica riding out the last leg of the voyage in her stateroom below.

Brigid stared straight ahead, her long lava-hued hair streaming straight out behind her in the gusts. The boat plunged into the strait between the slick walls of the narrow gorge. It pitched and jumped as it shot forward. Sun Fan took his vessel through, sliding with inches to spare past half-submerged boulders and jagged fingers of stone. The Yangtze broke over the bow and ran hissing over their feet and ankles, spilling over the port-side rail.

The concourse cut through gigantic tumbles of granite and basalt, huge boulders that had fallen from the cliffs over the centuries. Suddenly, the junk lurched violently. Everywhere sailors went staggering and stumbling and from starboard came a prolonged grate of wood against stone, but the boat still had momentum enough to drag free of whatever had snagged the hull. They heard Sun Fan swearing viciously in Mandarin as he fought the wheel.

The strait widened and the boat plunged between the cleft walls and into less agitated, but still violent, water. The white swells threatened to pile the vessel up on the shoals, but the foaming river calmed as the junk moved away from the throat of the strait. The storm lessened in intensity but rain continued to fall in a steady drizzle.

Exultancy swept the deck and the men shouted in joyful triumph when they realized they had emerged intact. Kane, although relieved, didn't feel like cheering. His point man's subtle sense of danger deepened as he stood up and took stock of their surroundings.

A light mist hung over the river and the surface glistened with an oily sheen, which only added to the hallucinatory quality of the scene spread out before and above the bow of the boat. Everyone stood up and stared.

"This has *got* to be the place," Grant said quietly, his voice hushed by awe.

The sight was not only strange, it was scarcely believable. On the right-hand face of the gorge, a group of small pavilions with brilliantly colored roofs clung to the slopes, sprouting like tenacious wildflowers. The structures carried their gazes upward from the upturned eaves to a gray crag upon which was perched a building out of an Oriental fantasy, like a page ripped from a storybook and somehow given immense dimension and breadth.

The huge pagoda dominated the stone bastions, the cloud-obscured afternoon sunlight winking from the gold-leaf spire rising from a roof gleaming with glazed tiles of green, blue and purple. A wide horned gate with a huge bronze disk suspended from the crossbar led to a shadowy portico. Golden dragons and fu dogs snarled down from the angles of the great gate.

Constructed of arches and angles, the temple looked ancient. Overlaid by a thick coating of bloodred lacquer, the support columns crawled with leering demons and slithering dragons. The temple looked beautiful, but there was something unnatural, even menacing about it.

"Yes," Erica said from behind them. "It's definitely the place."

Lakesh glanced over his shoulder at her, noting she was armed and dressed for the weather, wearing a black hooded cloak. Her one visible eye was fixed intently upon the pagoda. He said to her, "You've yet to explain sufficiently what kind place it is. Surely not the mausoleum itself."

"No," she replied. "More like the visitor's center or information booth to a cemetery. We should find the keys to the mausoleum there."

Both Grant and Kane turned, staring at her in disbelief. "The keys?" Grant echoed incredulously. "You mean anybody at any time could just stroll up there, grab a key and unlock the damned door to the crypt?"

"No," she said again, this time with an icy edge in her voice. "I don't mean that at all."

SUN FAN ORDERED the sail unfurled and when a breeze filled it, he steered the junk toward a stone jetty extending from the base of the gorge wall. Several quays and docks were built around a spit of rock that jutted into the Yangtze. A wide stairway stretched steeply up from the landing, the steps chiseled out of the rock.

Turning the wheel, Sun Fan held the junk's stern straight for the jetty. He ran alongside it, so close that the hull scraped the pilings. As the boat bobbed in the shallows, two of the crew leaped down to the pier and secured it to a cleat with a hawser, snugging the craft fast and tight.

A gangplank was put in place, and the outlanders disembarked carrying all of their gear. Lakesh had the interphaser securely strapped over a shoulder.

Sun Fan announced, "We will remain here for the night and wait for you until noon tomorrow. If you don't come back…"

His words trailed off, and he cast his eyes downward so as not to meet Erica's gaze. She said softly, "A wise decision, Captain. If we don't return by then, most likely we never will."

She affected not to notice the angry glare Kane directed at her as she added, "I am grateful to you for your service, Captain."

Sun Fan ducked his head reverentially. "It has been my honor, Tui Chui Jian."

He formally shook hands with the others who extended him words of thanks, then he walked back up the gangplank to the junk. Without hesitation, the five people began trudging up the damp steps. Erica took the lead, moving calmly between the crags of upright stone that had been carved by the elements into bizarre shapes.

Kane again felt admiration for the woman, but it was not evident in his tone when he asked, "You need to brief us about what we'll find at the top, Dragon Mama."

She glanced down at him over a shoulder, pushing the hood back on her cape and shaking her hair free. Tiny beads of moisture glittered on it, as if diamonds dusted her black tresses. Her face was austere, but made sinister by the black eye patch. "All I know are the legends."

"That's usually what we operate by anyway," Brigid said wryly. "I know a little about this region. It was central to the saga of the Three Kingdoms, which was a period between the disintegration of the Han Dynasty and the subsequent reunification of China under the Qin Dynasty. During that time, there arose three kingdoms and three sovereigns who vied to unify and control the nation."

"Yes," Erica said, sounding slightly surprised by

Brigid's knowledge. "The kingdoms were the Wei—based in northern China, the Shu—based in western Sichuan and the Wu—based south of the lower Yangtze. Allegedly, the temple was built on the site of the final battle to determine the fate of the Three Kingdoms."

The five people steadily scaled the time-pitted risers, picking their way carefully. In some places the steps were slippery and cracked. Erica's upward gait was a smooth, gliding motion, her legs invisible under the cloak. As she walked, she spoke, sounding not the least bit winded.

"The battle was very fierce," she continued. "The Feng-Shen text contains an account that all sides wielded weapons that were obviously not native to China five thousand years ago. So-called wind wheels launched hosts of silver dragons, mirrors on tripods radiated deadly heat, globes of fire and lightning darts. Immortals riding on flying dragons joined in the slaughter.

"At the end of the battle, seven hundred thousand soldiers died. Corpses were piled as high as mountains. Two of the sovereigns were dead. The third was appointed ruler of all of China."

"Let me guess," Grant grunted. "Shi Huangdi, who was really Huang-ti, and who now travels under the name of Wei Qiang."

"Who can say?" Erica replied. "The war between immortals and men ravaging ancient China may be only a fantasy...but the time frame for all of this to take place corresponds with the rise of the god-king system in Sumeria. Of course it was after that period the Chinese made the dragon a symbol of their civilization, believing that the celestial dragon was the father of the first dynasty of divine emperors."

Erica paused on a wide step, allowing the others to move up beside her and catch their breath. They were more than halfway to the summit. "The three sovereigns and all of their descendants are reputed to be buried here in a network of tombs, but if they were ever found, no official report was released, much like the secrecy surrounding the Xian pyramid."

"Are you claiming we'll find a necropolis up above?" Lakesh asked, inhaling deeply. "A Chinese version of the Egyptian Valley of Kings?"

"I'm not sure what we'll find," Erica answered frankly. "But ancient lore claims that only those with the bloodline of the first dynasty, the three sovereigns, can use the keys to enter the mausoleums. Almost all of the ancient birth and burial records were destroyed by Shi Huangdi, but one thing all Chinese believe is that there was an age of legendary immortals who accomplished fantastic things with the help of celestial beings."

Lakesh nodded in agreement. "Two thousand or more years before the birth of Christ, Chinese scholars reported sightings of *sui sing,* luminous globes that monitored the activities of the emperors."

Grant looked up, eyeing the sky apprehensively. The rain had all but ceased, but the sky was still overcast, covered by leaden clouds. He glanced behind him, looking at the countryside cut through by the Yangtze, the details lost in the blowing rain, and to the west and south, where the looming mountains bulked dark and grim. The Wuxia Gorge itself was like a giant water-filled crack through the center of the world. A movement at the mouth of the strait caught his eye, and he squinted at the distant shape of what appeared to be a wide, flat fan boat, but the rain intervened before he could discern any details.

Speculatively, he said, "If Enlil is behind all of this, why couldn't he have already picked up Wei Qiang, Musgrave, a squad of soldiers and flown them right to the temple…and they've been waiting to spring an ambush on us since yesterday?"

Flatly, Erica said, "You do not understand Enlil at all."

"And you do?" Brigid snapped, nettled by the undercurrent of superiority in the woman's voice.

"When he was in the guise of Sam," she said matter-of-factly, "we shared a dream of a new Earth. You couldn't comprehend it."

"I think we could," Lakesh retorted acidly. "He called it the Great Plan. His objective was to control all of humanity by turning everyone into extensions of himself. We put the brakes on it."

"Yeah," Kane interjected. "It was one of the high points of my life, if you must know."

Erica was silent for a long moment. "You're sure of that?"

Kane nodded, moving around her and continuing the climb. "More than anything."

Erica and Brigid walked side by side.

"Why are you so certain that Enlil won't jump us and just take the ring?" the former archivist asked.

"Because Enlil is testing Wei Qiang to determine if he is worthy of again serving as his viceroy."

"Supposition," Brigid snapped, tension and the physical exertion of the climb making her testy.

Erica didn't answer.

"You still love him." Brigid's tone was full of loathing.

Erica came to halt. "If I do, it's not a love you could possibly understand."

"I wouldn't want to," Brigid retorted. "My sleep is disturbed enough already without new disgusting thoughts floating around in my head."

"You *bitch!*" Erica whirled, her violet eye blazing, and she slapped Brigid across the right side of her face with furious strength.

Brigid staggered and caught herself just as Erica heeled sharply around to strike her again, cloak swirling about her. Brigid shunted Erica's blow aside and pounded a left hook into her midriff. The black-haired woman jackknifed at the waist and fell away toward the jetty two hundred feet below.

Chapter 26

Erica's cloak saved her. Brigid snatched its wide hem, and for a heart-stopping instant she held the tall woman suspended over the abyss, the toes of her boots barely making contact with the crumbling edge of a riser. For a long moment, as she held Erica over the brink, she stared into her wide eye. There was no fear there and the woman uttered no outcry.

Brigid couldn't even guess at the nature of the wild thoughts possessing her. Then she pulled Erica in, yanking her upward. She fell against her, then flung herself swiftly away and flattened against the rock wall, arms wide against the granite. Erica's face was chalk-white.

"Why didn't you let me fall?" she husked out.

"Don't believe for a second that I didn't think about it," Brigid shot back.

Erica massaged her stomach and grimaced. "I apologize for slapping you."

"As you should," Brigid replied, rubbing the side of her face. After a few seconds of silent glaring, she sighed. "We're both a little stressed out."

Erica smiled bitterly and touched her eye patch. "A little."

"Hey, you two!" Kane called down. "You expect us to carry you or what?"

Brigid glanced up to see an irritated Kane a score of yards above them. Neither he, Lakesh nor Grant had witnessed the scene between her and Erica. "We're taking a little breather," she shouted up. "Go on up without us."

"That's not going to happen," Kane countered. "You've got the food."

Erica and Brigid both shook their heads in weary exasperation at the same time and resumed the climb. The stairway led into a short tunnel under a retaining wall. They made their way up the steep slant, boots slipping on the wet stones. The stairs climbed through the passage and onto a rock-strewn plateau. The path widened into a miniature walled plaza, a flagstone path winding among the colorful pavilions. The five people followed the path toward the pagoda, moving in single file. There was the smell of wet vegetation in the air, and the faintest whiff of wood smoke.

The pavilions, arched bridges and red gates were like half-remembered dreams of imperial China, from a time of armored warriors, feudal castles, lords and ladies of the courts. The sound of bells in the air was constant. Thousands of them hung from the edges of the pagoda's tiled roof, clung to spires and girded the golden dome. They chimed with each passing breeze.

As they drew closer to the pagoda, Lakesh commented, "Chinese temple courtyards were built with traditional concepts of the five elements that were believed to constitute the universe and the eight diagrams of divination in mind. The underlying concepts of yin and yang, harmony and balance, and the *feng shui* principles of geomancy dominate all architectural activity—hence the preference for concentric or symmetrical construction."

"Yeah, I remember you talking about all that geomancy stuff from the Cambodian op," Grant said. "I thought I'd forgotten most of it."

Lakesh smiled. "You'd be surprised at the volume of information the mind can retain, friend Grant."

"Not really," he said darkly.

The arched entranceway did not have doors, so they strode in. The interior of the pagoda was cool, cavernously hollow and dim. The diluted late-afternoon sunlight slanted in from high openings, but did not illuminate much beyond where the shafts fell. Moving quietly, the five people walked through a huge audience hall with ancient frescoes on the walls, mosaic tiles on the floor and massive serpentine columns supporting the ceiling. Dead leaves were piled in corners like the nests of wild animals. Here and there the walls showed blackened soot streaks from cooking fires.

Two huge pillars stretched up to the ceiling. Gilded and jeweled carvings of ferocious, horn-headed demons guarded both of them. Ragged banners emblazoned with intricate calligraphy hung from the high crossbar, their colors faded. Between the columns, a broken prayer wheel lay amid a smashed row of stone tiger-dogs and a tipped-over statue of Buddha. To reach the opposite doorway, they had to pass between the pillars and wend their way through the wreckage.

Erica tilted her head up, gazing at the banners. "The Pillars of Heaven?" she murmured.

"I don't think anybody has been here in a while," Brigid said, unconsciously lowering her voice. "It almost looks like the place has been deliberately defiled."

"Who would do that?" Kane inquired, eyes darting from shadow to shadow.

"Perhaps someone who is protesting heaven," Lakesh whispered.

Then six dark figures lunged at them through the gloom. Kane sprang back and flexed his wrist tendons. The Sin Eater seemed to appear out of nowhere, but the rushing figures paid no attention to it. With a grunt of surprise, Grant unholstered his own pistol.

Their attackers were very short, scarcely more than four feet tall, squat and bowlegged, with sallow yellow skin and slitted eyes in their ugly, pushed-in bulldog faces. Matted, coarse black hair was knotted at the backs of their heads. They wore only red-dyed leather loincloths, and bizarre tattoos writhed over their ropy limbs and torsos.

Although small in stature, their arms rippled with knotted sinew and stringy muscle tissue. The dwarves snarled and hissed as they attacked, armed only with slender rods of ebony or some smooth black wood about two feet long, knobbed at both ends. The round balls gleamed with jade inlays.

"The Ba!" Erica shrilled in astonishment. "Have to be!"

"Anybody speak their language?" Grant demanded as the dwarves formed a circle around them. They spun the rods around above their heads in hazy, humming circles. The five people moved back to back, all of them drawing their weapons.

"I don't think there *is* a Ba language," Lakesh said, voice tight with tension. "Perhaps a local or tribal dialect, but they haven't spoken yet."

Neither Kane nor Grant wanted to shoot the stunted people, since they and their friends were the trespassers. The two men had killed enough indigenous peoples in their years as Magistrates and preferred now to find alternatives to violence if possible. However, it didn't appear as if the dwarves intended to give them another option. One of them charged forward, keening a war cry, black rod held out before him like a spear.

Grant fired first with a sound like a giant clapping his huge hands once. A 240-grain round caught the Ba in the chest and sent him reeling away to thud against one of the columns and slide down to the littered floor, leaving a smear of scarlet on the wood in his wake.

Then the dwarves were on them like rabid wolves. They were exceptionally swift and agile and very adept in the use of the rods. One laid a knob along Kane's wrist with a flickering stroke like that of a striking serpent. The black ball seemed only to graze his sleeve, but the shock of the blow numbed his arm from wrist to shoulder. He couldn't depress the trigger stud of his Sin Eater.

He snarled, "Watch it! Those things are like shocksticks!"

Even as he spoke, another rod struck Brigid's forearm, at the clump of ganglia on the inside of her elbow, and she cried out as her TP-9 fell spinning from her suddenly useless fingers. Her handgun clattered against the floor tiles, but she was not helpless. She had fought for her life many times in the past few years and been taught every trick of dirty fighting known by Grant and Kane. She kicked a dwarf in the groin and, as he reflexively bent to clutch at his crotch, she brought a knee up into his throat. He went down, gagging and clawing at his neck.

At the same time, Grant squeezed off another shot, the round catching one of the stunted creatures in the right knee. The dwarf's high-pitched scream rose toward the ceiling and he dropped to the floor, plucking at his maimed leg. If he didn't die from blood loss or shock, Grant felt certain he would be crippled.

As he bent to snatch up Brigid's autopistol, an ebony knob slammed against his temple with agonizing force, sending crimson flares of pain lancing through his skull and down into his neck. He was only dimly aware of falling, fighting to stay conscious.

Lakesh cried out in pained anger as a rod struck the barrel of his Colt, and a numbing shock was transmitted through the steel, into his hand, streaking up his arm to the shoulder socket. The pistol dropped from his nerveless fingers. "Those aren't just pieces of wood!"

"No," Erica blurted in a voice breathless with fear. "They're the keys to the mausoleum!"

Kane opened his mouth to voice a question, but it

turned to a hoarse cry as scalding agony lanced through his left leg from the back of his knee to his thigh. The muscles felt like they were seizing, the veins injected with molten lead. His leg buckled and he went down, barely able to catch himself on his left hand, his paralyzed right arm hanging at his side like a slab of frozen beef.

Erica's toylike Makarov cracked like the snapping of twigs, and two of the half-naked little men flailed backward, slapping at themselves. A black baton clattered to the tiles and rolled across the floor. Brigid stretched out an arm to grab it, but she caught a blur of movement from behind her. She twisted aside, taking the impact of a knob on her right hip. Pain shivered through her, but if the rod had struck squarely where it had been aimed, the impact could have cracked her spine.

Still, she reeled clumsily, overwhelmed by the sudden, stunning pain. She stumbled against Erica, who caught her and kept her from falling, but she was also prevented from shooting again.

Lakesh snatched the length of wood up, briefly examined it and swung it at a dwarf who had crept too close, smacking the hinge of his jaw with a knobbed tip. Although the blow landed solidly, Lakesh was surprised at the force with which the little man's head was jerked around.

The whole lower portion of his face skewed sidewise, the point of his chin skidding around and taking up position beneath his right earlobe. His teeth spewed from his mouth like a handful of corn mixed in with a torrent of blood. Life went out of his eyes with suddenness of a candle flame being extinguished.

"The thing transmits some sort of electromagnetic jolt on contact!" Lakesh exclaimed wonderingly. "Repeated hits are probably fatal."

"You think?" Grant bit out, shambling erect, kneading the side of his head. Reaching down, he secured a grip on the collar of Kane's coat and hauled him upright.

They heard the slapping of feet and more of the dwarves loped out of the murk, but they were armed with makeshift knives and clubs rather than the black batons. Kane clumsily drew his combat knife with his left hand, and Brigid fumbled with her Copperhead, holding it with one hand. The dwarves made a sudden, concerted rush, trying to bowl them over through numbers and momentum.

The five outlanders met the charge with knife, bullets, feet and fists. Within seconds, four little gnarled corpses lay on the floor, crimsoning the tiles.

The surviving dwarves drew back, black eyes glinting with malignant fires. They shuffled in a circle around the foreign interlopers, poised for another charge.

Lakesh, gasping as if he were learning the art of respiration all over again, due to a knobbed baton brushing his solar plexus, said, "I'm going to try something."

"I wish you would," Brigid said between clenched teeth.

"And do it fucking fast," Kane urged. Sensation was returning slowly to his arm and leg but both limbs felt distant, as if they were separated by miles from the rest of his body.

Reaching into the pocket of his field jacket, Lakesh extended his left hand, fist clenched tightly. The dwarves eyed it apprehensively, but did not retreat.

"Jun Zhu!" Lakesh suddenly shouted.

The Ba people jumped at the words, eyes widening in surprise for a second, then slitting again in suspicion and smoldering hatred. Like a conjurer performing a trick, Lakesh opened his hand with a flourish. The dim light gleamed on the nine Hydra heads of the ring he held between thumb and forefinger.

"Jun Zhu!" he announced again. *"Jun Zhu,* you ugly little warts."

The dwarves froze in place, staring intently at the ring. Then a hurried, whispered babble passed among them and they withdrew as silently as wraiths, leaving their dead and wounded behind.

Kane squinted into the gloom after them. "Interesting. *'Jun Zhu'* were the words Wei Qiang's soldiers were yelling."

Lakesh nodded. "It means 'true monarch.' That, in conjunction with showing the Ba people the ring, made them think we are acting in the true monarch's interests."

Brigid eyed the rod in Lakesh's hand and glanced over at Erica. "You say those sticks are keys to the mausoleum?"

"Yes," she answered, stepping over to pick up another baton that lay on the floor. "They look like the pictures I saw in the scrolls kept in the pyramid."

"And since the Ba people are associated with the role of gatekeepers," Lakesh put in, "the connection seems very obvious now."

Grant scowled, grimaced and rolled his shoulders impatiently. "Can we get the hell out of here and talk more about it outside?"

"I think that's a very good idea," Erica agreed, bending to pick up another of the rods. "I suggest we do it on our way to the Tomb of the Three Sovereigns."

Chapter 27

The trail cutting over the top of the plateau was difficult. Mist clung to the rocky escarpments, and it began to rain again. The downpour pounded them for several miserable minutes, then it ended. A long streak of golden sunshine shot through the rolling clouds, but Kane estimated they had less than an hour of full daylight remaining.

The paralyzing effect of the batons had worn off, although Grant occasionally winced and rubbed the side of his head. The analgesics he washed down with a swallow of bottled water hadn't alleviated the pain, only reduced it to a tolerable level.

Tugging back the hood of her cloak, Erica held up four black rods she had retrieved from the pagoda, clicking the knobbed ends together, producing tiny sparks.

Sounding enthralled, Lakesh declared, "I'm guessing that some kind of electronics are built into these things. Microcircuitry and tiny power packs, maybe like the CEM—chargeable energy modules—that we know the Annunaki employ."

"Yeah, but what good are they?" Grant demanded, still tenderly touching the side of his head. "Why would an emperor build a mausoleum and then make keys so people can get in and loot the place or snatch his body?"

Brigid smiled wanly. "You're forgetting that if Huang-ti, Shi Huangdi and Wei Qiang are all the same man, there are no bodies in there...but there's probably a lot of valuables, the least of which is the Armor of Immortality."

"Very true," Erica agreed. "Allegedly, the tomb of the Yellow Emperor was the most elaborate in all of Chinese history. To make it difficult for thieves, a series of traps were designed and installed. Only those taken into the confidence of the emperor's family would know the proper path to follow."

Grant snorted. "It still seems illogical to me."

"If you were a virtually immortal man," Lakesh said, "and wanted access to treasures in your tomb, wouldn't you want to safeguard them?"

After a thoughtful few seconds, Grant said, "I probably wouldn't leave them in places that would attract thieves."

"Actually," Brigid said, "the psychological effect of using a crypt or mausoleum as a vault was probably a strong deterrent against superstitious natives with thieving inclinations."

For the next mile, the path was open and clear. As the sun began to set, the air became cooler and the terrain rockier. Ruins like vague dreams of the ancient past rose from sandstone cliffs that thrust up like the prows of wrecked ships.

The five outlanders strode through a narrow ravine among immense outcroppings of dun-colored stone that were deeply scored and eroded by exposure to the elements. Grant and Kane scanned the perpendicular walls of the gorge. They blinked up at the strange statues cut into the cliffs. They were built to fantastic designs, colossal armored men with grim visages staring down forebodingly, calculated to frighten any who dared to intrude this far.

The path turned to the left, and they passed a shrine holding old Buddhist relics, bones both human and animal and a grinning statue of a devil with a horned head and protruding tongue. Kane felt the back of his neck flush cold.

The path turned sharply to the left and opened up on a flat, swept-clean expanse of ground. All of them came to a halt. They stood, the five of them, staring silently at the building squatting in the center of the barren plain. There was an alien quality about the structure, as if they somehow knew alien hands had raised it, although not even Brigid could have put into words exactly why she felt that way.

Kane drew in his breath and absently chewed on the inside of his cheek, studying the structure intently. It wasn't anything like he expected. Instead of an elaborate pagoda, the building was low, flat roofed and squat and solid, like a somewhat squashed, debilitated mountain rising up out of the ground. It reminded him of the structures he had seen in the underground kingdom of Agartha a few years before.

It did not look like a burial place, but more like a fortress or even a prison, all sharp angles and corners.

The fitted blocks that composed its facade resembled a porous, volcanic stone, glossy black with pitted surfaces.

As they continued to stare at the mausoleum, Kane's sense of dread and awe grew. He forced a half smile to his lips and inhaled deeply through his nostrils. "Smell that?"

"Smell what?" Grant asked, alarmed.

"The lovely aroma of a trap," Kane replied. He glanced at Erica. "This is the place, right?"

She gave him a look of scorn. "What do you think, Einstein?"

Kane affected not have heard her. He stepped forward. "Let's go. Everybody keep their eyes open." He cast Erica a glance. "Feel free to reject half that advice."

The nearer they came to the mausoleum, the vaster it became. At first sight, its dimensions hadn't been impressive, but the closer they moved toward it, the larger it seemed. There were no guards to be seen, nothing that could be interpreted as an alarm system. Kane felt fear rising in him, but he tamped it down, throttling it.

They halted and stared silently at the fifteen-foot-high doors. They appeared to be made of thick slabs of teak. Neither one bore a knob, a latch, a handle or even a sign of a hinge, but both portals were perforated with perfectly round holes, arranged in circles.

"Erica, those holes look to be about the same size as the keys you took from the Ba," Brigid said in an unsteady voice.

Stepping closer to the doors, she said quietly, "I was thinking the exact same thing."

Swiftly, she began inserting the knobbed ends of the

rods into the holes on the right-hand door. All four of them fit perfectly, but nothing happened. Erica stood and glared in baffled anger at the batons protruding from the perforations.

"Aren't keys supposed to be turned?" Kane ventured.

Erica first shot him a look of contempt, then her brow furrowed. She took the end knobs of the rods and twisted them counterclockwise. A faint electronic chirp and brief flashes from the jade inlays accompanied each turning. "Something's happening anyway," Erica announced.

"Whatever it is," Grant opined dourly, "I'm positive it's not a common feature of ancient Chinese tombs."

A grinding rumble slowly built, and then was overlaid by a series of squeaks, creaks and hisses. Long disused gears, pulleys and hydraulics slowly moved. The left-hand door ponderously began to slide upward. It slid into a baffled slot and caught with a loud click. The black mouth of the portal yawned opened, leading into the throat of a long passage. No one moved or spoke for what felt like a very long time.

Finally, in a subdued, almost apologetic voice, Lakesh said, "The longer we stand around out here, the more our imaginations will run away with us. If we're going in, we'd better do it while I have still have some nerve left."

Grant glanced over at Kane, then made a sweeping, grand gesture with his arm. "After you, point man."

Kane cast him a sour, reproachful glance, then stepped over the threshold. Nothing happened. He waited, breathing shallowly through his nose, aware of the dead, stale air and musty smell of long-dead things. He stepped farther into the passageway and saw a heap of bones in his path. It was the skeleton of an adult, very, very old, desiccated and broken.

The crushed skull was turned to face a niche cut into the wall and within it was a smaller version of the stone colossi they had passed in the ravine. The head of the statue was fashioned after the casques of armored Chinese warriors. Long arms ended in cruel curved swords crossed over its chest. Ten feet from toe to crown, the bronze giant towered. It looked like a mailed soldier out of a nightmare past, and its proximity to the smashed skeleton made Kane feel distinctly uneasy.

He unleathered his Sin Eater and cautiously eased past the statue, then called for his companions.

"Do you think we should take the keys out of the door?" Brigid asked.

Kane considered the question for a few seconds then said, "Bring them. They could come in handy later."

"For what?" Erica wanted to know.

"Just do it," he snapped tersely.

When Grant, Brigid, Lakesh and Erica had joined him, he began striding down the passageway, alert for any strange sound, but the sights were strange enough. Every few yards they passed small niches inset into the walls containing grotesque effigies of potbellied demons with monstrous leers and scowls.

The passage went straight, following a direct line toward a dim rectangle of light. Then the corridor took

a sharp turn to the left. Now that they were actually
within the mausoleum, Kane's dread and awe ebbed. As
usual while in a potential killzone, he walked heel to toe,
feeling fully alert, poised and calm. Every sense was
honed to razor keenness, his nerves steady, his heart rate
normal. He felt keyed up to his maximum potential,
totally in command of his reactions.

Around them, in wall niches, they saw more of the
giant brass soldier statues. When the five people reached
an archway, Kane gestured for everyone to pause. The
skin prickled at the back of his neck, and he felt a cool
draft of air against his face. From his war bag he
removed a magazine and thumbed out a 9 mm round.
He tossed it through the door and heard it clink and
clatter on the floor.

Almost instantly, huge swinging blades, like meat
cleavers welded to the ends of pendulum arms, swung
down from the shadowy ceiling, up from grooved slots
in the floor and the walls. There were at least six of them
whirling past, slashing at empty air. Erica murmured
something indistinct and shrank against Lakesh.

Grant, Brigid and Kane stood shoulder to shoulder
in the archway, observing the pendulums.

"With apologies to Edgar Allan Poe," Brigid
remarked softly.

Neither Kane nor Grant knew what she meant, but
Lakesh chuckled appreciatively. By now Kane was accustomed to Brigid's often cryptic comments, which
always seemed to center on dead zones in his education.

The three people scrutinized the swinging blades,

calculating the arc and torque of the movements, timing them. Brigid memorized the rhythm of the strokes and announced, "Got it."

"Got what?" Grant asked.

"How to get through them. It's a trap, but only for interlopers who can't do the calculations."

"And you can?" Erica challenged.

Brigid threw her wintry, over-the-shoulder smile, tensed her body, then sprang from the archway into the midst of the blades as they went hissing past. She stood between two of them and said, "I'll see if I can find some controls on the other side."

"Yeah," Kane said sourly, "if you don't get turned into sushi first."

"Wrong country and wrong species, Kane," Brigid shot back.

She maneuvered lithely between, around and under the pendulums. Although her movements were graceful, the undertaking was risky in the extreme. Because of the heavy weight of the supporting armatures, she seriously doubted her shadow suit would turn the edge of the blades if they struck full. At best, she would suffer broken bones, at worst, instant amputation.

Counting under her breath, Brigid slid among the flying scythes, stopping, ducking, twisting and stepping. Clammy sweat sprang out on her forehead. Although the journey took less than a full minute, it seemed like a chain of interlocked eternities before she stood on safe ground again, within the archway opposite.

For a long moment she stood breathing deeply,

waiting until her stomach no longer jumped in adrena-line-fueled spasms.

"Are you all right, dearest Brigid?" Lakesh's voice was heavy with apprehension.

"Why wouldn't I be?" she asked sardonically, looking around. "I always feel relaxed after a workout like that."

Walls of jade paneling met her eyes. The floor was tiled with alternating squares of green jade and yellow gold, and multicolored carpets were scattered about on it. From a brass tripod rose a wavering spiral of pale blue light. She saw nothing that looked like a lever on the walls, then her gaze was drawn back to the fluttering finger of light, remembering the tales of Huang-ti's miraculous tripods. She stepped over to it and realized the radiance was not flame or even an electric lamp. The light shone from a convex lens of a glassy substance, like a cloudy mirror.

On impulse she passed her hand over it and heard clicks and clacks from the room of blades. Turning her head, she saw the pendulum arms rising up to the ceiling, sinking into the floor and withdrawing into the floor. "I think I found the controls," she called.

"You *think* you have?" Kane retorted skeptically.

"Best I can do," she replied breezily.

When her companions crossed through the room, they followed the passageway again, which ran straight and unobstructed for a hundred yards. They stopped at another archway that opened into an area of flat, un-decorated flooring. Kane waved everyone back. He crouched, studying the room. Grant unsheathed his long combat knife and stretched his arm out into the room, prodding the floor with the tip. It made solid contact with a semimusical chime.

"What do you think?" he asked.

Kane shrugged. "You need to ask? I think the same thing you do."

He took out another bullet and with a thumb, flipped it into the room. It struck the floor and rolled almost to the center. He tossed another and another with nothing happening in reaction. When five cartridges lay scattered at various points on the floor, Erica said impatiently, "If that room is a trap, the mechanism must have malfunctioned after all these years."

Kane was on the verge of reluctantly agreeing with her. "One more, let's make it an even half dozen."

He threw the round across the room, toward the opposite archway. It fell short by a few feet and when it struck the floor a tiny flash was followed by the splitting of the entire floor down the middle in a precise line. The two halves of the floor slid quickly back into hidden slots at the base of the wall.

Kane, Grant and Brigid leaned forward to look down through the opening so as to follow the fall of the bullets. A shudder shook Kane's shoulders as he gazed down at the tips of a forest of sword blades, twenty feet below. The bullets fell among them, bouncing from the splintered rib cage of a cadaver sprawled on the knives. The two parts of the floor slammed back together with a sound like two wooden blocks colliding.

"Pretty damned diabolical," Lakesh said dourly. "There are probably pressure-sensitive sensors in the floor. The trap isn't sprung until the hapless intruder has almost made it across. Right at the moment of greatest relief, the ground drops out of from under them. Literally."

Kane's eyes darted back and forth, around the room, studying the corners. "If these traps were made only to snare the unwary, then it stands to reason there's a way through here."

Brigid nodded absently as she looked around herself, then she chuckled. "I think I've found it."

"You *think* you have?" Grant challenged.

Brigid moved into the room. "Best I can do."

She paused and glanced back at her companions. "You coming?"

Chapter 28

Brigid Baptiste's solution to the rigged room was embarrassingly straightforward and simple: to get across it without tripping the floor trap, she sidled along the wall to the opposite door. Since the tomb's traps were designed to kill the unwary, she hypothesized that people who actually were permitted entrance knew how to bypass the various deadfalls in the simplest and swiftest way possible.

Her four companions reluctantly mimicked her actions and when they were safely through, they moved on, entering a rotunda where three corridors met. Only one showed a glimmer of light, shining up from a tripod, and Kane led the way down it. The passageway dead-ended at an ornate, gold-leafed double door. Within wall niches to either side stood the statues of warriors, silent sentinels made of brass.

Kane and Grant eyed the door carefully, examining it for trip wires or pressure-sensitive floor plates. When they found nothing of the sort, Kane beckoned Erica forward.

"Do you want the honors this time?" he asked. "I have a feeling we've reached the end of the line."

She frowned at him. "Why do you say that?"

"No reason. Just one of my feelings. You can pass on it, but then you don't get first dibs on whatever we find inside."

Erica nibbled her underlip, thinking it over. Then, taking a deep breath, she placed her hands on the doors and pushed them. They opened smoothly on invisible hinges. She took a step forward and the four outlanders followed her—three thousand or more years back in time.

They entered a great, high-ceilinged chamber and came to a halt, staring around wide-eyed. The huge room was a museum of Oriental artifacts; everything looked as if it had been perfectly preserved from the days of the Yellow Emperor. The man may have been a ruthless tyrant, but even Grant and Kane had to grudgingly concede Huang-ti's taste in art and furnishings had been impeccable.

Taoist and Buddhist scrolls, sculptures large and small adorned the walls. There were delicately carved ivory screens, tiger skins, polished spears and swords, intricately woven patterns of colorful silk, jade masks, plaques and even dishes. Demons, dragons and monsters of all shapes menaced any intruders from the corners.

But it was the jade man seated on a lacquered black bamboo throne in the center of the room that caught and held their attention. Brigid's breath caught in her throat at the first sight of him, mistaking the figure at first for a mummy, then a statue. Then she realized it wasn't a mummy or a statue of man, but a breathtaking piece of art crafted almost entirely of jade, inlaid everywhere with delicate gold filigrees.

Every detail, from the noble facial features to the headpiece, had been molded with an obsession for lifelike rendering. Its perfectly proportioned forearms lay on the arms of the throne. The fingers were constructed of little half cylinders of the green mineral, the halves held together by a delicate webwork of gold wire. The expressionless face bore a disquieting resemblance to Wei Qiang's masklike features.

"Kai Bu Xiu," Erica husked out in a hoarse whisper.

"My sentiments exactly," Lakesh murmured excitedly, moving toward it. Erica followed swiftly at his heels.

At the apex of the ceiling, a cluster of spheres revolved in majestic procession around a central glowing Sun, three feet in diameter. Red, blue, green and even striped orbs glided back and forth in a dance of mathematical precision.

Tilting her head back and studying them, Brigid commented, "It's a mobile of our solar system...but there's one extra planet."

Kane eyed a small dark sphere cutting across the orbital path of Mercury on the far side of the Sun and said flatly, "Nibiru. I guess that cinches it as far as Annunaki involvement with Huang-ti is concerned."

"I didn't know there was any doubt," Lakesh commented distractedly, gingerly lifting the left hand of the jade armor and working the fingers. "Very impressive. Exquisite craftsmanship."

Erica examined the headpiece, turning it this way and that. "Impressive is a woefully inadequate word, all things considered." She thrust her hand into a small opening at the base of the skull. "I can feel circuit boards, so it's most definitely a machine."

Brigid said, "That machine in the shape of armor served as the template for a lot of superstitious practices over the centuries. Some Chinese families devoted their whole lives to accruing enough jade and gold to make crude copies of the Kai Bu Xiu in the hopes it would restore them or their loved ones to life."

Lakesh took the Hydra ring from his pocket and slipped it onto the index finger of the armor's right hand. The band fit into a round socket just above the knuckle. The fit was not tight.

"This is all so very *not* fabulous," Grant announced with undisguised sarcasm, "but without the other eight rings, that thing is just a very unfashionable and heavy suit of clothes, right? It won't function at all."

"We'll take it with us if we have to," Erica declared confidently, eye shining with a raptorial light. "Between Mohandas and I and the tech-heads you have in Cerberus, we ought to be able to figure out exactly how it works. Perhaps we can circumvent the operational protocols so we won't need the rings at all."

"I can assure you that you won't."

The cold voice spoke from somewhere behind them. They wheeled, hearts trip-hammering in their chests, Grant's and Kane's Sin Eaters questing for targets. Both weapons centered on a section of wall that had opened up, revealing a dimly lit passageway hidden by a silk tapestry. Wei Qiang, Werner Musgrave and three yellow-uniformed solders stood there, Calicos trained on Lakesh and Erica. The man and woman froze in mid-movement, staring at the intruders.

For a long moment, the tableau held, with no one speaking. Then Wei Qiang inquired in a flat voice, "Didn't any of you think I would have secret ways into my own mausoleum?"

"It occurred to me," Kane admitted. "I'd been meaning to raise the topic at our next strategy session, but everybody was so pumped about finding old Jade Jaws here—"

"Shut up, Kane," Musgrave snapped, jabbing the barrel of his subgun in his direction. The wooden box in which Erica had kept the rings was tucked under one arm. "You're not funny. Lower your weapons."

Slowly, Grant and Kane did so, but they did not holster them.

"A clever trick," Lakesh said sourly. "I really should have seen it coming."

"Yes," Wei Qiang drawled. "That you should. It looks like a very definite checkmate to me, Dr. Singh."

The tall Chinese crossed the room, his eyes fixed on the armor. Two of his soldiers accompanied him, making unmistakable gestures with their subguns that Lakesh and Erica should back away. Lakesh did so, but Erica stood her ground, face a tight mask of hatred.

Wei Qiang waggled his gold nail protector in her direction. "You still have one eye, Tui Chui Jian. Quite the lovely one, too."

Lips working as if she wanted to spit on him, Erica stepped back to stand beside Lakesh.

Clearing her throat, Brigid asked, "Why do you care, Wei Qiang?"

The man's slanted eyes flickered in brief, annoyed puzzlement. "What do you mean, woman?"

Brigid waved to the suit of jade-and-gold armor. "You've already lived about five thousand years. What can you do with more? What could you possibly accomplish with another thousand years or even a hundred?"

Qiang lovingly caressed the green likeness of his face and murmured, "Such a handsome, dashing prince."

Fixing his penetrating gaze on Brigid, he stated, "I had immortality, yes...but not youth. That was stripped from me over three thousand years ago."

"Why?" Kane asked. He surreptitiously watched as Werner Musgrave gazed around the chamber, doing a very poor job of concealing his awe and avarice.

In a dreamy voice, as if he were peering into the past, Wei Qiang said, "I displeased Changhuan. I did not do his bidding. I defied him, I disobeyed him."

"What motivated you to do that?" Lakesh inquired in a studiedly mild, inoffensive tone.

Wei Qiang turned toward him, showing the edges of his teeth in a savage grin. "Because I conquered the people of this land. I bound them to my will. I made them my slaves. I knew the guardian dragon had concealed wisdom vaults all over the world, so I decided to seek them out and claim them for myself, and not be content for the few boons he doled out when it served his purposes.

"When I stood upon the brink of power beyond limit,

Changhuan punished me. He denied me the Nine Rings of Eternal Return and the Kai Bu Xiu. He banished me because I dared to challenge his authority, to build my own empire instead of playing the puppet."

"Enlil still doesn't like lowly humans challenging him," Grant commented.

"Enlil?" Wei Qiang echoed, a hint of surprise in his voice. "He was not my guardian dragon."

"It was Enki," Musgrave interjected in a ghostly whisper. "Enki was Changhuan."

Realization rushed through Kane like a flow of cold water circulating through his veins. "I get it now...you were a pawn in the conflict between Enlil and Enki."

Wei Qiang nodded and said simply, "Yes."

There was no need for him to elaborate. They were all familiar with the story. Nearly five hundred thousand years before, Enlil, who commanded lordship over Earth, wanted humankind to be kept in as primitive a state as possible. The opposing group, led by his half brother, Enki, disagreed with this stance.

The Annunaki had set out to redesign the hominid inhabitants of Earth into a race of slave labor that would grow more intelligent and efficient with each successive generation. After several thousand years, the slaves became not only more intelligent and efficient, but also rebellious and intractable.

The ruling council of the Annunaki decreed that intermediaries were needed between themselves and the masses of humanity. A hierarchy was clearly defined, and for many millennia the Annunaki oversaw the welfare and fate of humankind. All the while, they remained apart from the people, approachable only by the high priests and kings on specified dates, communicating only with their plenipotentiaries.

A fierce rivalry arose between opposing factions of the Annunaki for the hearts and minds of people, partly because they had come to depend increasingly on human kings and their armies to achieve their ends. When this situation became too unwieldy, the Annunaki chose to create a new dynasty of rulers, known as demigods or god-kings, because of their exalted bloodlines.

As a bridge between themselves, a pantheon of gods and humankind, they introduced the concept of the god-king on Earth. They appointed human rulers who would assure humankind's service to the deities and channel their teachings and laws to the people.

Sumerian texts described how although the Annunaki retained lordship over the lands and humankind was viewed as little more than a tenant farmer, humanity grew arrogant. Fearing a unified human race, both in culture and purpose, the Annunaki adopted the imperial policy of divide and rule. For while humankind reached higher cultural levels and the populations expanded, the Annunaki themselves fell into decline.

The Annunaki ruler returned to Nibiru after arranging a division of powers and territories on Earth between his feuding sons, Enlil and Enki. Civilizations such as Egypt, Sumer and the Rama Empire were created by the two half brothers. Wars were fought by the extended families of Enki and Enlil, and the nations changed hands back and forth through different conflicts.

"Enki was grooming you to be his pocket god-king," Brigid said, "but he wanted you to be a civilizing influence, not a conquering one."

Wei Qiang smiled. "That tactic took too long. Five thousand years ago, the people of China were barbarians and peasants, immune to reason. They equated kindness with weakness. A swifter, more decisive plan had to be put into place to save time."

"What did you care about time?" Grant demanded. "Weren't you practically immortal?"

The smile fled from Qiang's face. "Only to a point. The maximum life span the Kai Bu Xiu can bestow is perhaps thirty thousand years, give or take, but it's youthfulness that matters, vitality...which I have not enjoyed in many centuries."

"And that is what the reborn Enlil has offered you," Erica said. She did not ask a question; she made a statement.

Wei Qiang inclined his head toward Musgrave. "So his agent has said, if I fulfill a few tasks."

Anger sent a sudden flush of heat to the back of Kane's neck and caused the blood to pound in his temples. "The consortium is working for the overlords?"

Musgrave sneered. "We're strictly acting as intermediaries in this situation, Kane. Or intermediaries of intermediaries, to be precise."

"Which I'm sure all millennialists always endeavor to be," Brigid put in sardonically.

Musgrave affected not to have heard the remark. "We're aware of the fall of the baronies, but not the specifics. A representative of the entity that calls himself overlord Enlil sought us out and proposed we arrange the displacement of Erica van Sloan from the Xian pyramid."

"Why didn't he do it himself?" Erica asked. "Is he afraid to face me?"

Musgrave made a scoffing noise. "Hardly. Enlil is too concerned with other matters to waste his attention and resources on such a trifling irritant as you. However, he did suggest we seek out Wei Qiang because at one time, the pyramid had been his home."

Qiang shrugged negligently. "More like a summer home and storage unit."

"The consortium supplied Wei Qiang with everything he needed," Musgrave continued. "It put quite a strain on our resources, but we feel the investment is worth the dividends."

Grant eyed Wei Qiang critically. "And in exchange for the rings and your youth, Enlil expects you to act as his puppet, like you did for Enki thousands of years ago. He wants you to lay claim to China and fight off any incursions from the other overlords."

"He has not expressed such a desire to me," Wei Qiang said, returning his gaze to the suit of jade armor. "But I imagine the arrangement he has in mind is something like that."

"So the mighty Huang-ti, the Yellow Emperor, is happy to serve as a slave of an inhuman monster?" Lakesh snapped. "You thought you would be ruler of a world empire once, and Enki ended that dream. Why do you think it would be in his half brother's interest to return you to your youth and revive all of that overweening ambition?"

Musgrave shifted position and snapped, "Be quiet."

"Why should we?" Erica asked, drawing herself up haughtily. "Could it be that the Millennial Consortium doesn't want Wei Qiang to know that the overlords are the resurrection of a monstrous evil and that Enlil's plan for him is to act as his chief human foreman of a slave and cannon fodder farm? He'll act as the straw boss, but he'll still be a slave. The only difference is that Wei Qiang will be an *immortal* slave."

Picking up on Erica's thread, Lakesh said calmly, "And of course, Mr. Musgrave here secretly conspired with Enlil to enslave you…didn't you, Mr. Musgrave?"

For a long moment, Wei Qiang stood motionless, face showing no emotion. Then he made a low, growling noise deep in his throat and he turned toward Werner Musgrave. The man cringed from the unreasoning fury that blazed from Qiang's eyes, the mad rage of a monarch who suddenly realized he had been duped into handing over his kingdom to an enemy.

Chapter 29

Wei Qiang slowly advanced on Werner Musgrave. In a low-pitched tone, made even more frightening by its lack of inflection, he said, "I'll be slave to neither god, demon or man. Not even for immortality."

Musgrave backed toward the door, swinging his Calico in short arcs to cover the outlanders and the soldiers. The yellow-uniformed men followed his movements with grim eyes and steady gun barrels. He said petulantly, "It was your vanity that caused Enki to turn against you all those centuries ago, Wei Qiang. Don't make the same stupid mistake again with Enlil."

Wei Qiang extended a hand. "Give me the rings."

Musgrave acted as if he hadn't heard, still stepping back toward the doorway. "Tell your men to drop their guns, and then we can talk about this like reasonable, pragmatic men."

Wei Qiang did not lower his hand. "The rings. Do not leave this room with them, Musgrave...if you wish to live."

"You're useful to Enlil, to the consortium," Musgrave said, a wheedling note entering his voice. "We can forge a great alliance...our combined power will bring us all the wealth and power we ever dreamed of."

"As a slave?" Brigid interjected. "The slave of Enki turned against the Annunaki once before. Why would Enlil trust him again? Once Wei Qiang has served his purposes, establishing a beachhead here in China, he'll be discarded. All Enlil really wanted was for Erica, the Dragon Mother, to be displaced from Xian. That's been accomplished."

"Yes," Erica chimed in, her tone brittle with undisguised mockery. "Enlil gave you the job as his eviction agent. Rather a steep career decline for the Yellow Emperor, don't you think?"

Picking up on the thread of playing to Wei Qiang's wounded vanity, Lakesh put in, "You served as a figurehead for brigands to rally around, but you know damned well Enlil won't allow you to take up residence in the pyramid again. He wants it and the Heart of the World only for himself."

Wei Qiang's face lost its masklike placidity and twisted into a rictus of homicidal fury. He dropped his arm to his side and hissed between clenched teeth, "I have changed my mind. You may depart, Musgrave."

The man's tense, scarred face relaxed with relief, then almost instantly locked tight with suspicion. "I can take the rings?"

"If you must." Wei Qiang inclined his head a fraction of an inch. "Take them and go."

The man made a move to step over the threshold, then paused. "You're coming with me, to make sure your men don't try to kill me."

"They will not," Wei Qiang stated. "Leave, before I change my mind and order them to shoot you down where you stand."

Musgrave glanced feverishly around at the furnishings of the room, licked his lips, then with a sigh of resignation backed away into the corridor. He called, "When you've had the time to think this all over, I'm sure you'll come to the most logical decision. Self-respect and service in exchange for immortality is the kind of deal I wish was offered to me. I know I'd accept it without a second thought."

Wei Qiang's lipless mouth creased in a smile and he whispered as to himself, "Of that I am sure, consortium man."

The clank of metal on metal, the rhythmic clicking of joints suddenly came to their ears as well as a howl of terror from Musgrave. Looking down the corridor, they saw a blurred pair of towering figures striding swiftly after the millennialist. A chill crept up Kane's spine as he watched the metal colossi lumbering out of the wall niches.

"Robots," Grant murmured. "Those statues are guardian robots."

"The automata are programmed to prevent anything from leaving this vault," Wei Qiang said. "I'm gratified to see that my mechanical men still work after all this time. It was one of the few gifts from Enki that I actually enjoyed."

Brigid gazed in awed wonder at the machine-men pursuing Werner Musgrave. The man sprinted in raw panic, uttering wild cries with every step.

When he reached the rotunda, he stumbled to an unsteady halt as more of the robot warriors marched out of the corridor mouths, tramping toward the place where Musgrave stood. Bleating in wordless horror as realization came to him, Musgrave dropped the box containing the rings and sprayed the automatons with full-auto fire from the Calico. The bullets bounced off the armored torsos and heads with keening whines, little sparks flaring at the points of impact. The robots' relentless pace did not falter. They closed in around him, swords lifting and falling.

The sound of metal shearing through flesh and bone was loud and ugly, but Musgrave stopped screaming almost instantly. Brigid winced, feeling her stomach roil. Absently she noted that all of the metal warriors bore small round holes in the centers of their backs, each one surrounded by a little raised collar of engraved metal.

Wei Qiang chuckled, a raspy sound as heartwarming as old bones rattling around in a tin can. His gaze, as well as that of his troopers, was fixed on the scene in the rotunda. Kane caught Grant's eye and the two men exchanged a short, almost imperceptible nod. Kane moved with the desperate swiftness of a man who has long lived by the speed of hand and eye.

He swung his right arm in a flat backward sweep, his Sin Eater weighted forearm slamming into a soldier's neck. There was faint, mushy crunch of cartilage. Like a man who has slipped on a patch of ice, the trooper's legs flew out from under him and he crashed heavily onto his back.

Wei Qiang whirled, shouting in anger, and the other soldier wheeled, raising his Calico. Grant depressed the trigger stud of his Sin Eater and the 9 mm round smacked into the lower belly of the trooper. The man staggered backward a score of feet, bent double around an agonizing wound. By the time he collapsed, nearly at the base of the bamboo throne, he was unconscious due to the double trauma of pain and hydrostatic shock.

Wei Qiang did not expend any time ministering to his injured trooper. A long sideways leap brought him beside Erica. His left hand tangled in her hair as he wrestled her in front of him. They grappled violently for a long moment, and Lakesh quickly tried to get behind Qiang. The four knob-tipped keys Erica had removed from the door fell from beneath her cloak and rolled across the floor.

Hissing in anger, Wei Qiang snapped away the golden cone from his thumb and pressed the razor-keen edge of his nail against Erica's throat, indenting the flesh over the jugular vein. "Stop," he commanded, "or she dies."

Kane aimed his Sin Eater at his head. "And you don't think you will, too?"

"I honestly don't know," Wei Qiang replied with surprising frankness. "I suppose we'll find out together."

"There's a better way to resolve this, isn't there?" Lakesh asked. "You don't want to serve Enlil's cause, and we don't want you to serve Enlil's cause. There's a great deal of common ground right there."

"I serve no master but myself," Wei Qiang spit autocratically. "Ever and always. No creature will ever trick me into acting as its pawn and live to reap the spoils of its duplicity."

"All right, then." Lakesh spread his hands wide in a conciliatory gesture. "Why do we have be at each other's throats?"

"Because," Erica said between clenched teeth, "his goals are the same as Enlil's...he wants to set himself up as a god, as he did in the old days."

Wei Qiang's drum-tight features stretched in a death's-head grin of appreciation. "Very astute, Tui Chui Jian. But this time I'd insure that mortals like you stayed few in numbers and poor in resources. Just like Enlil and the overlords, I wouldn't make the same mistake of letting your kind multiply to where you become threats again."

"What makes you think we're going to allow you inside that jade armor and wear the Hydra rings and renew yourself so you can put your plan into motion?" Grant growled.

The sound of heavy footfalls and metallic clankings and clickings echoed from just outside the door. Two of the robots lumbered into the chamber. One of them carried the wooden box with blood-wet brass fingers. Red photoreceptors glowed like coals dug out from the furnace of hell.

"It's not up to you to allow anything, Grant," Qiang said, his voice dropping to a throaty purr. "My servants here will make sure it happens as I wish it to happen. Dr. Singh, take the box and then set it down on the lap of the Kai Bu Xiu. Do it now, unless you would prefer to watch me carve an epic Wu poem on this whore's breasts."

Swallowing hard, Lakesh crossed the room to the robot and, after a moment's hesitation, removed the box from its grasp. He returned to the Armor of Immortality and placed the box exactly where Wei Qiang instructed him. "Now what?"

"Stay there." He backed up to the bamboo throne, still holding Erica in front of him. "The rest of you...go outside."

Grant, Brigid and Kane did not move.

Wei Qiang slowly drew the scimitar curve of his thumbnail across Erica's slender throat, leaving a thread of blood in its wake. "Do it. I have no compunctions about killing this pyramid squatting, Annunaki-loving slut."

"Please do as he says," Lakesh said quietly. "If not for her, then for me."

The three people hesitated a moment longer, then turned and started for the doorway. Wei Qiang returned to the bamboo throne, shifting his grip on Erica from around her throat and waist to her arms. "Dr. Singh, take the rings out of the box and place them on the fingers of the armor," he said.

Brigid cast a glance over her shoulder at Qiang. When she saw his attention was fixed on the wooden box, she lunged forward, tucking and rolling. She came to her feet directly behind one of the automatons, an ebony rod in her hand. She jammed a knobbed end into the socket inset in the robot's back and felt a surge of satisfaction when it caught fast. She gave it a twist and the metal warrior swiveled at the waist, arms swinging

wide. The edge of one brass hand swept across her
shoulder, bowling her off her feet.

The upper body of the metal warrior continued to
spin, its right fist bashing against the head of its companion with a deafening crash of jangling metal. Shock
rooted Wei Qiang in place, and Erica fought out of his
grasp, leaving her cloak clutched in his hands. She
rushed toward the concealed portal.

Rubbing her throbbing shoulder and scooting
backward to get away from the robots, Brigid shouted
to Kane, "The other keys! Grab one and cram it in!"

Without hesitation or question, Kane did as she said,
bounding forward, scooping up a rod from the floor
and slamming the knob into the socket on the second
robot's back. He twisted and then ducked, barely
avoiding a scythelike sweep of its hand.

The two automatons turned on each other, metal-
shod limbs rising and falling, smashing against each
other. The alloyed gladiators locked in combat. They
staggered and stumbled, crashing against the walls,
knocking loose plate-sized chunks of masonry.

Grant, Kane and Brigid scrambled out of their path,
moving to a far corner. The din of the battle was almost
stunning, as brass hands wrenched and tore at steel
limbs and sword-equipped extremities slashed rents in
metal skulls and plunged through mailed thoraxes.

Sparks showered from torn relay boxes, and power
packs burst with ear-compressing concussions. Thick,
harsh smoke seethed from the giant bodies. Hissing
skeins of electricity clung to their bodies and the giant

figures stopped. They heard the muffled thump of explosions and wreaths of black oily smoke squirted from the joints in the robot's exoskeletons. The red glare of their photoreceptors died.

The two metal warriors froze, limbs locked together. For a long moment, no one in the chamber did anything but stand and stare.

Then Grant's fingers groped over the grenades clipped to his combat harness. He gripped a metal-shelled canister, detaching it from the harness, thumb flipping the priming pin away and depressing the red arming button atop it.

He shouted, "Lakesh!" and lobbed it in a looping overhead throw then flung his body flat on the floor. Lakesh, his face registering startlement, caught the grenade on its downward arc, squawked once in dismay and tossed it toward Wei Qiang, who stood behind the black throne.

He yelled, *"Huang-ti!"* and hurled himself in the opposite direction.

Surprise stamped itself on Wei Qiang's face, due either to being addressed by his true name or the sight of the object flying toward him. Reflexively, his hands opened and he caught it. Realization and recognition gleamed in his eyes an instant before a blaze of light suddenly illuminated the area around the black throne and the Armor of Immortality with a white, incandescent glare. A tremendous cracking roar, half explosion, half windstorm, slammed against Lakesh's eardrums. The shock wave of the concussion was slight, but he felt invisible hands tugging at him, trying to yank him backward.

A gout of oxygen, smoke, scraps of silk and even an ivory screen swirled around him, irresistibly sucked back toward the wedge of instant vacuum created by the detonation of the DM-54 implode grenade.

He lunged behind a statue of the goddess Xiwangmu, who ruled eternal paradise, and for an eerie split second, his body hung motionless in midair, his momentum interrupted. Then the maelstrom effect created by the implosive device collapsed in on itself and he fell heavily, grunting in pain. At the same time he felt and heard tiny fragments of jade pattering down all around him.

Fanning smoke away from their faces and coughing, Brigid, Kane and Grant rose to their feet and apprehensively approached the epicenter of the implosion. They saw Erica creeping out from the concealed door and Lakesh rising unsteadily from behind the statue.

Grant and Kane lifted away the broken ivory screen. There wasn't much to see underneath it—the bodies of Wei Qiang and his soldier were mangled lumps of flesh, their eardrums shattered by the brutal decompression, their eyeballs pulled from their sockets, blood from ruptured vessels springing out from every orifice, their lungs flattened wafers of tissue. It was impossible to differentiate the mangled heaps of scarlet-painted flesh and splintered bone. Wei Qiang and his trooper were joined together forever, arms, legs and even organs entangled with one another.

The Kai Bu Xiu, the Armor of Immortality, resembled a shapeless lump of fused, half-slagged jade smoldering in the center of the floor. Nothing remained of it but scorched, dark green fragments and tiny puddles of melted gold wire.

"I think the immortal Yellow Emperor has met his mortality at last," Lakesh said hoarsely. "And he took the secret of his immortality with him."

He speared Grant with a sharp, accusatory glare. "An *implode* grenade?"

Grant heaved the broad yoke of his shoulders in a shrug. "In an enclosed place like this, an implode with a limited effect radius was the best bet."

Kane looked at Brigid, who rubbed her shoulder and winced. With a mock severity, he said, "Why didn't you tell me what those keys would do to the robots?"

"Because I didn't know until I tried," she replied. "But since the sockets on the robots were the same as on the outside door, I figured it was a standardized system." She paused, grimaced and added, "However, I had no idea turning the keys would make the machines run amok. I thought it would turn them off. I must have engaged some sort of preset combat program instead. If we run into anything like them again, I'll know better. I've learned my lesson."

Dourly, Kane said, "Just once I wish we'd learn a lesson without something blowing up."

"On the bright side," Grant commented, "Enlil will be royally pissed."

Erica knelt next to the clutter of smoking jade, poking and sifting through the shards. "Not too late," she whispered breathlessly. "Not too late."

"Too late for what?" Lakesh asked irritably.

Cupping her hands together, Erica scooped up a little heap of ash and jade. A Hydra's ring lay nestled among the fragments. The metal looked dull and lusterless, shot through with a network of hairline cracks.

Carefully, she stood up, holding the ring as if it were as fragile as spun sugar and eggshell. "We can analyze this one," she said in an urgent whisper. "Study it, find out how to make it work again. That's all any scientist needs, a starting point!"

"Give it a rest, Dragon Mama," Kane said wearily. "This kind of immortality the human race can do without."

She ignored him. Pursing her lips, Erica gently blew ash away from the jeweled eyes of the nine horned heads. Under the pressure of her breath, the Hydra's ring crumbled like a piece of ancient parchment and drifted to the floor in a scattering of dust.

JAMES AXLER

DEATH LANDS

Cannibal Moon

Compassion is a luxury in a brutal land where life is cheap, but Dr. Mildred Wyeth holds fast to her physician's oath to show mercy. Now she's stricken by a plague that brings on a deep craving for human flesh. Unwilling to lose one of their own to this pervasive pestilence without a fight, the companions follow the trail to Cajun country, where the mysterious Queen of the Cannies is rumored to possess the only antidote to the grim fate that awaits Mildred...and perhaps her warrior friends.

Available March 2007 wherever books are sold.

AleX Archer
THE CHOSEN

Archaeologist Annja Creed believes there's more to the apparitions of Santo Niño—the Holy Child—luring thousands of pilgrims to Santa Fe. But she is not alone in her quest to separate reliquaries from unholy minds who dare to harness sinister power. A dangerous yet enigmatic Jesuit, a brilliant young artist and a famed monster hunter are the keys to the secrets that lie in the heart of Los Alamos—and unlocking the door to the very fabric of time itself....

**Available January 2007
wherever books are sold.**